Champagne Book Group

Presents

Children of Neptune

By

Makenna Snow

Champagne Book Group
www.champagnebooks.com
Copyright 2017 by Jill Keene, Jodi Keene
ISBN 1-94712-809-4
July 2017
Cover Art by Jake Clark
Produced in the United States of America

Champagne Book Group
P.O. Box 467
Oregon City OR 97045
USA

Acknowledgement

Nothing worthwhile is accomplished alone. We owe tremendous thanks to Angelle Pilkington for editing too many drafts to count and her positive support through the process. To Nikki Andrews for her exceptional editing and support leading us to publication.

To our families for their support and belief in us, thank you.

Finally, to our mother: quite simply this book wouldn't have happened without you.

The World of *Children of Neptune*

People:

Alcandor, KingFirst of Neptune's line. Commissioned Quadrivium

Angela Lorente - Student at Quadrivium

Archer Miles - enComm professor at Quadrivium

Bertrand Cox - Student at Quadrivium

Bevan - Head of palace security

Chace Traven - Student at Quadrivium

Charlotte (Charlie) Houndswood - Student at Quadrivium

Declan Newcastle - Chancellor General of Council of Seven. Will's father

Elliot Bennett - Student at Quadrivium

Ellis Stemp - Human Studies professor at Quadrivium

Eric Furax - Student at Quadrivium

Eveleen Houndswood - Charlie's grandmother

Jaiette, Princess - Jet, the princess

Judith Saberton - Morwenna's mother

Lilly Parmenter - Student at Quadrivium

Maddox (farmer) - Lives below in Aurealia

Magnus, King - Jet's father and King of Pelagiana

Merrick Donovan - Array inventor. Famous Alum of Quadrivium

Minerva - Goddess of Wisdom

Morwenna (Morrie) Saberton - Student at Quadrivium

Neptune - God of the sea

Phoebe, Queen - Jet's mother and Queen of Pelagiana

Glaucilla Wolverhampton - Scholarch, Head of Quadrivium

Roger Saberton - Member of the Sagesse and Morwenna's father

Rosamund Hyde - Hydroshifting professor at Quadrivium

Sabrina Newcastle - Will's mother

Salacia - Neptune's wife

Tempesta - Wicked goddess in love with Neptune

William (Will) Newcastle - Student at Quadrivium

Zephania Ruecroft - Movement professor at Quadrivium

Places

Aquatheater - Outdoor seating. Used for the Aquaticup

Aquatica - All the water of Earth

Arctic Hall - Residential hall at Quadrivium

Atlantic Hall - Residential hall at Quadrivium

Atrium Quadrivi - Main Atrium in Quadrivium

Aurea Regia - Palace of the royal family in Aurealia

Aurealia - Village under the Shield below the Surface of Indigo Lake

Cocoa Cup - Café on Quadrivium and in Indigo City

the Eripium - Hospital for Pelagi and animals on Quadrivium

Grand Foyer - Entrance of Quadrivium

Hall of Reflection - Mirrored hall in Quadrivium

Hippio Strata - Rail system throughout Indigo City

Indian Hall - Residential hall at Quadrivium

Indigo Beach - Beach on Quadrivium Indigo City City built around the surface of Indigo Lake

Indigo Lake - Lake in the center of the Island of Pelagiana

the Ordinary - Main dining room/cafeteria at Quadrivium

Pacific Hall - Residential hall at Quadrivium

Pelagiana - A secret island hidden in the Indian Ocean. Gift from Neptune to the Pelagi in exchange for their defense of Aquatica

Persecutio - Historical time when ancient Romans persecuted Pelagi for sport

the Proprietary - Main building on campus

Quadrivium - School at the surface of Indigo Lake

Saberton Reading Room - Quiet room off the main library

Sofana Beach - Beach outside the palace in Aurealia

Southern Hall - Residence hall at Quadrivium

Animals

Atlas - Maddox's sea mink
Cinnsy - Schipperke
Clio - Queen's lowchen
Delphinius - Neptune's dolphin
Giselle - Eric's honey badger
Growler - Arctic Hall mascot
Jax - Tiger shark
Macaroni - Southern Hall mascot
Norman - Chelsea Brooke's sable
Onyx - Lilly's dog
Peppercorn - Jet's sable
Rorqual - Pacific Hall mascot
Stella - Hippocampi
Storm - Elliot's warrah
Svashi - Will's sea mink, mate to Viktor
Titan - Pacific Hall mascot
Viktor - Will's sea mink, mate to Svashi
Volucris - Indian Hall mascot

Miscellaneous

Aquaticup - Annual competition celebrating Pelagi history
the Array - Main power source, housed in Aurealia
Aurealian - Pelagi who live in Aurealia
Aurea Regia Guard - Palace security
the Baroque - Magical giant pearl from Neptune which protects the Shield
the Boards - Posted schedule and scores during Aquaticup
Cloak and Veil - Secret Society. Operates in the tombs.
Civis Sagesse (the Sagesse) - Governing body of Pelagiana
Dunamai - To have power, the basis for the study of Movement
Echolocation - Locating objects by reflecting sound
Eelfare - Main communication network, powered by the Array
Electrocyte - Modified muscle or nerve cell that generates electricity in electric organ of certain fishes

Elver - Communication device for note taking, research

Encephalic Communication (enComm) - Telepathic communication between Pelagi and their animal partners

Family Faire Weekend - Parents' weekend during first term

Hecaton - Unit of measure for land on Pelagiana meaning 100

Heliopons - Helix bridge from surface to Aurealia

Hydorian Terebra - Form of martial art used in Movement

Hydroderm - Class which teaches how to properly use hydroshifting

Hydroshift - Skin shift to water form

Keeps (pets) - Animal partners who live with Pelagi

MotoPearl - Transportation. Modeled after a noble pen shell, powered by the Array

Naumachia - Mock naval battle staged by the ancient Romans

Noble Order of Fin and Feather - Government/political Agency. Operates missions given by Neptune

Pelagi - People populating the island of Pelagiana

Regia Guard - Palace security

the Shield (the Paragon) - Protection around Pelagiana

Springtide ball - Annually held dance celebrating the season

Wave and Wing - Academic Society. Only the top two students from each year may be invited (entrance is not guaranteed)

Wintertide break - Week long break between terms at Quadrivium

One

"Get me out of here," she whispered. Jet crept along the ancient stone passage and waited for instructions. Inky blackness closed in as her heart hammered in her chest.

"Come on," she said, teeth clenched. She had no choice but to stop—if she took a wrong turn, she'd be discovered and her plans ruined. At last, a voice reached her.

"It's the next left, and you're free all the way to Sofana Park." There was no audible sound with his words, just what Jet could hear in her own mind. She followed the dark tunnel until she reached a wall with iron rungs forming a ladder. She climbed to the top and pushed away the large stone blocking her exit. Blinking against the harsh sunlight, she emerged from the tunnel, then returned the stone and hurried along the path leading away from her prison.

Shell fragments crunched under her sandals, and the wind whipped her long, dark hair around her head. The promise of the sea hinted the air, and Jet ran, her heart skipping with excitement. At last, her co-conspirator's sleek, black body emerged from the forest, and Jet grinned.

"Peppercorn, now isn't the time to hunt. You have to help me get back so I'm not late."

Her pet sable stared at her with his brown eyes and snorted. Peppercorn's entire body was covered in luxurious, black fur, save for a tuft of white on his head. *"You're the one who needed a break."*

Jet rolled her eyes at Peppercorn's admonition. She had been able to enComm—communicate with him telepathically—for years, and he never missed an opportunity to set her straight. *"You sound like the king. We've been through this. I need to get out of there occasionally. If I don't, the walls close in on me."*

Peppercorn darted along the path in front of her. *"The king and queen have a lot to worry about right now, but I will always help you, Jet."*

"You take good care of me. Thanks, Peppercorn...though it sounds like you're eavesdropping through walls again?" she said.

"Besides, I know you like to hunt too much to be satisfied with palace food."

He had no response but another snort. They hurried along the path. Jet flung off her sandals as the shells gave way to pink sand. They'd emerged from the cover of forest onto a deserted beach. She ran to the water.

She dove into the surf and swam. Feeling the familiar pull at her core, her body hummed, her skin tightened and smoothed, and her heart rate slowed. She shifted to her water form and became stronger, faster, and lighter. She let the powerful sensation envelop her, relishing the sense of belonging she felt in the water. She found one of the underwater tunnels leading to the world outside her safe bubble.

Exiting the stone tunnel, she entered larger body of water called Indigo Lake. Cutting through the clear water, the village of Aurealia sat below, protected in the half bubble of air beneath the crystalline Shield. Neptune had provided the Shield to safeguard her people—the descendants of Neptune himself.

And safe was just what Jet's life was. As a princess, she had trained since childhood for the duties she'd one day assume as queen. At sixteen, those duties seized center stage, with public appearances ruling her days. She pushed the limits of her breath, her chest tight as she picked up speed before swimming to the surface. She'd be late for today's session if she didn't get back home. After sighing, she took a huge breath and dove down, headed for home.

~ * ~

"You're late," Bevan, her head of security, said.

Jet blinked. Her wet hair was pinned back, water dripping down her back under the heavy velvet robe. The massive throne room doors loomed in front of her. She prayed she wouldn't throw up.

"Their majesties, King Magnus and Queen Phoebe of Pelagiana, present their daughter, Princess Jaiette," the footman announced to the hundreds of people anticipating her arrival.

Jet swallowed hard and trudged through the doorway. The room was divided by a long aisle constructed of intricate stone mosaics, leading to three thrones on a platform at the far end. The hundreds of people bowing to her on either side of the aisle terrified her. Her hands were damp, and she couldn't stop her racing heart. Her cheeks burned and sweat drenched her forehead.

She kept her pace measured, remembering her training for once. She chanced a glance at her father. The king's expression remained passive, except for the tic in his jaw. Jet knew that expression. He was mad or perhaps worse—disappointed.

When at last she'd climbed the four steps up to the platform, she turned too fast and tripped on the ridiculous robe she'd been forced to wear. She'd scarce caught herself before she fell. Her mother gasped. Jet's maneuver wasn't graceful and, for certain, wasn't "princess worthy."

She stood, faced the crowd, dreading her father's introduction. Several seconds ticked by before King Magnus cleared his throat.

"Ladies and gentlemen of the Civis Sagesse, thank you for convening today. Your efforts on behalf of our world are appreciated. I would also like to extend the appreciation to you all as you help guide our future queen in her training," he said. "Your past and future lessons ensure her success and our world's continued safety."

No pressure there. Their world's entire fate lay in her hands, and she was covered in flop sweat.

"Princess, please acknowledge the governing body," the king instructed.

Jet cleared her throat, willing her voice to sound strong. "Ladies and gentlemen, as the king indicated, we thank you for your invaluable procedural lessons. As the future queen, I look forward to working with you to ensure the well-being of all of Pelagiana—both here below and at the surface of our great island."

There was an approving murmur from the crowd. *There, that wasn't too bad.* She had even remembered to mention the population who lived above the Shield, near the surface of the lake in Indigo City.

"Please proceed with this month's lesson." She prayed it would be an easy one this time.

Jet recognized both men who stood on either side of the aisle. Her father's most trusted advisers and friends each held senior positions in the Civis Sagesse. The first to speak, Roger Saberton, was tall and strong, with dark hair and facial features like a hawk. He bowed low.

"Princess Jaiette, it is an honor to see you again. Member Newcastle and I have spent the last month working on this lesson." He acknowledged the other man. Distinguished by his sandy-brown hair and kind gray eyes, Declan Newcastle bowed to Jet as well.

"Yes, Your Highness," he said. "We had a wonderful lesson on parliamentary procedure from the country known as England. It was a practical lesson as well, since many of our own procedures are similar. However..." He stopped speaking, and both men stared at one another.

"However?" the king questioned.

Roger Saberton answered, "However, an issue of national security has come to light, and while this may seem like trial by fire, we thought to give the princess a crack at it. With your lasting good health, Your Majesty, and the young princess's own reign many years away, it was decided to see how she might handle this situation. Of course, the ultimate decision is yours. We didn't think the exercise would hurt either way, since she will need this type of training when she rules."

"Proceed," her father said.

Jet's stomach dropped. She had studied parliamentary procedure. She wasn't prepared for a surprise.

Saberton cleared his throat then said, "A villager outside the Aurea Regia has reported his animal is missing. Atlas, a sea mink, has gone without telling his partner. The villager's name is Maddox. His concern should be obvious. Atlas was one of only three sea minks left on the planet." Dressed in his own ceremonial robes of black, he paced before the platform as he delivered the news. He faced Declan Newcastle.

"Member Newcastle, since you are the guardian of the other two minks, perhaps you can add something to this?"

"Of course. Atlas is unrelated to my minks, and I needn't remind anyone here that without these animals and the many others that partner with us, we cannot do the job set forth by Neptune—protecting the waters of all of Aquatica."

"Yes, yes." Saberton waved Newcastle's comment away. "The princess is aware of her sacred duty, and this isn't the time for me to remind you that rest of the planet doesn't particularly need us watching out for them in a modern world. The humans are doing just fine without us. I am more concerned with what's happening on our island and why some animals are missing." Saberton stared at Jet. "That is where you come in, Princess Jaiette. How would you propose to handle this?"

Her stomach launched to her throat and stuck there. She had no idea what to say, what to do. She couldn't imagine her life without Peppercorn. Tears sprang to her eyes. *Come on, Jet! Think.* They were all staring at her, expecting an answer. Saberton and Newcastle offered smiles while her father's face revealed nothing, not even a nod of acknowledgement. A minute passed until she stared into her mother's warm, blue-green eyes and found what she needed. Jet straightened her spine, lowered her shoulders, and unclenched her fists.

"I would favor an investigation into this matter." She thought she sounded somewhat confident, but recognized her misstep when the crowd erupted in expressions of protest.

Saberton raised his hand to quiet the members, and simultaneously his inky-black eyebrow arched at Jet. "How would you propose to conduct said investigation, Your Highness? Which section of the Regia Guard would you employ to do this?"

Newcastle moved to the center aisle. "Member Saberton isn't trying to put you on the spot, Princess, but the questions he asks need answers before you can even speak your first thoughts. Such is the burden of the crown."

Without warning, a man shouted from the back of the room. "How does the princess plan to keep the other animals from panicking? If we launch an investigation into this, the other animals may think they are in danger and stop working with us." The rumble from the crowd signaled their agreement.

I should've thought of that.

The anonymous voice from the back erupted again. "Perhaps she's the first in Neptune's royal line who isn't fit to rule. She didn't even show up on time for—"

"Enough!" the king roared.

Jet jumped. Her father never shouted. He seldom had an emotional reaction at all. The crowd stood frozen. Tears threatened, and she pushed them back.

"Clear the room. I want to speak to my daughter and Member Saberton." Magnus focused his attention on Declan Newcastle. "Declan, Member Williams was out of order. I trust you will address the situation." Newcastle followed the remaining stragglers out of the throne room, leaving Jet to face her fate.

Two

After Bevan had closed the doors behind the last member of the Sagesse, Jet confronted the king. "Father—"

He cut her off with a wave of his hand. "Later," he growled. King Magnus stood before Roger Saberton. "All right, my friend, tell me what this is all about."

"Exactly what I was saying the other day, Magnus," Saberton said.

"Roger, I agree that the princess was wrong in suggesting an investigation."

Jet's stomach dropped again. Her father was taking Saberton's side. She didn't believe she was wrong. It *was* weird that the animal had disappeared. She clenched her fists.

"I do not agree with the public humiliation of my daughter, however."

"Of course you don't. Member Williams was out of line, but if the princess isn't tested, she will never be an effective ruler. She is too closed off down here from the real problems of our world if she believes the animal disappearances are important enough for an investigation. There is just one member of the Sagesse who agrees with her—Declan Newcastle."

"I hold Declan and his family in high esteem, Roger. I also believe the animal disappearances are unusual. Animals are our window to the world beyond us. They scout for us. They let us know what is happening outside of Pelagiana. Our sworn duty to Neptune requires we try to save and protect the world's near-extinct animals. We have failed in that endeavor too many times."

"Of course, Magnus, but this isn't the point. We have real problems, and these little ceremonies are wasting our time." Saberton's smooth voice echoed in the empty hall. "Your Majesty, I know you understand my position. As one of the first families in Pelagiana and a leading member of the Sagesse, it is my duty to protect Neptune's gift. There are those who believe the princess is…ahem"—Saberton cleared his throat and corrected himself— "that the *monarchy* has closed itself off from the problems facing our people."

Jet trembled. There were Pelagi other than Williams who believed she was an idiot? This was a disaster. She couldn't rule if people thought she didn't know what she was doing.

Her father paced the platform. "As the king, my family has been entrusted for thousands of years to guard Pelagiana and all who dwell here. The royal family is provided special advantages to accomplish this goal. The young princess has not been privy to all—her education is incomplete."

What did Neptune provide the king or queen of Pelagiana that Jet didn't know about?

"I do not question Neptune's wishes in this matter. Nor should you," her father said.

"But I do not, Your Majesty," Saberton said. "You have made my point. Neptune's gift of the island of Pelagiana and this secret kingdom below the lake's surface is in danger. Above us, Indigo City and its inhabitants lie in peril from discovery by the humans—because of what you have allowed."

Her father stopped on the platform. "Must I remind you that we Pelagi began our time here on earth charged with duties from Neptune? Protect the waters of this planet and its inhabitants. We have brave Pelagi out in the world doing just that—in secret. We need the animals to do this, and we need to save the animals that need us. And Roger, we *are* half human, or have you forgotten? We once lived among them, and I cannot stop any member of our country—whether they choose to live in Indigo City or here below under the Shield—from going out in the human world. We are a free society, and I must continue that tradition."

Saberton shook his head. "The humans almost wiped us out! That is why we are here in the first place. Neptune gave us this world to stop the ancient humans from using us for sport. Now, two thousand years later, you are allowing Declan Newcastle to work among them. You are allowing human studies to be taught at Quadrivium. Our next generation is learning *none* of the dangers the humans pose. I haven't forgotten anything. I remember my lessons well. The humans are responsible for the slaughter of almost all Pelagi. We were not always half human. We were once gods." The bitterness resonated through the massive hall.

"Roger, I've heard this argument from you before. Let's focus on the matter at hand. What was the outburst from Williams really about? Other than a few flubs, the princess hasn't shown herself to be the fool he claims."

It wasn't close to a sterling defense, but at least her father said something in favor of his daughter.

Saberton drew himself up, his voice calm. "As you heard today, there are some who believe that your allowances are leading to the destruction of our society, that you indulge the princess down here by not exposing her to all of Pelagiana. There are also many who believe you should allow the Array to be housed in the city instead of under the Shield."

Her father would refuse to move the Array to the surface as he had many times in the past. The Array was their power source and had been since the Pelagian biologist Merrick Donovan extracted the power of the electrocyte from an eel. Jet had heard rumors that there were those at the surface who wanted to control the Array, especially since it powered the precious Eelfare network. But it was also the duty of the royal family—of her people—to protect it.

"We've been over this. The Array is safest down here. We have excellent people maintaining it, and it is easier to control here. I have allowed the Sagesse to send out its information through Eelfare. We are a well-connected world, whether a citizen lives above or below the waters. If we allow the Array or Eelfare to be controlled by the Sagesse, private interests could overrule the good of all Pelagiana. While the Sagesse enjoys all the benefits of the Array for communication, the security of the Array is so critical to our society I cannot allow its possible compromise." He stopped in front of his throne. "And I do not indulge my daughter."

"That doesn't stop the rumors," Saberton said.

"I have heard the rumors. They are rather dramatic, don't you think?" The king lifted a brow.

"I do not," Saberton snapped. "No monarch in two thousand years has allowed such free rein among the Pelagi. You know I don't agree with complete freedom in interaction with humans, but I realize it is necessary. I just worry, Magnus, that this small number who doubt you and the princess will grow larger. They believe it is dangerous and reckless."

"It is progress." The king fisted both hands. "Or should we stop using MotoPearls and Elvers? Ask your 'growing number' if they are willing to give up all we have gained from our *careful* foray into the human world. That includes saving animals. I am willing to wager that no one would want to give up the conveniences my *reckless* ideas have garnered. And finally, we cannot fulfill our duty to protect the waters of earth by hiding on our secret island. My daughter will do her duty when the time comes."

"This is easy for you to say."

"What does that mean?" The king's eyes narrowed.

"It means, *Your Majesty*, that you have no vested interest. No skin in the game, so to speak."

Jet did not like the look in Saberton's dark eyes.

"Get to the point, Roger."

"You and your family live here under Indigo Lake, protected beneath the Shield. You have no worries. It's clear your daughter needs further education if these trivial animal disappearances register her concern. The dangers of interacting with humans should command all her attention. It shows her lack of training."

"My daughter's education is excellent and a two-thousand-year tradition. The royal family cares a great deal for all the people of Pelagiana and our animal partners. How could anyone believe otherwise?" the king asked.

"Your Majesty, pardon the insolence, but you hole yourself under surface. You visit Indigo City with your wife and daughter for ceremonial reasons only."

Jet's stomach clenched.

"Leave my wife and daughter out of this," the king said.

Saberton threw up his hands. "You prove my point again! Your daughter is heir to the throne and yet she, as all monarchs have been, is educated here. The children of Neptune are water warriors, trained at Quadrivium in case we are ever at the mercy of the humans again. Yet Princess Jaiette has never visited the school and has no working knowledge of Indigo City! She knows nothing of the risks these ideas of yours pose on the real people of Pelagiana. There is an entire society above the surface that is in danger, and you can't see it,"

"Enough! We will speak no more of this."

Saberton lowered his eyes. "I apologize. You asked what the outburst was all about, and I am telling you." He paced in front of the thrones. "Your Majesty, the people are seeking something from you. Something more than what you have been willing to give. They want reassurances. I fear for the future of the monarchy if you don't come up with something to appease them."

"Roger, I appreciate the fact that you are a good and passionate man. You come here for love of country, and I cannot find fault with that."

Jet did not agree with him. Right now, she could punch Roger Saberton. Her body hummed with rage.

"Magnus." Saberton's tone had softened. "It is not dire, but I like to worry. Just do something new or different. You could use Princess Jaiette somehow," he suggested. "Give her a project that brings her to the surface. Lord knows she could use some training. It is painful to see a future monarch so insecure. I know she will outgrow this, but a project could speed this along." Saberton directed his attention to her. "Princess, I apologize for my blunt manner, but you'll have to get used to it as queen. There will be far worse than me to contend with when you rule. Everyone will criticize you from time to time. Gaining confidence is part of the training."

She said nothing. Saberton might be right, but that didn't tamp the lump forming in her throat. Her father and Saberton strode from the throne room and closed the door behind them.

Of course she was insecure, but did everyone else see it as clearly as Saberton? Worse still was the suggestion that they "use" her somehow. Roger Saberton's words echoed in her mind and filled her with dread. What project could they possibly give her?

Three

Jet and her mother stayed behind in the throne room until her father returned. It was his duty to officially dismiss the members of the Sagesse, and she doubted he would linger. The lecture she was about to receive wouldn't be pretty.

Her mother reached over and held her hand. "He loves you a great deal. This is difficult for him."

"But not for me?"

"I know it's awful, Jet, and you can't imagine what it's like watching members of the Sagesse question your abilities. As your mother, it is horrible having to hold my tongue as they attack. But you must be strong and steel yourself. It is the only way."

"What if I can't? What if I am the first in the royal line to be a failure?"

"That isn't possible. Today's lesson was a setback, yes, but you'll learn from it. However, a tiny bit more confidence would be ideal. You'll get there; you just need to accept that you'll be queen one day."

"Mother, I know."

"Then why did my daughter, the future queen, arrive late to this lesson? You have not yet accepted your destiny. That isn't unusual in someone your age, but try to remember this—accepting that which you cannot change isn't a weakness. It is the opposite. You can't change the circumstances of your birth. When you accept you will be queen one day, things will fall into place for you."

"I wish I could believe that, Mother." Jet wasn't ready to be queen. She knew it, and she had no doubt her father would agree.

At last Magnus came back to the throne room, his imposing frame taking up the width of the aisle. He ascended the platform and stood in front of Jet. She stood still, ready for a battle. He took her hand in his. "I love you, little one."

"I love you too," Jet said.

"We don't have time for a big talk right now. For the most part, you did nothing wrong today, except you show a remarkable lack of respect when you appear late. I can't even lecture you on that. We haven't the time."

"I didn't mean to be late, and I'm sorry. Why don't we have time, Father?" she asked. "You enjoy lecturing me."

"Because tomorrow you are enrolling at Quadrivium as a second-year Beta student, and we have precious little time to get you ready. You'll continue your studies among the other children of Pelagiana—the 'children of Neptune,' as Roger calls them."

Jet jerked backward, tugging her hand free from her father's.

"Magnus!" Jet's mother cried, her shock echoing in the empty hall. "They ask too much. You can't be serious."

"We have no choice, Phoebe. She must do it."

Grim determination rang through her father's words, and Jet's nails bit into her palms. Could she change his mind? Appeal to the Sagesse in person? Run away? Panic gripped at her throat, making it difficult to breathe. "I won't do it."

"You will." The king towered over her.

"How is this supposed to solve anything? Sending me to a strange place to make a fool of myself in front of everyone? If you think I'll do better at Quadrivium than I did in court today, you're wrong. I'll do worse and bring shame to your legacy." Jet's breath huffed out in great, terrified gasps.

"You place too little importance on your brain and your instincts. You might not believe it, Jet, but I wouldn't send you unless I believed you could do it." His eyes softened. "I need you to do this—for your future—as it is your legacy also at stake."

The tears threatened, and she pulled them back. "You are so wrong about this. There has to be another way."

"There isn't. Jet, this decision isn't careless. But it *is* a royal mandate. You are required to obey."

"Of course I am." She didn't try to keep the bitterness from her voice.

"I know you have grown weary of your time in the palace. Neptune alone knows what you get into when Bevan isn't aware. Approach this as an adventure Can't you see the opportunity it presents?"

"I see the opportunity for thousands of modern Pelagi, not to mention all the other students, to mock the foolish princess as she stumbles her way through Quadrivium."

"First, just because we choose to live a quieter life beneath the surface does not make you unsophisticated. You will find your way, and that is the whole point of this exercise. You must show we still matter and that we care about our people. I am showing I care by sending the heir to the throne and my only child away to school for the first time in our history. My sacrifice is a great one. I love you so much. *We* love you so much." Magnus regarded her mother.

Jet wanted her mother to come to her defense, but Phoebe said nothing. Maybe this was what her mother meant by accepting that which couldn't be changed, but Jet wasn't through fighting yet. "There has to be a different solution."

"I have no more time to convince you. You will do this. There is no other way. There is too much grumbling about the monarchy. They will make us break a promise our family made to Neptune thousands of years ago. You have to convince them you have what it takes." He stiffened his spine. "I have one more request."

"You have not requested anything of me, Your Highness. You have given me an *order*." Jet crossed her arms. "Whatever you 'request,' I am, of course, your servant." Hot tears threatened.

"However you choose to see this, it is imperative you succeed. I could use less sarcasm and more cooperation."

"And I could use more choices."

"That is not an option, and you know it. It's time you grew up and accepted that reality."

"Fine. Anything else, Your Majesty?" she bit out.

"You will have a *mission*, so to speak, while you are there. Besides absolute success in your studies—and I mean perfection, Jet. They must not question your competence. I also need you to keep your eyes and ears open for us. The Sagesse meets in the compound that houses the Quadrivium. You will let me know what you hear and who is doing the grumbling about your failings and my allowances. I would like names."

"My failings?" She swallowed hard, fearing the answer before she asked the question. "It can't be that bad. I was only late once."

"It has less to do with punctuality and more to do with self-confidence and presence. You haven't proven yourself to these people, and unfortunately, whether we like it or not, they can choose to pledge their loyalty to another if you don't seem up to the task."

"And I don't seem up to it?"

The king cleared his throat. "It is obvious your heart hasn't been in it. That is not to say you aren't capable. You are more than that; you just haven't exhibited the behavior often."

"I see."

"No, you don't see yet, but you will. There is no choice here but perfection."

Hot anger churned inside her. Jet hated having no control over her future.

The king returned to his throne. "Find out anything you can about the animals, Jet. You have a gift with them, and they might tell you why some have stopped speaking to us or why they are leaving. You must do this in secret. I need to know everything."

She put her hands on her hips. "So the missing animals do matter? Why didn't you defend me to Saberton?"

"I don't have the luxury of defending my daughter in court. If I proclaim in public that I am concerned about the animals, can you imagine what might happen?"

"The animals might leave for somewhere safer," she said, remembering Williams's outburst in court.

"At last, you understand. I am not permitted to voice every concern I have, insomuch as it might cause panic. However, there are procedures in place for investigations should I desire that route. You will one day learn that this job has secrets beneficial to all. Right now, you will do as requested and keep this to yourself."

Jet had never encountered this side of her father. She hated the dark determination in his eyes as much as she hated him at this moment and what he was forcing her to do. And on a whim, at that! He had spent only a few minutes with the Sagesse, hammering out this plan for *her* life. Her mother was wrong; accepting her fate didn't lead Jet to a sense of power. It led her to rage.

Her pulse pounded in her head, and her eyes watered as she answered her father, "Certainly, Your Highness."

Four

"Your Majesty, we have some serious concerns about this." The head of Jet's security team was trying to convince her father and mother of the best way to get her to Quadrivium. The family met in the offices of the Regia Guard a few hours after her father ordered her enrollment, and her time in the beloved palace Aurea Regia was nearing its end.

Bevan pointed to a graphic showing the school grounds. "Security at Quadrivium is an issue. Part of the training at the school is allowing the population to lead their own lives. They are not monitored in a way we would like for our princess. We can provide a detail or secret guards."

"I hate both those ideas," Jet said.

"We will have subtle security, Bevan. The princess should not be seen as special. She must accomplish her goals like any other student," the king said.

"Magnus, she isn't like other students," Queen Phoebe said.

"She will be safe, Phoebe, but she must not appear to be privileged. Keep it private, Bevan. Use secret guards. I want no one, including the princess, to know who is watching her."

"I don't like that idea any better." Jet folded her arms and leaned back in her chair.

"We have little choice, my daughter. Besides, I imagine you'll find a way around the guards, just as you do here."

She said nothing. She figured her father meant for her to sneak around Quadrivium to gather her information. The guards could make it difficult.

Bevan put that fear to rest. "Our guards will not be effective around the clock. It would not fit with the ideals of Quadrivium for students to be followed. We will do our best, but as I said, there are concerns."

The king reached for the silver pitcher of water in the center of the table and poured a glass then took a sip. "Let's move on for now. I've reviewed the options for getting to the surface. While the princess is magnificent at hydroshifting, we will not be swimming to Indigo City. That would require us to ride the hippocampi—which are for ceremonial use now—and that isn't the message we want to send. Using the tunnels and passages that lead to the surface would send the wrong message as well since they were first carved into the lakebed beneath us for use as escape routes to evade humans. What about the final option, Bevan?"

"The most popular way to get to the surface is via the Heliopons. If we choose the bridge up to the surface, that puts us in position to ride the Hippio Strata to the station at Quadrivium."

Jet liked this option. She had seen the Hippio Strata on visits to the city before, but she had never ridden the train. She would love to have the chance.

The king got up from his chair. "I will not allow anyone to believe we were forced into this decision to save the monarchy. Princess Jaiette attending Quadrivium will appear to be another way the royal family embraces change without fear." Her father paced. "Therefore, we will opt for the Heliopons and the Hippio Strata—one of the benefits of our careful interaction with the human world."

And with that, the plans for Jet's departure were complete.

~ * ~

Two hours later Jet sat on her bed, staring at her room, which was decorated in deep blue and pale yellow. It did little to calm her. She had no idea what to pack, wear, or even do once she got to Quadrivium. She felt clumsy, inept, and unsophisticated. It reminded her of what she experienced when she addressed court or the members of Sagesse.

Suddenly a ball of fur darted through her room. She recognized the incessant yapping of her mother's pet Löwchen.

"Clio!" Jet said. "I've asked you to stop sneaking in here. You belong with the queen." The yapping persisted, and Peppercorn chimed in. Hopping down from a brocade chair near her window, her pet sniffed.

"That dog is a nuisance. It doesn't listen," Peppercorn said.

"She's only a baby, and she isn't ready to enComm yet. When she's ready, she'll listen to reason."

"Until she does, send her back to the queen. She's so loud."

A knock on the door interrupted their conversation, and the queen strolled in.

"Okay, Clio, out you go." Queen Phoebe scooped up the tiny puppy, patted her soft fur then handed her to a palace guard outside the door. "Isabelle, please make sure Clio stays in my rooms this time." The guard took the barking puppy away.

"Now, let's sort things out." The queen sat next to Jet on her bed, took her hand.

"What is there to sort, Mother? Father took away all my choices."

"Ahh, my baby girl, he took many, and the fact that you are the only heir to the House of Neptune took many others, but you still have the most important choice."

The queen hugged Jet to her, and she inhaled her mother's scent—a mixture of the sea and hibiscus. How could Jet leave the one person beside Peppercorn she could talk to? "I have no idea what choice I have left."

"You can choose *how* you accept your fate," the queen said. "You have yet to decide to accept it all, but it is important—the most important thing, in fact—how you become the next ruler of Pelagiana. Everyone is watching, and if Roger Saberton is to be believed, many think you will fail."

Her shoulders dropped. "I don't think I can pull it off."

The queen squeezed Jet's hand. "You'll figure it out. You must. Your mind and your heart are ready. You should try trusting them and yourself."

"Mother, I've never talked to anyone my own age. I've been surrounded by elders my entire life. Not only do I have to prove myself to the Sagesse, I have to figure out Quadrivium and everyone there. I don't think my mind and heart are ready to fail on such a huge scale."

"I hate to echo your father, but we don't have much time. You must get past the fact that you have to do this, and instead focus on a way to do it well."

"Is it that bad?"

"I think so, my love. There are many who have stopped trusting the monarchy altogether, and your father fears the animals are missing because they have lost faith too."

"No! That can't be true." Jet jumped off the bed and paced. "We would have heard something."

"Perhaps, but this gives you a chance to solve the mystery on your own terms." The queen stood and folded the clothes spread on Jet's bed.

"I'd like to help. I just wish it didn't have to be this way."

"Accept what you can't change, remember?" the queen reminded her.

"That's easy for you to say."

The queen laughed, went to Jet. With a gentle stroke, she brushed Jet's hair away from her forehead. "How wrong you are."

She raised her eyebrows.

A slight twinkle lit her mother's eyes "Did you know I didn't want to go to the Springtide gala when it was time for the future king to choose a wife?"

"No."

"I hated the idea of being paraded in front of someone as if I were a horse at auction. The whole idea of it seems quite stupid to me."

"Why did you go then?" Jet asked.

"Because, just like you, I had no other choice. My parents would never have defied an order from the monarchy. I fought bitterly for my right to choose, but I was outvoted."

"But you might not have been chosen by the king."

"You're right, but that didn't matter to me. It was the point of the whole exercise that irked me. No choice and dictated by some unknown entity. Sound familiar?"

"Yes, but you didn't fail as miserably as I have."

"You haven't failed anything yet, Jet. And don't be too sure about how I handled things back then. Seventeen-year-old, headstrong young women seldom handle all challenges with grace and dignity. There were some missteps, in particular when your father chose me." She snatched a blouse and shook out the wrinkles. "It still irks me a bit. You come by your stubbornness naturally. In the end, it all worked out. Once I accepted my fate, I fell deeply in love with your father and the important work we do."

"This leaves me to ruin a two-thousand-year tradition."

"Enough of that talk," the queen said. "You haven't ruined anything. The talk of ending the monarchy didn't begin with you. It's been around for years. It can, however, end with you. You can choose."

"Grace and dignity?" Jet asked. "I'm not so sure, but I might need a brain transplant to achieve that."

"You need to trust yourself, and all will be well."

"I have to figure out why the animals are missing, save my job as future queen, *and* try not to behave like an idiot, all while surrounded by total strangers in a completely foreign place. I'm not sure I can handle so much."

Queen Phoebe wrapped her arms around Jet. "Trust me, you can handle it. Besides, you don't have a choice."

Five

As the royal family made their way outside the walls of Aurea Regia and into the town of Aurealia the next morning, the crowd cheered. Jet's mother waved from the open carriage to the excited crowd. Her father, regal as usual in dark gray robes, acknowledged the crowd.

"Jaiette, you look as if you are attending a burial. Snap out of it," her father said under his breath.

Jet hated when her father told her to snap out of it, as if her feelings could change in a moment. She gritted her teeth and forced a fake smile.

"I'm sorry, Father. I'll try to be more cheerful as I leave behind everything I know and love because it's a good move politically."

King Magnus' eyes flashed, but Jet's mother stopped the brewing argument.

"Jet, we know you are sad about Peppercorn, but that doesn't give you to right to share your upset with the crowd. It is not their fault your pet didn't say goodbye. If you aren't enthusiastic, the Aurealians will worry you are being forced to do this. You know that's acceptable."

"I just don't know why he didn't come to see me off. I won't see him until Wintertide break. That is a long time." Jet's cheeks ached as she forced the grin and wave.

"I know, my love. And we are sorry."

Her father said very little on the ride to the Baroque. When they reached the pearl at the bridge, the Aurealians had doubled in number and were waving and cheering at the royal family. They exited the carriage and walked to the Baroque, the giant pearl Neptune gifted the people of Pelagiana. With its magical properties, the pearl protected the people beneath the Shield. Jet and her family then passed through the magic pearl to the entrance of the Heliopons.

She couldn't stifle her excitement when entering the Heliopons. A giant, helix-shape bridge, the Heliopons swirled for almost a mile up to the surface of the lake. According to her father, the Heliopons was much like a train or airport terminal in the human world, a hub with shops and food kiosks, bridging people from one destination to another.

Outside the enclosed walkways, the water of Indigo Lake swirled from a deep blue to light turquoise. The fish and freshwater mammals became less dense as the royal family ascended. Outside the glass-covered promenade, Jet could just make out the Shield covering

Aurelia. The kingdom and its little village were invisible to her now. An otter swam by, and it reminded Jet of Peppercorn.

She caught a glimpse of herself in the reflection of the glass. With her eyebrows drawn together and lips tight, she looked worried. Too many thoughts swirled in her head. She missed Peppercorn. How was she supposed to spy on the Sagesse? How could she fit in at Quadrivium, especially when her class had been there a year already? And how was she supposed to make people believe she could handle the job of being queen if she were already this nervous? What would the people at the surface think of her?

Finally they reached the platform enclosed in glass at the surface. Squinting against the sun, Jet took in the bounty of Neptune's gift and the magnificence of their secret island. Indigo Lake was vast, and beyond its beach to the east stood towering mountains covered with lush foliage and cascading waterfalls. Grottoes were built into the rock of the island and subaquatic caverns, but she had never explored them. She might get that chance during her time here.

To the west lay the powdery-pink sand beach and billowing marsh grasses. Beyond that was Indigo City. The massive city was built into the rock of the mountains behind it and kissed the shoreline of Indigo Lake. The mountains surrounding the entire lake were another protective measure Neptune had employed to keep their population from discovery.

Beyond the mountains was the sea, which held crashing waves, forbidding rocks, and treacherous coral reefs, making Pelagiana inhospitable to the human eye. But Neptune left nothing to chance, making the island visible only to creatures possessing Pelagi blood.

The aboveground train system known as the Hippio Strata came to life before her eyes. From the gleaming stone buildings of Indigo City, an enclosed train bulleted on the tracks above the water of Indigo Lake, coming to rest outside the glass doors of the platform where they stood.

The train was automated, with gray bench seats lining the inside of the car. The royal family, along with Bevan, entered. No other Pelagi traveling to Indigo City were permitted in this car. Jet figured it had to do with security, and Bevan confirmed this, his wide shoulders taking up almost the entire doorway of the train, blocking the entrance.

"Since the train is powered by the Array, we have no worries of hijacking, Your Majesty," Bevan said to King Magnus. "The car has been swept for danger, and the fact that there is no driver helps us maintain safety for the time being."

"Excellent," King Magnus said. "Since we are alone for a bit, why don't you tell us about your classes, Jaiette?" Her father was a little too cheerful to her ears, but she didn't have the heart to spar with him right now.

As the train lurched and began its climb from lake level to high above the water, Jet could think only of the impending stop at Quadrivium. She glanced at the stunning skyline Indigo City had to offer from this vantage point. Below was her beloved Indigo Lake, the beautiful Shield, and the kingdom it protected now hidden from her view.

"Yes, Jet, tell us about it. I know your father was able to get your schedule for you," her mother said.

Jet swallowed and tried to focus. "I have five classes this term. I am studying enComm, Movement, Human Studies, BioEcology, and World Literature."

"That is very exciting. What a wonderful opportunity to show your talents." Queen Phoebe brushed a hand through her hair.

"One of her tutors is also a professor at Quadrivium," the king said to his wife. "Archer Miles is one of the enComm teachers up here. He, along with several other professors over the years, have split their time between Quadrivium and the palace to see to the royal family's education."

Professor Miles was her favorite tutor at home, and enComm was her favorite subject. With only one day to prepare for school, Jet had been too busy to visit the professor before she left. At least now she wouldn't be quite so alone.

"Perhaps you can speak to Professor Miles before classes begin tomorrow, and he might be able to answer some of your questions about Quadrivium. You didn't have a lot of time to research," her mother said with a pointed glance at the king.

"Well said, Mother. We had no time to get used to this idea." Jet shot her father a look.

King Magnus stared at the floor. "Both of you are right, and I am truly sorry, Jet, but our positions don't leave us many choices. I was left with little choice too, yesterday, since this idea seems to be the will of the people." He cleared his throat. "But understand this, this was the most difficult decision I've ever made."

"I am going to fail."

"You will not. You only think you will. The blood that runs through your veins is worthy. For over two thousand years, when this family has been tested, we have never failed."

"No pressure there."

Bevan masked his laugh with a cough and stared out the window of the train.

The king's lips thinned. "The burdens of the gift Neptune left us are great, but I believe you will one day cherish the honor of serving. Only a royal can harness the powers necessary to keep Pelagiana and the waters of the world safe. You know who you are, Jaiette, and of what you are capable. You just have not realized it yet. I have faith that you will not let us down."

She said nothing. What could she say to solve anything? The tremendous weight of a two-thousand-year tradition lay on her shoulders, and her father was wrong. She could not live up to that tradition. How could she, when the idea of just going to school petrified her?

Her mother gave her a gentle nudge. "Jet, we've arrived."

She moved her wooden limbs and stood to exit the train. The platform and station were just outside Quadrivium's walls. Her breath hitched as she exited. Having no escape or alternative, she squared her shoulders. It was time.

Six

As Jet exited the train and moved through the station, several palace guards surrounded the small building. Outside the station, more palace guards flanked the family as they made their way to the gates of Quadrivium. Huge groups of people had gathered and were cheering.

The crowd's enthusiasm contradicted Roger Saberton's claims that the royal family was irrelevant.

Her mother drew Jet's attention and pointed to the enormous ivy-covered walls guarding the entire campus of Quadrivium. She couldn't see anything beyond their substantial height.

She wasn't prepared to be excited at seeing Quad for the first time or for her curiosity about a group of students entering the massive iron gates ahead of them.

When Jet, her family, and the entire cumbersome guard detail finally made it to those gates, she couldn't contain a small gasp. The opening revealed an extensive, poplar-lined avenue leading to a gleaming, white building.

"It's immense!" She slowed her pace.

Her mother tugged Jet's sleeve. "Come on, Jet, the hippocampi are ready."

She almost rolled her eyes at the ancient, magical sea horses sometimes still used in royal ceremonies. Able to survive in and out of the water, they were unwieldy, difficult, and an indication that the royal family clung to tradition too much.

She stopped the eye roll in time and said fast. "Perhaps it would be better to walk the avenue, Father? It will give us a chance to tour the grounds like the other students."

"Good idea," the king said.

Bevan let out an audible groan but did not harp about the security issues for once. Her family strolled the length of the campus on the broad path toward the white colossus in the distance. On one side of her strode her mother, holding her hand for reassurance. Jet tried to see it as the prison sentence she had believed it to be for the past day, but fell under the spell of the idyllic surroundings.

Grassy fields with students crossing them or resting on blankets soaking in the sun captivated her. She couldn't fathom the freedom of just lying in the grass. She rarely had free time in Aurealia. The breeze blew across her cheeks, and the leaves rustled overhead. The smell of the sea beyond the mountains floated in the air.

The royal party encountered a roundabout, in the middle of which stood a marble statue depicting Minerva and the Venerated Owl. Beyond these guardians of wisdom lay the Proprietary, the main building on campus. Upon seeing the steep, white staircase leading to the main entrance, Jet was relieved to have her family by her side. Two sentries clad in blue-and-green uniforms attended the entry.

Bevan signaled the sentries, and the ancient wooden doors swung wide, offering a view of an imposing foyer. They entered through a set of double doors to the right, which opened into a spacious sitting room.

"Queen Phoebe ran her hand along the wall. "The stone is the same ivory color as in Aurea Regia—a reminder of home."

Her mother was trying to be cheerful, but the fear Jet had lost touring the grounds had returned to burn in the pit of her stomach.

A footman entered the room. "Your Royal Highnesses, may I present the scholarch of Quadrivium, Madame Glaucilla Wolverhampton."

At first glance, Madame Wolverhampton's appearance was severe. Her red-and-brown hair was short and spiky, and she wore thick, horn-rimmed glasses low upon her angular nose. The scholarch had bright eyes and a small mouth.

She leaned forward and bowed. "Good afternoon, and welcome to Quadrivium. We are truly honored. I will be conducting your private tour and orientation today. Please stop me if you have questions or concerns along the way." They exited through the doors from which they entered.

"This is the Grand Foyer, in which we host a multitude of curricular and extracurricular affairs, such as presentations, lectures, exhibits, and social events." The Grand Foyer was embellished in polished glass, gold, and marble carvings of classical motifs. Leading them toward the main staircase, the scholarch paused.

"I supposed I hadn't thought of this until now, but how do you wish to be addressed here at Quadrivium, Princess?"

Jet hadn't thought of this either. "How do you address the other students?"

"We address the students as miss or mister, and their surname."

She swallowed hard. "Then please call me Miss Lennox."

"Excellent." The scholarch led them to the top of the staircase. "This is the Hall of Reflection. The stained-glass windows depict historical events. The largest window above you shows King Alcandor signing the Royal Charter creating the Noble Order of Fin and Feather."

Jet clasped her hands in front of her as she followed the scholarch and her parents through the massive hall. Each step led her further from her old life.

The scholarch steered them into a large atrium. "The name, Quadrivium, expresses our mission. This institution is a crossroads of higher learning. The indestructible walls of these buildings are built with adamantine, which is quarried from deep within Indigo Lake. The main building contains classrooms, faculty offices, student common areas—such as the Ordinary—and the residential houses. Outbuildings situated on campus and all the estate lands belong to the Quadrivium Trust and include additional housing, alternative dining options—such as the Cocoa Cup—specialty libraries, theaters, chapels, stables, gymnasia, and gardens. The grounds also contain a building for the Civis Sagesse when they are in session. We rarely interact with its members. We also maintain a separate full-time security detail on the grounds."

In the center of a large atrium punctuating the Hall of Reflection, the scholarch said, "This is the Atrium Quadrivi. This room commemorates the ancient curriculum of astronomy, mathematics, music, and geometry. Our education system is founded in human traditions of antiquity, as we had lived in harmony with humans prior to their ancient persecution of our people. However, as centuries passed, the Pelagi and human educational traditions blended to become what Quadrivium is today."

Jet bit into her bottom lip as the scholarch guided them through the Ordinary, the Saberton Reading Room, and Goddrick Library. Madame Wolverhampton assured her that negotiating the grounds of Quadrivium was quite manageable.

"We realize students transition from home to school at differing paces and there are unique circumstances surrounding your specific matriculation. We shall endeavor to make your transition as easy as possible."

"Thank you, Madame Scholarch," Jet said.

They made their way down a corridor lined with picture windows exposing a view of a tree-lined courtyard, the focal point of which was a three-tiered adamantine fountain honoring Neptune. Catching the light of the sun, the dribbling water shone like diamonds. They reached the end of the corridor and were met with a dark, metal gate.

"Welcome to Arctic Hall, your residential house here at Quadrivium." Madame Wolverhampton paused until Jet reached the gate. "A word about security—we are not jailors or babysitters at Quadrivium. Students are encouraged to explore the grounds freely with our trust. You are all almost of age, and a student has that trust unless they give us cause to withdraw it." She cleared her throat. "That being said, I will tell you about your Elver. The Elver is directly connected to the Eelfare network and powered by the Array, but even the Elver will not trace your whereabouts. I'm assuming you need some information on this since typically royals do not need Elvers.

"Because of the sustainable power of the Array, the Elver will never die until its owner does. As with all Elvers, it will respond only to one Pelagi's touch. This one has been manufactured with you in mind. Your specific information was fed to Eelfare, and this Elver will only ever work for you. Pelagi receive their Elvers here at Quadrivium but take them wherever they go once they graduate. You have access to all the information posted to Eelfare, and that includes Quadrivium library and the news and announcements published by the Intelligence System." The scholarch resumed the tour. "We weren't always so lucky. Until our greatest student, Merrick Donovan, could get an eel to trust him with its secrets, we Pelagi used parchment and texts just as students all over the world still do. But with the invention of the Array and Merrick's other inventions, Eelfare and the Elver, we have lightened our loads."

The scholarch held the Elver. "Now as you can see, I am touching the Elver, but nothing is happening. But when I give it to you, Miss Lennox, you shall learn its secrets."

Jet grasped the offered dark gray device. Hinged like a clamshell, the Elver was roughly the length of a young lobster and smooth like dolphin skin. From the moment the scholarch put it in her hands, it vibrated, and the Elver opened like a book.

"One side of the Elver will show your schedule or the day's events sent from Eelfare and the Intelligence System. The other side is yours to navigate. You may take notes, access information, or turn in assignments. You may even communicate with others. It is alive, but it isn't, if that makes sense. It's quite magical, and most learn it as they go."

The scholarch led them through a large salon with numerous sofas and chairs intimately arranged. Lamplit, wooden, private rooms surrounded the perimeter of the salon. The ivory walls were decorated with banners, flags, and numerous strange artifacts, including an oversize tapestry of an angry growler.

"The growler is your residential hall mascot. Each hall has one. This is a good time for me to explain this. As I said before, our system is a hybrid, so to speak, of all the best educational systems from the human world, and the commands of Neptune. Borrowing ideas has enabled us to come up with the best solutions to instill loyalty, love of learning, and school pride.

"There are five residential halls at Quadrivium, each named for one of the oceans of Aquatica. It is our sworn duty to protect all the waters of earth, and this is a reminder. Each residential hall boasts a mascot with which you will identify. Artic Hall is the growler. Your color is cobalt. Pacific has the rorqual and their color is silver. Indian Hall has a volucris, scarlet in color, while Atlantic Hall is represented by the color emerald with titan as their mascot. Finally, Southern Hall's mascot is a macaroni, and their color is yellow.

"These will become desperately important to you right around the time of the Aquaticup, Miss Lennox." At the king's raised eyebrow, the scholarch explained, "I know you're all quite familiar with the games, but Miss Lennox will be attending this year as a participant, and residential hall loyalty plays a part in the festivities. Many of the events are full contact and quite brutal. We deem the games excellent training for your more physically demanding classes here at Quadrivium."

Jet's hand's shook as she held the Elver.

"At any given time, we have between four and five hundred students spread over the five residential halls at Quadrivium. We like to offer you the comfort of home, and the common area and separate halls give our students that. But your classes are mixed, and you are encouraged to enjoy your meals in the Ordinary with the entire student body. There are residential tables, and you will find your loyalty will lie with the Artic Hall," the scholarch said.

Jet couldn't imagine caring about school rivalries at all when she was so terrified of what lie ahead.

After a stop to tour the pantry, the scholarch led them to Jet's room. Madame Wolverhampton addressed the king and queen. "We were able to accommodate your request for a single room. While traditionally Betas do not occupy singles, an exception was made. Generally, Betas choose their roommates and then participate in a lottery for room selection. Miss Lennox will be afforded this privilege next year as a Gamma."

Jet was disappointed she had received special treatment but at the same time, couldn't help feeling a sense of relief knowing she didn't have to stumble through meeting a roommate. She hated that her emotions were so conflicted.

Madame Wolverhampton rounded toward Jet. "Do you have any questions for me?"

She didn't want the special treatment. "Actually, I was curious— is next year the earliest I could be assigned a roommate?"

"All of the students are already paired up this year, but that doesn't mean we don't allow for changes. However, I think we'll navigate those waters when we face them, Miss Lennox," Madame Wolverhampton answered, though it wasn't really an answer at all.

"Now, Miss Lennox, if you please," she motioned toward a door. The door had to be hundreds of years old, but it gleamed golden.

"Welcome to your home for the next two terms," the scholarch said.

Seven

Jet's dorm room had white marble floors warmed with two cobalt rugs of related designs. Three oriel windows overlooked the courtyard outside Arctic Hall. She had to admit—the room was lovely. The walls were bare, ivory stone and begged for pictures, or anything else she could think of to hang. She couldn't stop her heart from leaping at the sight of a wooden desk facing the windows and two upholstered chairs inviting company to sit and talk.

The only other furniture was a four-poster bed with canopy, set against the wall opposite the door. It was decorated in curtains and linens complementing the area rug before it. Upon closer inspection of the bed, "Peppercorn!"

She rushed to the bed, tripped on the rug, and fell into the pillow. She scooped Peppercorn into her arms and gave him a fierce hug. *"How did you get here?"*

"Your mother's idea, of course. They brought me in a separate carriage with your luggage as if I was chattel." Peppercorn snorted.

She choked back the tears. "Thank you."

The queen stroked Peppercorn's white tuft. "You're welcome, Jet."

The king put his arm around Jet. "Of course, dear."

Madame Wolverhampton coughed. "All students are encouraged to strengthen their encephalic communication skills. Thus, we encourage them to bring their keeps to Quadrivium. Your pet will have run of the grounds as well. I find that most animals have the resources to see to their own comforts, but if you have issues, don't hesitate to ask. We are hopeful this helps ease your transition as well, Miss Lennox." She reached for the door handle. "This concludes our tour. When you have additional questions, you should consult your residential House Master. That would be Professor Ruecroft. She is also the Movement Instructor, and you will find her to be quite knowledgeable. Professor Ruecroft has also earned the distinction of holding her position at Quadrivium the longest. The school wouldn't be the same without her. Please use her extensive knowledge of the facility when you have questions."

Madame Wolverhampton bowed to the king and queen.

"Your Majesties, if you will excuse me now, I will let you say your goodbyes. As tomorrow is the first day of the new school term, the other students will be trickling in soon, and I must prepare to greet them.

It has been a pleasure, and please let me assure you, as I do all our new parents, your daughter will be well cared for here. And one final bit of information—I should remind you that Family Faire Weekend is scheduled five weeks from today, and we encourage you to come and support the students. The Newcastles are hosting the Welcome party at their home in Indigo City, and this is a wonderful opportunity for you to meet your daughter's new friends and other Quad parents."

King Magnus glanced at the queen. "We would be delighted to attend."

"You have been most helpful and thoughtful in taking this time for a private tour, Madame Wolverhampton. We shall rest easier now, having seen firsthand what good hands Jaiette is in," Queen Phoebe said.

"Thank you." The scholarch left the room and closed the door behind her.

Alone with her family, the optimism Jet felt earlier was now overshadowed by an overwhelming sense of sadness. Tears of uncertainty rolled down her cheeks.

Phoebe took her daughter in her arms, the queen's dark eyes awash with tears as well. "We are proud of you, Jet. It isn't every day someone decides to forge a new path."

"I didn't decide this. I know it's a mistake."

"It's never a mistake to try something new, Jet," her father said. "This could end up the best thing that happens to you, if you can just embrace it. Your attitude will define your success." Her father stared at her a moment. "You remind me so much of your grandmother, Jaiette. The black hair and green eyes are replicas of hers. They say Neptune himself had a hand in her beauty. Be proud and remember who you are."

Queen Phoebe withdrew a sea-silk bag from her pocket and handed it to Jet. "Just a little reminder of home and how much you are loved. Never give up on yourself, my love."

With careful hands, Jet removed a delicate silver chain, upon which hung a pink, iridescent pearl. A thin coil of silver wrapped protectively around the pearl. When a royal was born or married into the line, a piece of the Baroque appeared at the palace the same day—a gift from Neptune. Her father's words confirmed this was hers.

"That pearl is special, Jet. Every member of the royal family is required to have one on their person when they are of age. Your mother and I wear ours embedded in our wedding bands. Since you are leaving us, we thought you should have yours now. Only the Baroque or pieces of it can heal the Shield should it become damaged. Please don't take the necklace off. It is another duty, I am afraid."

She understood this all too well. "What happens if the royal line stops or a royal loses the pearl?"

"That has never happened in two thousand years, but I imagine Neptune has a contingency. Only you would worry about that." Her father rolled his eyes. "Concentrate on that which you *can* control. Learn the powers of the pearl, and it will become a comfort rather than burden."

She had no idea what he meant.

Her father clasped the pearl around her neck on its whisper-thin silver chain. It warmed against her skin.

"Oh, and by the way, speaking of comfort, I snuck some extra pomegranate candy sticks in one of your bags. I know they're your favorite." Her father placed his hands on Jet's shoulders. "For my final instruction, have some fun."

She hugged her parents tight. Despite her anger at her father, she knew she was loved, and no matter what happened, that would never change.

~ * ~

Jet didn't venture out of her room after her family left. She wasn't ready to face all the students and teachers. She was behaving like a coward, but it was all too much, and the quiet of her room offered a little peace before the storm of her first day tomorrow. As she unpacked, Peppercorn searched for an exit from her room.

"Why can't I just open the door and let you out?"

"I like to come and go as I please. Besides, it isn't convenient for you to open the door for nighttime hunts when you might be sleeping," her pet huffed. *"Perhaps, for now, I'll use the window."*

She folded her uniforms and kept one eye on Peppercorn's progress. Finally, near the stone fireplace, he stopped sniffing.

"While you're out and about, can you start to scout around? You can be places I can't right now, and I am going to need your help to find out what the Sagesse is doing,"

"Of course you need my help. I'm not living in this tiny room because you need help with enComm." He snorted. *"You and I will need to formulate a plan, but just now, I am too hungry to bother."* His sleek body patrolled the length of her room. *"There's a draft down here…ah, excellent, a little hole I can just fit through."* Peppercorn forced his body into a hole way too small for him.

A knock sounded on the door. His head peeked out of the tiny hole, as Jet reached the door. Just outside the door stood three girls staring at Jet.

The tallest, a girl with short, blonde hair and brown eyes, said. "Hello, Your Highness. My name is Lara." She gestured to the girls behind her. "This is Amber and Gillian. We're all Betas and Arctics, just like you. We thought you might want to join us for dinner?"

Should she join them? What would they talk about? What if she messed up and said something awkward? "No, thank you." Jet closed the door to their confused faces.

"That was not friendly and definitely not a good start," Peppercorn said.

She slumped on her bed. "I know but I panicked," she said. "Oh, I should've just said yes! They must think I'm so rude. Why would anyone want to be my friend now?" She couldn't believe she hadn't said something more to the girls. She turned to her pet.

Peppercorn was pacing in front of the hole now. He didn't like to repeat himself and he never lied to her. He said nothing, so she enCommed.

"I know it's a waste of my time to sulk about this situation. I have very little choice in this, so I'll try harder, I guess."

"I had no doubt you would come to this conclusion sooner or later." And with those words, he again stuffed his body into his exit until his sleek, black body disappeared from her view.

Alone in her room, darkness surrounded her and, as she listened to the other students settle into their own rooms, she thought again of her promise to Peppercorn. Despite her poor first attempt at speaking to students, she hoped that one of them might end up being her friend.

Eight

Jet skipped breakfast the next morning. She was too nervous to eat. Her schedule had appeared on her Elver the day before. She stood in front of the full-length mirror on the back of the door. Even if she wasn't ready, she had to fake it until she could figure out what she was doing.

"Well, do I look like I belong here, Peppercorn?" she asked as she tucked the Arctic Hall cobalt neck sash under the collar of her white blouse. Her long, black hair was braided behind her neck, her pearl necklace hidden under her blouse. The black skirt of her uniform fell below her knee.

He met her gaze, offering an approving twitch of his nose. Jet tousled his tuft, packed her Elver, and headed off to Movement class.

Lara, Amber, and Gillian chatted in the hallway as Jet passed. She wanted to say something, but Amber pounced. "Oh, Lara, it's Her Majesty. I can't believe she's going to class. She must think she's too good to do something we normal students have to do."

The girls laughed, and Jet's face heated. What had she expected? She had been rude. She tried to think of something to say, but didn't know where to start. She should apologize.

"I, ah…" She swallowed. "I was out of sorts last night."

The girls ignored her and sauntered away. Jet stood in the corridor, trying to calm her racing heart. This wasn't starting off well.

As she ran to find her first class, Movement with Zephania Ruecroft, Jet couldn't help wishing someone else was in the same predicament—late. But the huge stone and marble corridor leading to the classrooms of the Humanities Wing was empty. This was terrible. She didn't choose to be here in the first place, and now she was starting her first day late. She hated appearing stupid. She breathed in panicked gulps and, as she reached the door to the classroom, she told herself to stop behaving like an idiot. Squaring her shoulders, she turned the knob.

She rushed in, hoping to escape notice, but instead the instructor stopped her at the door. She was a small woman with iron-gray hair pulled back in a harsh bun, and her black gaze was sharp through round spectacles. Her skin showed the ravages of time and, despite her petite frame which Jet towered over, the woman still intimidated her.

The professor addressed the class in an icy tone. "Ah, Her Royal Highness has deigned to grace us with her tardy presence."

Muffled giggles from the other students filled the air. Jet's palms dampened as the professor raised a single finger to quiet the class.

"I do hope whatever kept you was worth it, Princess. Now that you are five minutes late and have held up my class, perhaps you wouldn't mind taking your seat? Or do you need an engraved invitation?"

The giggles erupted into snickers. Jet ignored the other students. "I'm sorry, Professor Ruecroft. It won't happen again."

"We shall see, Princess. And to give you some motivation, you just earned your first rip." A low murmur rumbled among the students. Jet didn't know what a rip was, but could guess it wasn't good. The professor smirked as she motioned Jet toward a vacant seat.

Lara, at an adjacent table, muttered, "She is so stuck up. Now she thinks she doesn't have to follow the rules."

This was a disaster. Jet slunk next to a girl with bright-green eyes and hair the color of cork.

"I'm Charlotte Houndswood, Your Highness," the girl said under her breath and held out her hand.

Jet grabbed it like a lifeline. She wasn't sure if this girl was being kind or not, but she had little choice but to try to recover. "Please call me Jet."

Her hand shook, and her heart still boomed in her chest from the confrontation with the professor. She was upset with herself for getting off to such a poor start. She clutched at her necklace under her blouse. It warmed when she touched it, and she calmed as she thought of home.

The class snapped to attention when the professor tapped the podium. "As I was saying before I was interrupted…" All eyes once again focused on Jet, and her stomach leapt to her throat. Jet kept her gaze on the professor.

"My name is Zephania Ruecroft. I will be your Movement instructor this year. However, some of you may also know me as Master of Arctic Hall." She paused for a moment and directed her attention to Jet. "For those of you just joining us, Movement training for sport and competition is the focus of Beta Year. As you should know, Movement is based on Dunamai. Dunamai translates loosely from the ancient Greek 'power flow.' Some say it also means 'to have power.' Either way, it developed as a synthesis of human and Pelagi martial and movement arts—Greco-Roman wrestling, water grappling, East Asian martial arts, Hydorian Terebra, and fencing. Its highly stylized, fluid body movements require specialized training and rigorous practice. Dunamai intensifies in speed and endurance when practiced for competition or defense. Each student is required to compete in two tournaments, one of which must be with a partner in Synchronized Fight Flow. The other event may be of your choosing. By the end of Beta Year, you will be prepared to study Movement self-defense training." She narrowed her eyes. "Any questions?" No one responded.

"Well then, on to our first lesson. Any volunteers?" The professor's inquiry was met with silence.

Jet froze in her seat.

The professor moved from behind the podium. "It appears I shall be forced to choose...how about Her Highness?"

Jet bumped her knee on the desk as she stood and limped her way down the aisle to the professor.

"Before diving into Movement Two, the princess will demonstrate a review of last year's curriculum. Princess, assume neutral position then lead us through the Thirty-Form Fluidity Flow."

Thank goodness I learned this last year. Jet slowed her breathing and released all physical tension. Unifying mind and muscle, she abandoned all thoughts of Professor Ruecroft and her classmates. She transitioned from one stance to the next feeling her long, clean movements. From a low bow, she flowed into the final form, the thanksgiving stance. Tired but a bit more confident, she met the professor's chilling stare.

"Now the princess will assume and hold hippocampus stance with arms extended. Each of you will be required to demonstrate proficiency of this as well. It is a basic Movement Two stance, used for strengthening the legs and back and practicing strikes. While there are several variations, the princess will demonstrate the front-facing hippocampus." Ruecroft motioned her to begin.

Exhausted from the previous flow, which had taken almost twenty minutes, she did as she was told. She dropped in low and extended her arms out to the sides. Immersing herself in the position, she tried to breathe her way through the burning in her legs and back. For a bit, she could coax her muscles into submission. But then Ruecroft talked about the importance of the hippocampi stances and how holding them well demonstrated one's commitment to attaining proficiency. She droned about the importance not only of endurance, but groundedness achieved through mastery of the stances.

Jet's arms were the first to betray her. Heavy and aching with exhaustion, her back and legs soon followed. Unable to hold the position any longer, she surrendered to fatigue.

The professor stopped her lecture and addressed Jet. "Your Highness has some difficulty with commitment and groundedness. Perhaps this is to be expected."

Her nails bit into her palms. Was the professor this malicious with everyone? Jet said nothing, believing protests would be pointless.

Ruecroft crossed her arms. "I suggest you find someone who knows what they are doing to help tutor you, Princess." She dismissed Jet with a wave of her hand. "That will be all. You may return to your seat."

She refused to show her anger and embarrassment despite the titters from the students. She mustered as much dignity as she could on her way back to her seat next to Charlotte Houndswood.

Professor Ruecroft surveyed the room and asked, "Who's to be my next victim?" Her expression softened.

"Oh, yes, Miss Saberton, please join me and show the class how it's done." Ruecroft purred her introduction, "This young woman mastered Alpha-level Movement under my tutelage, passing with perfect marks. Class, Miss Morwenna Saberton is the one to watch. I wager her to be the front-runner for induction into the Society of Wave and Wing."

Miss Saberton stood at the professor's side now. "Thank you, Professor," she said.

Morwenna was stunning. Pixie in appearance with flaxen hair flowing behind her, her eyes were ice-blue and framed by the darkest, longest lashes Jet had ever seen. Morwenna melted into hippocampus stance. Her body was small but strong, athletic, and compact. She held the stance with ease. Her performance was flawless. Jet couldn't help the flash of envy inside her as she watched with the rest of the class.

The professor praised Morwenna's graceful power and inner stillness. "Thank you, Miss Saberton. That's the way it's done. You may return to your seat." Amidst energetic applause, Morwenna glided back to her empty seat.

The boy next to her said, "You do love to put on a show, Morrie."

She teased back, "The show is all for you, Will. And stop calling me Morrie. We aren't seven anymore."

Jet wished he would turn around so she could put a face to the back of his sandy-brown head atop broad shoulders and strong back.

The lesson ended without another embarrassing moment for her. She breathed a long sigh of relief when Ruecroft dismissed them. As she packed her belongings, she thought about the events of the morning and her poor performance. She was angry with the teacher for calling her out in front of everyone, and she was disappointed with herself. Lost to her thoughts and distracted, Jet rushed to leave the room and plowed straight into a solid wall of chest.

"Whoa there, Princess. I'm afraid I'm in your way."

Strong hands held her shoulders and prevented her from falling backward. Jet looked up into slate-blue eyes. Her breath caught in her throat. This was the boy who sat next to Morwenna. Will.

She croaked out an apology, "I'm sorry. I wasn't watching where I was going."

"Well, Princess, that much is obvious. But we're not so formal out here in the hallways." He released her shoulders, and she tried to recover her wits.

Her heart hammered in her chest when his grin revealed the dimple in his cheek. The lingering bad mood from Movement class melted away. She forced herself to act like everyone else and relax. "If that's the case, then maybe you could drop the 'Princess' and call me by my first name?"

"Princess Jaiette, it would be my pleasure to call you whatever name you'd like," he said. He gave her an impish bow of his head.

"I think 'Jet' will work. What should I call you?"

His left eyebrow winged up "Sorry, I should have introduced myself right off. I'm William Newcastle. Everyone around here calls me Will."

"Nice to meet you, Will. Sorry again for the collision." She thought she sounded somewhat normal, and her heart rate was leveling.

"No problem, happens all the time. Hey, what classes do you have?"

After she rattled off the list of classes, he said. "I have enComm too. Maybe we can have lunch together after class on Thursday?"

Before she could answer, they were interrupted. "Will, were you planning on keeping the princess all to yourself?"

Jet and Will pivoted toward Morwenna Saberton. She was even more beautiful up close. Standing next to her was Jet's tablemate from Movement. Charlotte was a pretty girl, but she paled in comparison to Morwenna. That would be true for anyone standing next to her.

"Morrie, she doesn't like to be called 'princess'." Will gestured to Jet. "This is *Jet*. This is Morwenna Saberton, the bane of my existence, next door neighbor, and best friend since before we could talk. I call her Morrie."

Morwenna poked him in the shoulder. "But I don't like it when he does." She flipped her hair off her shoulder. "Now, Jet, I think you met Charlotte, my roommate?" She spared the girl a glance. "And now that we have been introduced, what are you two talking about?"

"It's nice to meet you, Morwenna. Will was asking me about my classes. Speaking of class, your performance in Movement was impressive."

"Thank you. So, what classes are you taking?" When she heard Jet's schedule, Morwenna scrunched her nose. "Oh, you have enComm too? I decided not to enroll again."

Will nudged Morwenna. "That's because Morrie can't make the animals talk to her, and she's used to getting her way everywhere else."

Her eyes darkened. "Come on, Charlie, let's get to Human Studies, and maybe we'll catch up with these two later." The two girls left Will and Jet in the hallway.

Jet, surprised she had been absorbed into their little group so fast, forgot about Movement and the fact she didn't belong at Quadrivium. She wished Will would bring up having lunch again.

He picked up his bag. "Come on, I'll show you where your next class is." They strolled along, amidst a sea of students rushing to their classes. He greeted each one by name. He gestured toward a door on his right.

"Each of the classroom wings are dedicated to the four original academic disciplines Quad was founded on, but they've changed the names to reflect a more modern approach. This is the History wing, but you'll see classes here like Movement and enComm because they didn't know where else to put them. We have our meals with everyone in the Ordinary, unless you're planning on being a shut-in?" He raised his eyebrow at her, and she shook her head. He proceeded with his impromptu tour. "I think there are about a hundred and twenty Betas this year."

"And you know them all," Jet said.

He shrugged. "I like people. It would be a waste of my time at Quad if I didn't get to know them."

She hadn't met anyone like him. But who was she kidding? She hadn't met that many people in her safe haven below the Shield. She struggled to come up with a response, but was saved when he yelled to someone down the hall.

"Hey, Traven! Get back here." The boy trotted back to where he and Jet stopped.

He was tall and broad-shouldered like Will. He had dark eyes and hair, and an easy grin as he approached them. He dropped his heavy pack with a thud onto the marble floor in front of them. He bent over and grabbed an Elver from his pack. "Yeah, Newcastle?"

"Let me introduce you to the princess," Will said. "Chace Traven, meet Jet."

"Yeah, okay." Chace made a formal bow, peeked up from the bent position, and winked at Jet. "A pleasure beyond comprehension, Your Majesty." He straightened and chuckled with Will.

She blinked and rushed to answer as the stares from the other students in the corridor were growing embarrassing. "Just 'Jet.' Please, don't be so formal."

He shook his head. "Uh, I was kidding. Newcastle here is a lord or something, but I don't stand by convention."

She felt like an idiot. Of course he was joking with her. She could think of nothing to say to recover.

Chace checked his Elver. "We need to meet real fast about debate practice. Do you have a minute?"

"Yeah, we do. You need serious work, Traven."

"Thanks for the assessment, Captain Newcastle. I'm giving my best."

"Your best needs to be better. I don't plan on losing any matches this year."

Chace rolled his eyes. "Everyone is waiting in the atrium."

Will leaned closer to Jet. "Sorry, I've got to go, but I'll see you around, Princess." He gave her a wink.

Her two classmates sauntered away. She'd acted like a moron when Chace made his joke. As she made her way through the bustling corridor to her next class, she tried to ignore the stares from the students passing her. Peppercorn's advice to relax echoed in her head. She had to try.

Before she'd left her room this morning, the only thing she experienced was dread. And while Ruecroft's class had cemented her fear, she'd lost it with Will. Jet realized she was actually excited about what came next. Maybe she could pull this off.

Nine

"I didn't see any obvious way that could lead us to the Sagesse chambers unless we stroll over there and knock," Jet complained to Peppercorn. "It's been one week, and I don't have a lot of time during the days to wander around either. I have no idea who is following me, and on top of that, every person at this school watches me wherever I go. They aren't all friends either."

She thought of Lara and Amber as she settled at her desk. She had an essay due tomorrow for Ruecroft, and she needed a perfect score. She couldn't afford to give Ruecroft another reason to pick on her.

"Your complaints grow tiresome. You're here to do a job."

Jet counted to ten before she responded. "I realize that, Peppercorn, but I have three jobs to do at the same time, none of which I can neglect." She inhaled. His honesty could be exasperating, but still, she realized she was taking her frustration out on him. "I'm sorry. This isn't ideal for you either."

"I've quite enjoyed my time here so far, actually. There are more animals for me to visit with, and the hunting is excellent. And I believe the same holds true for you with those your own age and the freedom you have here. You've settled in. It's time to work."

"Okay, what do you propose with my current limitations?" Jet asked.

"Your newness will wear off soon. At that point, you might become more anonymous. Until that time, I suggest you query your fellow students about their parents and their position on the monarchy. Also, ask about the animals. But be subtle, Jet."

"I'll try. How about in the meantime, you scope out the tunnels again and see what you can find? I know you didn't have a lot of luck earlier this week, but maybe there will be fewer animals in the tunnels and you can be more anonymous too. If Bevan is to be believed, there is a labyrinth beneath our feet, leading everywhere including the Sagesse chambers. Can you investigate some more?"

Peppercorn snorted his answer. Jet took it as a 'yes'.

~ * ~

Jet walked into enComm—by far her favorite class already. Admittedly, it helped quite a bit that Will took the class too. She had met a few more people but none she felt as comfortable with as him. As she chose one of the empty chairs, placed in a circle today, she kept an eye on the door for him. When he arrived, his expression was creased with a deep frown. A boy she hadn't met yet came in right behind him.

"All I'm saying, Newcastle, is that your delivery needs work."

Will whipped around to the boy and poked him in the chest. "Back off, Furax. You don't know what you're talking about."

"No, I know plenty. You just don't want to hear it," the boy said. His white-blond hair hung like a mop in his eyes, which were the color of burnt straw. He pushed the scraggly strands off his forehead.

"I'm team captain, Eric, and if you don't like it, take it up with Stemp."

"You don't accept any constructive criticism, Will. You won't lose your edge if you listen to feedback from the team." Eric crossed his arms. "And I'm not complaining to our faculty rep. You should be able to handle this situation better as debate team captain. We're a team, and that means all of the members are important."

Furax slid into the seat on Jet's right. Will dropped into the seat on her left. Jet fidgeted with her Elver.

Will grabbed a water from his bag. "Hi, Princess. Are you settling in pretty well?"

"Yes. Thank you."

"Listen, I'm sorry about all that. Sometimes I can get a little intense." His ears reddened.

"It wasn't just intense; it was autocratic." The words were out of her mouth before she could stop them. She was about to apologize when Furax covered his laugh with a cough, and Will's brow furrowed.

"I'm sorry. It's none of my business," Jet said.

"Don't be sorry. It's on me." He leaned forward and peered around her desk to Furax. "Hey, Eric, she's right. I was being a bully. I'll do better."

"Whatever, Newcastle," Eric said.

To try to ease the tension between the two boys, she said, "Eric, I'm Jet. I saw you with your keep in the last class, when we practiced last year's curriculum. Her name is Giselle, right?"

"Yeah," Eric said.

"She's a honey badger, isn't she?"

He shifted in his seat. "She's mean too. They live up to the reputation."

Before she could ask him about Giselle and the animals disappearing, the door closed behind the professor with a clack.

"All right, class, welcome back to all of you. Last session we reviewed Alpha year curriculum. Today we will go with something a bit more advanced."

Jet was forever grateful Professor Miles was teaching enComm. She had known him most of her life.

"As I reviewed previously, Encephalic Communication— enComm—is not only an important practical skill, it is also a precious gift. This special bond between Pelagi and animals connects us as protectors, partners, and friends. Over the past few centuries, enComm partnerships have been responsible for advances in medicine, biology, physics, and linguistics, just to name a few. Yet, many Pelagi opt to forsake this rare gift. Some do not even communicate with their keeps. Your keep is your animal partner. It requires work, diligence, and focus to uphold this partnership. And I will not mislead you—there is an element of talent.

"Last year we worked solely with keeps, and judging your work from our last time together you all mastered that quite nicely—your badger being the exception, Mr. Furax, but that is not unusual in the species."

Professor Miles entered the circle beside Jet's and strode to the center of the circle of chairs.

He stood beside a massive, draped rectangular object on a platform. He removed the drape. "We will begin with our reserved, aquatic friend here."

Everyone except Jet let out a gasp. At last, something she was good at. The clamorous protest intensified around her.

Someone said, "He's out of his mind."

Another agreed, "It's hardly been done."

Professor Miles held up a calming hand. "No, I have not gone 'round the bend. And Mr. Traven, not only has it been done, it has been done quite frequently by advanced enCommers. So without further ado, everyone meet Jax. He is a juvenile tiger shark from South Africa."

The shark circled through the greenish-blue water. Jet guessed he was about two meters long, and the tank would soon be too small for him. Light green skin counter-shaded with a pale yellow underside, Jax still had the dark lines and spots of a young shark.

Will raised his hand. "And you believe this thing is going to talk to us?"

Professor Miles rested his hand on the tank. "Perhaps our first lesson should be referring to the animal as *Jax*, and not 'this thing'," he said. "To succeed in advanced enComm, there must be mutual respect, regardless of whether you like one another. Jax may not connect with anyone today, but there is a lesson in that. If we wish to advance our studies, we mustn't stop trying.

"We have had frequent, positive outcomes with juveniles, and working with Jax will help improve our skills so we can advance to adult sharks. Yes, the average adult shark is reticent and resistant to enComm, but communication with adult sharks is far from impossible. Actually, it is well documented in the scientific community. All of you need to remember that enComm is imperative. If we can't partner with the animals, we can't guard the waters. This is especially true of sharks. With the greatest electric sensitivity of any animal on this planet, sharks are an invaluable asset in the navigation of currents, in finding people lost at sea, and one day, I believe they will help us predict earthquakes. Even now, studies are being done to test whether electromagnetic fields given off by rock beneath the planet could predict seismic activity months in advance. Sharks can detect trace fields. If they trust us, imagine the outcome—advance warning to save entire communities at risk." Professor Miles rubbed his hands together.

Eric shook his head. "No one will succeed at this lesson. I doubt anyone in this class is going to get that thing—I mean, Jax—to tell us anything."

Jax shot to the surface, and his conical snout cut the water with a splash. He remained there for several seconds. Then, he swam to the side of the tank, snout to glass, facing Jet, Will, and Eric.

The shark's piercing eyes focused on her. The classroom, the students, Professor Miles, floated far off into the distance. She was alone with the shark now. He was the first to speak.

"All of them are afraid of me. I can hear their hearts racing and feel twitches and trembles. But you—you aren't afraid."

She slowed her breath. *"I know you won't hurt me, or anyone for that matter, so I have no reason to be afraid."*

Jax stayed there for several minutes, snout on glass, talking with her. Then, as suddenly as he had come to the glass, he plunged and began swimming in circles again.

Will tapped her arm. "Where were you? You totally were in a zone."

"Sorry. I was out of it for a second."

The other students resumed their protests to Professor Miles.

"That's enough. I've heard your concerns. I doubt it will change my goals for this class, however. Now before we begin our visualization exercises, I wish to ask Miss Lennox a question."

The entire class focused on her.

"What did Jax say to you?" he asked.

Eric sneered. "Please, Professor. There is no way the princess got that beast to tell her anything."

She raised her chin. "Jax told me his mother was wounded in a shark-finning attack, but fortunately she escaped. She and Jax were rescued and brought here by Fin and Feather. His mother is recuperating at the Eripium. The scholarch is keeping Jax temporarily until his mother recovers." She paused. "Oh, and he would like some salmon."

The class laughed.

"There is no way to prove anything she said is even remotely true," Eric said. "Besides, juvenile sharks don't spend any time with their mothers. They are on their own almost immediately after birth. Sharks aren't pack or herd animals. The princess doesn't know what she's talking about."

"Mr. Furax, I have heard about enough from you today," snapped Professor Miles. "Your information is quite wrong. The sharks surrounding Pelagiana exhibit heightened maternal instincts and clan behavior. This has happened in rare instances elsewhere on the planet. We try to talk to them so we can understand why some behave this way and some don't." The professor moved around the circle of chairs. "Mr. Traven, would you be so good as to retrieve the sealed note from my desk and bring it back to your seat?"

Jet bit her lip.

Chace returned to his seat with the note.

"Mr. Traven, please open the envelope and read it aloud to the class."

Chace ripped open the letter, an official Quadrivium missive. He cleared his throat and read aloud:

Dear Professor Miles,
I thank you for taking Jax to class with you today and taking care of him. I will be at the Eripium checking on his mother if you need to reach me.
Yours Most Gratefully,
Glaucilla Wolverhampton

Ten

By the time Jet and Will arrived at the Ordinary for lunch break, the entire student body was buzzing about her ability to communicate with sharks. She tried to shake off the stares of the other students. She'd dealt with worse growing up in the palace compound.

The Ordinary was a common area in the main building of Quadrivium where all residential houses could dine together. Each house also had what was called a family dining room for meals exclusive to its residents. Will and Jet decided to eat in the main dining room so they could catch up with Morwenna and Charlotte, who were members of Pacific residential college.

The food was served cafeteria style. Jet went through the lines with Will before they chose their table. Since she'd skipped breakfast, she was starved and chose a cheese tray and a wakame and cucumber salad. Most Pelagi food had evolved from their history interacting with humans. The cheese came from the cows on the dairy farms that dotted the countryside at the surface of their island outside Indigo City.

Food was cultivated in a similar fashion to humans' crops and farming techniques. At the surface of the lake opposite of Indigo City, there were many rural communities, which provided milk, cheese, and eggs to all Pelagiana, both above and below the surface. The Pelagi had also learned the benefits of seaweed consumption far earlier than their human brethren, and Jet made it a point to eat the nutrient-rich sea grasses as often as possible.

Will gestured with his tray to the tables. "Where would you like to sit?"

"No idea—wherever."

"Let's sit at the Arctic table," he said. "It'll annoy Morrie that she has to sit here with us instead of us sitting at Pacific with her."

The five long tables each had a runner of a different color denoting to which residential college the table belonged. Jet and Will headed for Arctic, with its long, cobalt cloth in the center of the table.

Her curiosity got the better of her. Now, she thought, how to be subtle? "Umm, how long have you and Morwenna been seeing each other?" *So much for subtle.*

He squirmed in his seat. "It's not like that with us. I've known Morrie for as long as I can remember. She was always running the show when we were kids. Our parents live next door to one another, so it was inevitable we were thrown together a lot. We travel to and from school together during holidays, and besides, it's nice to have someone to hang with."

He picked up a piece of bread from his tray. "It's always nice to make new friends." He tilted his head.

His words warmed her from the inside out, and it dawned on her she should say something nice too. "Thanks, Will. I completely agree."

Morwenna and Charlotte arrived with their own lunch trays. "Why do you force me to sit at this table, Will?" Morwenna slipped into the seat next to him.

"Because it's important you get out of your comfort zone." He put an apple on Morwenna's tray. "Besides, it'll do you good to sit at a winning table for a change, Morrie."

"Please. When it's time for Aquaticup, your growlers don't stand a chance against my rorquals." She placed her napkin in her lap. Charlotte sat beside Jet.

"You got me last year, but I don't make the same mistake twice. You'd better make sure you're ready. The growlers will dominate the games this year," he said.

Charlotte unwrapped her silverware. "We heard you talked to a shark, Prin—uh, Jet. Sorry. It'll be a while before I get used to thinking of you as one of us."

She squeezed a lemon into her tea. "Don't worry. I'll answer to pretty much anything, Charlotte."

"Call me Charlie, everyone else does. So, did you *enComm* with a shark, or was that a rumor?"

The Ordinary was crowded, and again people were gawking. She tried to ignore it. "Yes. I did. His name is Jax. He's just a baby, and his mother was injured. He was hungry."

Will jumped into the conversation. "You should have seen her, Charlie. Her eyes got all serious and focused. No one in the class knew what the hell was going on because they were all whining about having to try to talk to it in the first place. Then, out of the blue, Professor Miles asked Jet what it said, and the entire class went crazy when she says the thing was hungry."

"That doesn't seem like too much of stretch. Aren't all sharks hungry all the time?" Morwenna tapped her fingers on the table.

"Don't mind her, Jet," he said. "Morrie's just jealous because she can't get any animal to talk to her after the first conversation." He nudged Morwenna with his shoulder.

"I don't understand why talking to animals is such a big deal," she said. "I mean, really, what good is that skill anyway?"

"I know a lot people don't think it's important to keep up the old traditions, but I think we need to keep them alive. Our relationship with the animals helps foretell storms even before our modern technology can. The animals become our allies in our sworn protection of Aquatica in so many ways. We partner with whales and dolphins to help with the Guardianship of Aquatica. A side benefit is they help protect us when we are below in the waters or out in the world among humans. We are able to find out what the humans are doing because of these animals, and knowing what is going on outside Pelagiana is invaluable. If we lose the ability to speak to them, we are losing a precious connection." Jet couldn't fathom life without Peppercorn. She hated the thought of the animals not trusting them and what that could mean.

Morwenna and Will sat stone-faced. She must sound stupid to them. She hadn't remembered her own warnings to just relax, and now they probably thought she was crazy intense.

Charlotte broke the silence. "You sure are passionate, Jet."

"Yeah," Will said. "It can't be a bad thing to believe in something so strongly." He grinned. "Although I'm not sure I like being lumped in with this surface dweller next to me." He nudged Morwenna again.

"Very funny." She focused on Jet. "I get what you're saying, but our life in Indigo City is a lot different than what you're used to in Aurealia below. Once you visit the city, you'll see how antiquated the idea of our sworn duty to Aquatica is. You have to understand that we have changed. Aquatica really doesn't need us. The humans have evolved to survive on their own. We embrace modern technology, and we don't care what the rest of the world is doing or why. We just want to *be*. Besides, my father says it's dangerous to venture outside in the human world and thinks there should be laws against it."

Will and Charlie said nothing, and Jet had no idea if they agreed with Morwenna. Jet reached for the conch pearl at her throat and thought of home. It wasn't her job to change Morwenna's mind. But she could ask Morwenna about the animals and monarchy. She was Saberton's daughter, after all.

"So you think Pelagiana doesn't need to bother with the ancient laws?"

Will answered, "I guess some people think that way, like Morrie, but I don't think it's a big deal if people disagree with the Sagesse or the monarchy. My father says that's been going on since Neptune created Pelagiana. I doubt it matters much either way."

Jet figured this was how a lot of people felt if the decisions being made didn't affect daily life. Unfortunately, she wasn't so lucky. Every decision the Sagesse and her father made had the potential to ruin her future. She didn't think she could ask any more questions without arousing suspicion. "Well, I guess there is a lot I have to see and learn in Indigo City."

Morwenna brightened. "That would be amazing. Showing the princess around the city for the first time would be very cool." She pressed her lips together for a moment. "You'll have to explore the city and see the beach, and—"

Will laughed. "Whoa, Morrie. Give her a chance to breathe."

Charlie giggled. "She probably needs longer than a week before she makes plans to visit anywhere. Besides, her first free weekend she might have other ideas of how to spend her time?"

He responded before Jet could. "That's true. I have an idea. Everyone is supposed to come to my parents' house for the Welcome party during Family Faire Weekend. We'll make a weekend of it, and you can explore with Morrie. I was going to ask you to visit anyway."

He planned to ask her to visit his house? Morwenna's answer explained his reasons.

"That's a great idea. Now she can find out what the problem is with Svashi." She patted his forearm.

"Who is Svashi?" Jet asked.

"She's Will's pet sea mink." Morwenna wrinkled her nose. "Everyone makes a big deal of the sea minks because they are extinct everywhere else, and Will's family is entrusted to care for the last two. Now that Atlas is missing from below the Shield, it's an even bigger job for the Newcastles." She sat up straight. "Hey, that should appeal to you, Jet, because his family is one of the original guardians of Aquatica and they take that pretty seriously—in his house, anyway."

"Anyway..." Will shot Morwenna a pointed glare. "Svashi has been acting strangely the last couple of weeks, and I figure since you can get a shark to talk to you, you might be able to do the same with my mink. I'm not the best enCommer, and my parents are okay, and Svashi is keeping to herself. She says she's okay, but it'd be great to have your opinion."

"I'd love to talk to Svashi for you," Jet said.

Morwenna shifted and peered around the table. "Good, it's settled. I get to show Princess Jaiette off to Indigo City, and she can help Will figure out that stubborn animal. You're coming too, Charlie."

Morwenna was bossy. Jet tried not to let it bother her that the only reason Morwenna suggested the visit to Indigo City was to show her off. Morwenna deserved a chance. She couldn't afford to offend anyone at this point. She was trying to accomplish a mission.

Morwenna interrupted her thoughts. "I'm not trying to be rude, Princess, but what exactly are you doing up here anyway?"

"Come on, Morrie! That's a terrible question to ask her," Will said.

"I'm sorry. I was just curious. I mean, I know the party line from my father. The princess is supposed to be learning among the people, blah, blah. But what does she have to say about it." She cocked her head at Jet.

She wasn't prepared for this question. She had no idea how to answer it, since she really hadn't chosen to be here in the first place. She reminded herself she was smart and forced her brain to work. "So, your father is Roger Saberton?" Deflecting the question by asking another was a good idea.

"Yes. Daddy is extremely well respected in the Sagesse and all Indigo City, actually. It's strange we haven't met before, since Daddy and King Magnus are such good friends. They do keep you royals sheltered down there, don't they?" Morwenna raised her eyebrow.

Anger spiked. "My father was following a tradition Neptune himself established. I'm here now because things change." Her teeth clenched.

"Oh, I'm not trying to offend you, Princess. It's just I'm a terrible gossip, and I love to be the first with the story."

She tried to let go of her anger and searched her mind for a subject change. "Before your sea mink stopped talking to you, Will, she didn't tell you anything about the other animals disappearing, did she?"

"No." He scratched his head. "Why would she?"

"Atlas is missing, and he is one of the last sea minks as well. It's curious."

"It's no big deal. My father says it's up to the animals when they come back, and it's a waste of time to worry about them," Morwenna chimed in.

Will scowled. "Of course your father thinks that, Morrie. None of you have any luck with animals."

Before Morwenna could reply, Scholarch Wolverhampton appeared in the huge, arched entryway of the Ordinary. "Students, please, may I have your attention?" She clapped her hands to those still talking.

The scholarch remained still until the few hundred or so students quieted. When at last she had silence, she began her daily announcements. "As you are all aware, the orientations for the various student societies begin next week. If you are interested in joining, you will find information for each in your residential common rooms." Madame Wolverhampton drew herself up. "As there are so many from which to choose, I would caution our new students to research extensively for that society or club which is the best fit. Joining one of these organizations is quite rewarding, of course, but also requires a time commitment. Any of you unsure if you can handle both society membership and your studies mustn't feel pressure to join. Our primary focus should remain on our training." Her smile widened. "Now, our most exclusive organization, of course, is the Society of Wave and Wing. Orientation will be held next week in the atrium. Membership for SWW is by invitation only." Madame Wolverhampton's face darkened, and she clasped her hands in front of her. "A cautionary word about the secret societies here at Quadrivium. I realize there are traditions thousands of years in the making that must be upheld, but I encourage our society leadership to act responsibly. The recent rash of pranks and hazing has gotten out of hand to the point of severe injury to several students. This sort of behavior will be met with swift and severe punishment."

Scholarch Wolverhampton scanned the crowd and brightened again. "Now, as I believe your afternoon classes begin shortly, I encourage you to finish lunch quickly. Thank you."

As Jet finished her salad, she thought about the Society of Wave and Wing. If she were invited, she would be the first royal. She couldn't believe she was even contemplating joining anything, but if she did, it would go a long way to proving she belonged here at Quadrivium.

Morwenna handed Charlie her glass to fill with water. "Well, Jet doesn't have to worry about beating everyone out for SWW. What about you, Will? Are you going to the orientation?"

Jet broke in. "Why don't I have to worry about getting into the Society of Wave and Wing?"

Morwenna shrugged. "I mean, why would you even try? You are going to be the queen. Any reason for joining SWW is moot for you. It's supposed to help us with connections and getting internships after

Omega year. I can't imagine why you'd steal the opportunity away from one of us when you have all that already."

She hadn't thought of this. Was Morwenna right?

"Don't listen to Morwenna," Will said. "She's fiercely competitive and tries to get in anyone's head that might beat her for something." He beamed down at Morwenna.

"Will Newcastle! You are the most competitive person I know. I don't come close to your intensity."

"Are you interested in membership into SWW, Jet?" Will asked.

"I'd like to earn a spot because of something I did on my own. Not because I'm a royal."

"I think that's really admirable," Charlie said.

He nodded. "I agree with Charlie. You should try it."

Morwenna sniffed. "As long as it doesn't bother you that some people will think you're being unfair, it certainly doesn't bother me. I like the idea of competing and beating a princess. Besides, after your performance in Movement class the other day, I doubt any of us has anything to seriously worry about."

Jet had never met anyone so bold and outright aggressive.

He raised his hand. "My god, Morwenna. Leave her alone. She doesn't know your personality yet or that you're joking most of the time."

She shrugged again and picked up her fork. Jet hadn't noticed what Morwenna had brought to the table to eat until that moment. She speared the barramundi and ate with gusto. Clearly, she didn't share Jet's objections to eating animals they could communicate with.

She met Jet's stare. The smile didn't quite reach her glacier-blue eyes. Jet thought for the first time that he read his friend wrong. Jet recognized fierce determination when she saw it. Morwenna would do whatever it took to beat Jet for a spot in the Society of Wave and Wing. In this instance, she realized, Morwenna wasn't joking. Jet was up for the challenge.

Eleven

A couple days later, as Jet headed to another class, she was still thinking of her interaction with Morwenna. Jet's classes met every other day so she hadn't seen Will or Morwenna again since. She had passed Charlie in the hall a few times but hadn't had a chance to talk to her.

Buoyed by Charlie's and Will's easy attitudes, Jet determined to stay positive. Everyone was different. Some were more serious, competitive, or friendly than others, and all this experience at Quadrivium was going to help her better read different personalities. Her mother had often warned Jet to judge others on their actions, not their words. Morwenna was probably just being friendly in her own way. Jet would try to avoid negative judgments.

By the time she turned down the hallway of the Sciences Wing, she felt better. Someone called her name from behind her. Pivoting fast, she bumped into Charlie and Morwenna.

"Ugh, sorry," she said. "I can be a bit clumsy." That was an understatement, but she didn't need to advertise it.

"Shouldn't a princess be more graceful?" Morwenna asked. The other girl flitted down the hallway.

Charlie straightened her collar. "Don't let Morwenna bother you."

Jet shifted the pack on her shoulder. "She didn't. Why would she?"

"Oh, good. Sometimes she comes on too strong or talks without thinking, like the other day at lunch, but that's just who she is. She's not a bad sort at all. She just likes to get her way, and most times her way is better anyway. This is the second year we are rooming together, and I just wanted to let you know she doesn't mean anything by it. She is amazing at almost everything she tries—being competitive comes naturally to her. She was first in our class of Alphas last year. She even beat Will by a point. No one thought that was possible. It still bothers him. He's determined to win this year."

"I don't mind competitive people at all, and I like Morwenna. I like the idea that knowing her will bring out my best too." They stopped outside the classroom. "Is that why you two are roommates?"

"Morwenna can be very persuasive, and I like being on her good side," Charlie said.

"I get that."

"Great. Now what's your next class?"

"Human Studies with Professor Stemp."

Charlie's nose scrunched. "I've heard some Gamma years say it's a bore. I've got a free study period now. I'll see you later. Good luck."

Jet didn't know anyone in this class. She retrieved the Elver from her bag, placed her palm on it. It connected to Eelfare immediately, and she read the day's scheduled events. The other students found their places, and everyone was talking to one another.

She was grateful for the distraction when the door slammed shut behind the professor, and then her mouth dropped open at the sight of him. Professor Stemp was easily six and a half feet tall with a barrel chest and flaming-red hair flowing down his back. His beard grew long below his chin. He had several silver rings on his massive fingers, and a blue stone glinted from his ear. His robes were purple, which clashed wildly with his hair and beard. At least his appearance wasn't boring.

"All right, you monkeys, let's get started," Professor Stemp said.

At the tittering of laughter, he lifted a bushy, red eyebrow. "A monkey is an animal with several different varieties not indigenous to our island but is widely prolific almost everywhere else on earth. They are silly, loud, sometimes destructive, creatures. Therefore, I find the comparison to your population quite apt."

Jet wasn't sure what to do with this information.

"In this class, you'll learn about life outside our little island. That tidbit about the monkey is just an example." Professor Stemp lumbered across the room and threw a battered canvas bag onto the ancient desk at the head of the classroom.

"Now, because I am required by the Sagesse to teach you our grisly history with the humans—even if I think we're dwelling on ancient history…" The professor snorted. "I'll get that part over with today before we move on to the amazing wonders the outside world holds for us."

He grabbed his Elver from the canvas bag. It appeared like a tiny deck of cards in his massive hands. He touched it. "Your Elvers should now connect to mine through Eelfare. Please use it to let me know you are here."

Jet touched the side of her Elver, indicating her presence for roll call in *Beta Human Studies, Time: 1405, Instr.: Stemp.*

"Now, who can tell me why we're here?" the professor asked.

Finally, someone raised his hand.

The professor checked his Elver and said, "Bertrand Cox. Unfortunate name there, Bertie. Go ahead and answer."

Bertie Cox was a slight boy with pale hair. His voice quavered as he responded. "We're here to learn about humans?"

"A little too literal for my taste, Bertie. I was referring to the fact we didn't always hole ourselves away on this island. I was asking how did we get to be here, in this situation?" Professor Stemp waved his hands in the air. "Never mind. I'll do the telling, and you all just take notes. We'll get to the good stuff sooner this way."

He winked at the class. He kind of reminded her of her father—a lot of bluster with very little bite.

"You all know our history, but I'm required, like I said, to review it. So listen up and know that this information might crop up on a future exam." He lowered his large frame onto the desk, which creaked under the weight.

Jet touched her Elver and a transcript of the professor's words appeared and would be saved for her to study.

"Neptune used his divine powers to create our island. From a magical conch shell, he brought forth a giant pearl. Neptune lowered this Baroque below the surface of the water, and from it our island of Pelagiana was born. Also from the pearl came our Shield, or Paragon, guarding the bubble of life which houses Aurelia below Indigo Lake."

She listened, although she understood why some people said the class would be boring. Everyone in Pelagiana already knew their origins. Still, she clasped the necklace beneath her shirt. The tiny piece of the Baroque was safe where it was supposed to be, and she was keenly aware of her duty to it.

He clapped his huge hands together, startling the class. Several people jolted in their desks. "So, Neptune gave us Pelagiana as a place to come and live away from prying human eyes, but to do our sworn duty to protect the waters of the earth, it was necessary to live among them. We all went on quite nicely for a long stretch of time. This should be evident, as we are now half-human."

The class laughed, and he waved a hand to silence them.

"Most of our ancient ancestors were smart and kept the fact we had special talents to ourselves. This was easy, since we appear human. Living side-by-side with humans, naturally, they learned of our abilities. We helped with navigation and saved sailors from sinking ships. Before modern technology, we even used our ability with animals to warn the humans of impending storms. There were some humans who wanted control of that gift. That's when the trouble began."

He cleared his throat. "As an aside, you all should know by now that, just as with our population, there are evil individuals among the humans. So around two thousand years ago, power-thirsty men decided they wanted to use us. That time period is what we call the Persecutio."

Again, while she was well aware of all of this, she had fallen under the spell of Professor Stemp's storytelling.

"Can anyone tell me what *naumachia* means?" He narrowed his eyes and homed in on Bertie again. "What about you, Cox?"

"A mock naval battle staged by the ancient Romans for sport."

"Ho, ho, ho, I might have misjudged you, Cox."

Professor Stemp put his Elver on the desk. "Once our gifts were discovered by the humans, and we were still too naïve to hide them, the Romans had the perverted pleasure of capturing Pelagi among them and forcing them to perform in these battles. Those of our ancestors who survived the battles were killed anyway."

He stroked his beard. "An interesting aside in all of this is that the ancient Romans were quite advanced. They built tunnels below the surface of the earth for sewage or escape passages. We Pelagi employed this idea underneath the lakebed and Indigo City itself. Anyway, back to ancient Rome...with some good humans helping, the remaining Pelagi escaped detection in these tunnels and moved on." His hands fell to his sides.

"And that is how our dwindling numbers ended up here back on Pelagiana. We've had a good, long sulk for over two thousand years and replenished our population to the point I think it's damn crowded in Indigo City. Besides, hiding here was not Neptune's intention for us. 'Least, I don't think it was, since we're supposed to be guardians of Aquatica." He hefted his weight off the desk. "Hard to guard anything when you aren't in the middle of it. Wouldn't you say, Cox?"

"Yes, sir."

Jet thought Roger Saberton would not agree with Professor Stemp's opinion at all. She wondered if he knew that Professor Stemp was condoning Pelagi leaving the island to fulfill their duty.

The professor picked up the Elver and touched one side. On the giant wall screen behind him, a model of the Earth appeared and revolved. She leaned forward.

"Well, now that we have all that nonsense over with, let's get on to the exciting stuff." He gestured to the Earth behind him. "We'll begin with simple geography and go from there."

Twelve

"I couldn't believe it, Mother. The class was so boring. The professor just sat at her desk and watched us read. She didn't move the entire hour! We didn't even get to discuss the play."

In her room, Elver in her lap, Jet filled her mother in on the rest of her day after Human Studies.

"But what about your other classes besides World Literature? How is Peppercorn settling in? What about the other students?" Queen Phoebe asked.

"I like Human Studies and enComm best. I did meet one boy named Will Newcastle, and he's very nice." She couldn't stop the smile.

"Oh? Your father and I are well acquainted with his parents. He's a nice boy. Tell me more."

"Nothing to tell. He was friendly, and it was nice."

Her mother didn't say anything, only raised her eyebrows.

"Anyway, Peppercorn is doing well. He must have found access to food because he came back early this morning, fat and sleepy. He's been asleep on my desk chair since I got in the room. Haven't had a chance to ask him if he met any more animals in his travels."

"That reminds me," Queen Phoebe said. "Your father would like you to check in with him late tomorrow."

"I'll be sure to clear my schedule."

"Jaiette, this is difficult for him. We miss you, darling. Try to understand his side of things."

"Mother, let's not do this right now. I'd rather talk about something else." She avoided talking about her mission, as so far she had failed miserably in coming up with any information.

"All right. Tell me more about what you think of Will Newcastle? Is he smart?"

She could tell where this line of questioning was headed. A knock on her door saved her. "Mom, we have to talk later—someone's knocking."

"Okay. But one more thing before we hang up."

"What, Mother?"

"You like it there, don't you?"

That was a loaded question she wasn't ready to answer. "I love you. Bye!"

Queen Phoebe was still laughing when Jet clicked the conversation closed.

She bounced off the bed and opened the door. Morwenna and Charlie stood in the corridor. Jet gestured them in.

"Hi, Jaiette." Morwenna said. "We didn't see you for dinner in the Ordinary, so Charlie thought we should check on you to make sure you weren't buried under a mountain of books."

Jet shook her head. "No. I just decided on something quick here."

Morwenna strolled around the room, and paused at the stack of books and papers on the desk by the window. She made her way to Jet's bed. "I hope you aren't one of those serious people who study all the time. You could get boring." She smirked and lowered her pixie-like frame onto the mattress.

"I don't know what I am yet since this is still my first week."

Charlie leaned against the door. "Cut yourself some slack, Jet. My first year I was so homesick for Indigo City, I left every weekend I was allowed. But I found out that wasn't really helping me adjust."

"She was practically invisible the first term, and I had to teach her the error of her ways before it was too late," Morwenna said.

"Yes, it was Morwenna who bullied me into joining whatever I could and getting involved with the student groups open to Alphas," Charlie said.

"We're here to do the same to you."

"So you admit to being a bully?" Charlie teased.

"Of course I bully, but only when it's for the other person's good."

Morwenna must have been a great roommate to Charlie, since she was so shy.

Jet fixed a pillow. "How do you propose to keep me from burying myself in here?"

"Well, we were curious if you'd chosen any other groups or societies to go after?" Morwenna asked.

"I haven't made any final decisions other than the Society of Wave and Wing, but I was going to read up on them tonight before I decided. What about you two?"

For once, Morwenna let Charlie speak first. "Well, I am already a member of the Apollonian Octet. It's really fun, and we rehearse two days a week. We sing at all formal school functions. I'm also interested in the Society of Wave and Wing. I'm going to the orientation to check it out." Charlie wandered over to one of the chairs by the window and settled herself in.

She stretched out her legs. She was, in fact, quite pretty—golden skin and chin-length tawny hair with sparkling hazel eyes. Her slightly crooked teeth were appealing behind a warm smile.

"What about you, Morwenna? Are there any societies or clubs that interest you?" Jet asked.

"Every one of them interests me, but I haven't centered on one in particular." She looked down at long fingers and elegant pink nails. "Of course, I fully expect to be tapped for a secret society." She glanced over at Charlie a mischievous light sparkled in her eyes. "I'm hoping it will be the Society of Cloak and Veil."

Charlie gasped. "Morwenna, that isn't funny. Cloak and Veil meets in the tombs and, if the rumors are true, they might be behind all the animals disappearing! Why would you want to be tapped by them?"

"Why wouldn't I want to be tapped by the oldest and most secret of all secret societies?" Morwenna smoothed her blouse.

"Who said Cloak and Veil has something to do with the missing animals?" Jet hadn't heard this before. This could be a lead.

Morwenna waved it away. "If all rumors are to be believed, then Will and I are secretly engaged, and you, Princess, are at Quad because your parents kicked you out of the palace. You have to be careful what and who you believe."

"Got it. I just wondered about the animals and if anyone had any thoughts on them."

"Not any serious thoughts." Morwenna shrugged. "It isn't that big a deal. And Cloak and Veil and the other secret societies have far more important things to worry about than some silly animals."

Jet held back from questioning her further, for now. She couldn't be too obvious. She switched the topic. "I don't understand what tapping is?"

"During the rush period, you spend time with the society you'd like to join. If you're chosen, they 'tap' you in the middle of the night. Traditionally we call this 'tap night.'"

"It's a big deal, and even the professors and staff get involved," Charlie said, her eyes bright.

Morwenna tossed a lock of silvery-blonde hair over her shoulder. "No one knows when they're coming to tap and no one knows who's in the society, because when they tap you, the members wear masks. The new pledges are blindfolded, whisked off to their lair, and sworn to secrecy. The secret societies in Pelagiana are some of the most influential and powerful organizations we have. And membership remains a secret even after members graduate." She kneeled on Jet's bed. "My father told me that the politics of Indigo City is overseen by more members of Cloak and Veil than any other society. That kind of influence guarantees success." Her eyes glittered.

"So I have to assume your dad is a member?" Jet asked.

"How would I know?" She crossed her arms. "If my father is a member, he wouldn't tell anyone, including his children." She tilted her head. "When it comes to it, I wouldn't tell my kids either. They choose their members carefully, and no one has betrayed Cloak and Veil in over two hundred years. I wouldn't like to be the first one to do so."

Jet shivered. "This all sounds kind of dark and serious for a school club, especially if Cloak and Veil has something to do with the missing animals."

"I don't think those animals are missing. They are just being difficult. And it might seem silly to someone who has their entire life mapped out like you do. I mean, really, you're going to be the queen."

"Really, what does that mean, Morwenna?" Charlie asked.

"It means that the princess doesn't have to worry about her future after she finishes here at Quadrivium. But we do, and membership in one of the clubs can benefit us with connections when our time comes."

Charlie snorted. "You have a lot of room to talk, Morwenna. You're a member of one of the first families in Indigo City. I can't think you'll have a tough time getting help along the way when it comes time for you to choose a direction in life."

Surprised at her outburst, Jet added, "I understand what Morwenna is saying. I don't have to make many choices when it comes to what I'll do for a living. My only choice is *how* I'll do it. That's why I'm here. To learn all about things like secret societies and Indigo City and to remember that not everyone has it as easy as I do."

"I couldn't imagine having every decision about the future already made. You must feel trapped sometimes." Charlie leaned forward.

She made herself more comfortable and sat cross-legged on the area rug. "I am lucky, because my family is amazing. But who wouldn't mind a little more independence now and then?"

Morwenna spied something on the desk chair. "What is that fur ball over there?" She scooted back further on the bed.

"Oh, sorry, that's Peppercorn, my friend." Jet rose and pulled out the chair. She shot Peppercorn a warning glare that meant "be nice" and picked him up to introduce him to her new friends.

Charlie bounced up out of the other chair. "Oh, he's so cute! Are we allowed to hold him?" She reached out then dropped her hands.

Jet lifted a shoulder. "I'll ask him." As usual, Peppercorn took his time answering.

"If they jostle me too much, I'll bite," he said.

"You will not. You like the attention too much."

He flicked his tail in answer, and Jet faced Charlie with Peppercorn in her arms. "He says no problem,"

She handed the soft creature to Charlie. "Hello, Peppercorn. You are beautiful, aren't you?" Charlie said. "Something tells me you already know how lovely you are, though."

"You certainly understand his personality quickly enough." Jet faced Morwenna. "Would you like to hold him?"

She hesitated. Then she said, "Why not?"

Charlie carried Peppercorn over to Morwenna and rested him in her arms.

She gasped. "Oh, he's not just cute, Charlie. He's gorgeous." She stroked the luxurious inky-black fur, her eyes glowing with pleasure. "His fur is like silk and velvet at the same time. I have to ask Daddy for one."

Charlie snorted and shook her head. "I have no idea why I am surprised at you sometimes, Morwenna, but still you manage to catch me off guard." Rolling her eyes, she took the same position on the rug Jet just vacated. "You don't even talk to animals all that well and now you want one in our room?"

"I just haven't met the right one yet. If I had a beautiful pet like Peppercorn, he'd talk to me all the time."

"Not sure that's gonna happen for you, roomie," Charlie said.

All the girls laughed together, and an overwhelming sense of belonging washed over Jet. This was something she had never experienced before, having a group of people her own age around her, and reveled in it.

They spent another hour together before they called it a night. As she readied for bed, she thought about the animal disappearances and her true purpose for being at Quad. After talking to Morwenna and Charlie about Cloak and Veil, Jet needed more information. She had to figure out a way to infiltrate the secret society. She'd have to give it some more thought, but it could be a connection to the animals disappearing. She'd ask her father and Peppercorn. Reviewing it over in her head, she also decided to help Morwenna find an animal she could communicate with. The girl was ambivalent about animals, but maybe Jet could help her appreciate animals more. There had to be one willing to talk to her.

Thirteen

Several weeks of classes sailed by, and Jet was more at home at Quadrivium. She spent most of her free time with Morwenna, Charlie, and Will. She also set about familiarizing herself with the entire campus. It wasn't long before she could find her way around the grounds without getting lost.

Most of her courses were challenging, but manageable, and she thrived in each. But it was Movement with Professor Ruecroft that had become a dreaded start to the week. Jet had no clue why the woman hated her, but her attitude wasn't a secret. Professor Ruecroft made no bones about singling out Jet in class.

The more she tried, the less she could relax for the required lessons. If she wasn't relaxed, then she didn't have a prayer.

It was on their way out of class one morning when Will said, "Ruecroft has it out for you."

"Nonsense," Morwenna said. "She's just trying to get Jet to perform under pressure. If you can't succeed in Movement class, how can you expect to perform when it really matters?" She spun to Jet. "You have to get better. You really don't have a choice."

"How do you propose I do that?" she asked. Knowing you were bad at something was one thing. Having your friends openly comment on it was quite another.

"Ooh, princess getting testy." Morwenna pushed her hair back.

"I'm not testy, and I'm aware of the problem," she snapped.

"Easy, Jet, it's just constructive criticism. I think I speak for all of us when I say we all want you to pass Movement class."

As the group made their way down the hallway toward their next classes, she nudged Jet. "If you were sweet and positive all the time, you'd be a bore."

"Sorry for the overreaction. I'm a little sensitive about this." Jet exhaled. "Hey, who's meeting for dinner tonight before the Wave and Wing meeting?"

"I'm there," Will said.

"Me too," Charlie said.

"I'm sitting with Angela and Piper, so don't wait for me," Morwenna said. "I'll see you all after."

~ * ~

When Jet and Will strolled into enComm, she had forgiven Morwenna for calling her out about her Movement issues. She was sure Morwenna just wanted her to do well.

He gave her a side hug. "Try not to let Morrie rattle you. She doesn't mean half the stuff she says, you know. Morwenna really can't help herself sometimes, especially because everything is so easy for her. She thinks it should be just as easy for everyone else."

They sat next to one another. As usual, Jax the tiger shark, stared at them from his huge tank in the center of the room.

She rested her chin on her hand. "Why won't animals talk to her then? She *is* good at everything else."

"Don't take it personally. Her parents have really high expectations, and she hasn't let them down once." He raised one shoulder. "I think the reason animals don't communicate with her is because her parents haven't put any emphasis on that kind of thing, so she doesn't try very hard. Don't get me wrong, her parents are traditionalists and are in tune with the old ways, but I think they envision Morwenna doing something on a grander scale than talking to dolphins to predict the weather. The only reason for animal communication in the Saberton household would be for interaction with the human world, and that is a big no-no. What about you? Do your parents have big plans for your future reign?"

He swiveled his body, and when he looked at her with those slate-blue eyes, her face heated. She made herself focus on answering his question instead of his eyes.

"I think my parents want what all parents want, and that's for me to be happy." She shrugged. "Obviously there's a tad bit more pressure on me to make good decisions and succeed. Really, my parents are mostly concerned that I am up to the challenge ahead of me and that I'm content." This wasn't exactly the truth, since her parents had forced her to be at Quad in the first place, but she suddenly realized she wasn't angry about this anymore.

"That's cool. Not all parents are so concerned with the happiness part for their kids. It certainly doesn't feel that way with my father." His eyes darkened, and she was about to ask what he meant when Professor Miles strode in, carrying a large, covered bucket, and shut the door behind him.

"Students, today let us focus on getting a response from Jax using visual stimuli." Professor Miles hauled the large container and plopped it onto the table next to Jax. When Professor Miles opened the top of the pail, a putrid smell filled the classroom. He picked up the dead fish and showed it to Jax.

The young shark stopped swimming in circles and faced Jet. *"They play a game with me, and I want to see my mother."*

"They really don't mean anything by it. They are trying to learn from you. But I understand. I'll pass it along for you," Jet said.

"This is just a way for the princess to show off again," Eric said.

She frowned. She had started to believe they thought of her as one of them. She raised her hand. "A moment, Professor Miles?"

"Yes, Miss Lennox."

Jet confided to Professor Miles what Jax said to her, and knew Professor Miles would do something about it.

By the time class was over, she had completely forgotten about asking Will what he'd meant about his father not caring about his happiness. When she remembered, he had already left. Wasn't Will happy? Was there anything she could do to help?

~ * ~

After dinner, the Ordinary remained abuzz with excitement. Jet sat with the rest of the Betas for the informational meeting to begin. Will joined her at the growlers' table, and Charlie waved from the rorquals' table, where she sat with Morwenna and two other friends. Morwenna didn't wave, but she gave Jet a wink.

Madame Wolverhampton appeared out of nowhere. "Ladies and gentlemen, I know you are all looking forward to the commencement of this meeting, but I need to remind you that membership into the Society of Wave and Wing is exclusive. It is also the only society to confer membership at the end of the year rather than at the end of the rush period as our other student societies and organizations do." She straightened her spine. "We encourage your interest and hard work over the following two terms but must caution you against high hopes. Membership is limited." Madame Wolverhampton cleared her throat, as Declan Newcastle hurried in. "Wonderful. You've arrived.

"Before I introduce our special guest, I would like to provide a bit of background. The gentleman you are about to meet is a descendant of one of the pioneer families of Indigo City. For his work and charitable service, he achieved an unprecedented unanimous invitation to the Noble Order of Fin and Feather, where he holds the rank of Grand Commander. If that isn't impressive enough, he is also the inventor of the MotoPearl."

A soft murmur broke out among the students. The MotoPearl was a small vehicle people used to get around the city. The vehicle's construction was based on the shape of rare, giant clamshells, and the composition was similar to that of an abalone shell for its incredible strength.

"May I present Mr. Declan Newcastle, our liaison to the Noble Order of Fin and Feather, and advisor along with myself to the Society of Wave and Wing."

The applause was thunderous as Newcastle shook Madame Wolverhampton's hand. Jet clapped and nudged Will. "Why didn't you say something about your dad?"

He stiffened. "No big deal to me. He's just my dad."

"Thank you, Scholarch Wolverhampton, for your kind words, and I am so thrilled to be here to offer any help to these potential recruits." He rounded toward the audience. "Let me begin by telling you all a story before we launch into the requirements for membership into the Society of Wave and Wing." Stuffing his large hands into the pockets of his trousers, he paced. "Sit back and relax, and I will answer all your questions when the story is over." He cleared his throat.

"Salacia, the goddess of the oceans, was kind, gentle, and beautiful. Neptune fell in love with her and planned to ask her to become his wife. Tempesta was in love with Neptune and, enraged, set out to destroy Salacia. Tempesta conjured a storm of thrashing wind and crashing waves to capsize the magical, hippocampi-led chariot in which Salacia traveled. She was violently thrown into the sea and, upon waking, found herself in an unfamiliar grotto attended by a magnificent osprey. The osprey had heard her telepathic cries and plucked her from certain death, for Tempesta had also unleashed her sharks to kill Salacia in case she escaped the monstrous storms.

"Neptune commanded Tempesta to confess and reveal Salacia's location. Tempesta, facing Neptune's trident, lied and said she had nothing to do with it. He angrily extended his trident toward her, turning her to stone—a statue we call the Tempest.

"Secreted in the safety of the grotto, the loyal osprey, named Sofana, kept vigil for the weakened queen, while Neptune, believing his love to be lost forever, entrusted to Delphinius, his loyal dolphin, the task of retrieving her body for a proper burial. Delphinius searched all Aquatica for signs of the lost queen, until he came upon the ruins of her chariot at the bottom of the Atlantic. He kept searching, employing careful use of encephalic communication and echolocation.

"Sofana heard the silent pleas of Neptune's dolphin and guided him to the grotto. Delphinius retrieved Neptune's beloved queen and her loyal Sofana. Sofana soared above, watchful of the open sea and Tempesta's shark army. Delphinius braved the towering waves, the queen upon his back, and returned to the Golden Palace, where Salacia wed Neptune.

"Delphinius's and Sofana's heroism restored harmony to the House of Neptune and peace to all of Aquatica. Confronting mortal danger, they demonstrated bravery, loyalty, and perseverance. The pair became inseparable and spent the remainder of their lives in service to the House of Neptune. Their adventures have been depicted in arts and literature over the centuries, and they remain a symbol of our cultural identity to this day, as they united Neptune and Salacia."

Applause erupted as Newcastle finished the tale. He lifted his hand to quiet the crowd.

"Now a bit more recent history for you—hundreds of years ago, King Alcandor founded the Noble Order of Fin and Feather to advance the work of Delphinius and Sofana. Membership in this order, the highest honor of Pelagiana, is restricted to those extraordinary individuals elected by the College of Companions who demonstrate exceptional bravery, loyalty, and perseverance in service to their country.

"The Order of Fin and Feather is the parent group of the Society of Wing and Wave. Madame Scholarch, as the faculty advisor to the Society of Wave and Wing, recommends two students—one male and one female—in the spring of their Gamma Year to intern during their final year at Quadrivium with the Order of Fin and Feather. This prestigious internship by no means guarantees invitation to membership," he said. "However, it goes a long way toward being considered.

"Requirements for invitation to the Society of Wave and Wing are similar to those of the Noble Order of Fin and Feather. We require tremendous bravery, loyalty, and service. Your academic success weighs heavily. Additionally, we require expert proficiency in encephalic communication, Movement, and hydrodynamic facilities, which"—he glanced at Madame Wolverhampton— "I believe is covered for all students in second term of this Beta year. You will continue these studies until graduation."

Jet's shoulders slumped. Expert proficiency in Movement didn't seem likely for her anytime soon, and if she wanted to join SWW at the end of this year, she had to figure out a way to improve.

"We also require participation in one of the events at the Aquaticup, such as rescue swimming, free diving, finswimming, or hippocampi show riding. These events honor our history." Hands back in his pockets, he stopped and said, "Now who has a question for me?"

Arms shot in the air. Jet raised her hand too.

Mr. Newcastle pointed at her. "Nice to see you again, Princess."

Her cheeks burned at his use of her title. All eyes on her, she forgot her question…until Madame Wolverhampton intervened.

"Ah, yes. Miss Lennox is a welcome addition to the student body." She emphasized the *Miss Lennox,* and Jet was grateful.

"Yes, I imagine she is. Now, Miss Lennox, you had a question for me?"

Swallowing her embarrassment, she ignored the eyes still staring and asked, "Yes. How is 'expert proficiency' defined in each subject?"

"Good question, Miss Lennox," Mr. Newcastle said. "We require expert proficiency for each subject, as defined by your yearly requirements, and would in most cases coincide with perfect scores on final proficiency examinations. We do not expect Betas to achieve proficiency beyond their Beta curriculum and so on."

She thanked him with a nod, the information swirling in her head. She still had a chance. There had to be a way to get better at Movement. She needed to get past her fear of Professor Ruecroft. If she could just figure out why the woman hated her, maybe she could get some extra help from her.

Jet decided the best way to approach the problem was head-on. There would be no better way to prove the monarchy relevant and worthy than getting into the most challenging society available. There was no other choice but to schedule a conference with Professor Ruecroft and ask for help. Perhaps the professor hating her was all in her head.

Jet stole a peek at Professor Ruecroft, who was standing in the corner of the Ordinary. Her pinched expression aimed in Jet's direction offered her little reassurance her plan would work.

Fourteen

Professor Ruecroft's office was cramped and overflowing with books. Jet had signed up for an appointment during her normal afternoon office hours. A slit of sunlight shone through a narrow crack in the afternoon drawn drapes. Dust motes swirled in the beam, the only activity in the depressing space.

The professor sat behind a mahogany desk, writing notes and didn't acknowledge Jet's entrance. Knowing she needed the professor's cooperation to succeed, Jet waited for her to speak first. And waited. And waited.

Finally Professor Ruecroft lowered her pen and glanced up, giving Jet a nasty smile. "Ah, Princess, good afternoon."

She flexed her fingers. "Good afternoon, Professor. Please call me Miss Lennox. All of the other professors do, as does Scholarch Wolverhampton."

"I will not. Thank you very much." She capped her pen with a click. "You will find, Princess Jaiette, that I am unlike most professors here, as I do not buy in to your little performance."

Jet gasped.

"Don't behave the innocent with me. Most of the staff and students have been taken in by your little act. Coming to Quadrivium and playing student when the circumstances of your birth afford you everything you could learn here and more." Her chest heaving with anger, Professor Ruecroft stood. "What could you possibly achieve here except a bit of fun at our expense? See how the other half lives, perhaps?"

Her vitriol stunned Jet; her mouth hung open.

"You, a pampered, spoiled excuse for an heir, think it's funny to come here and act out some little fantasy when you and your family belong in Aurealia with the rest of the country bumpkins. You have no idea what it's like to live at the surface. The dangers, the decisions we have to make daily—you have no idea." The veins stood out on her neck.

Jet swallowed hard. She had to convince Ruecroft her motives were pure. "Please, Professor. I have no idea what you're talking about. I'm here to learn."

Professor Ruecroft snorted. "But you haven't improved at all. If that doesn't scream spoiled princess, I don't know what does." She strode around her desk and stopped right in front of Jet. "Neither I, nor this institution, will be made a fool of by your preposterous experiment."

Tears threatened but she would not cry in front of this woman. With no thought of getting in to the Society of Wave and Wing, Jet drew herself up, glaring into the professor's eyes. "Professor Ruecroft." Her voice shook. "No one has ever spoken to me the way you just did."

"I imagine they haven't, *Your Highness.*" Ruecroft sneered.

"You won't speak to me that way again. I came to Quadrivium to learn as much as I could about our people. I came hoping to learn so I could help. I came to your office hoping to persuade you to tutor me for your class." She took a bracing breath. "I realize now that is never going to happen." She hated the triumphant look on Professor Ruecroft's lined face.

"You may have won today, Professor Ruecroft, and you may think you have driven me from your class. But I will not only succeed in your class, I will be the best." She spun and headed toward to the door. She turned back to the professor. "The only thing you've done today was make me stronger."

She closed Professor Ruecroft's door and stumbled from the office, hot, angry tears streaming from her eyes. She plowed straight into Will.

"Come with me."

Too upset to worry, she let him direct her, wishing for the first time since she'd arrived at Quadrivium that she hadn't run into him. She wished she could sob into her pillow and punch something.

They walked outside and stopped at the shore of Indigo Lake. The water was placid today, and what few waves there were glinted in the late afternoon light. Jet caught her breath. It was beautiful, and her breathing slowed.

The pinkish-silvery sand welcomed them, and they settled themselves down. She kicked off her sandals and dug her toes in, enjoying the warmth.

He broke the silence. "Go ahead." He grinned at her, and she burst into tears.

"Come on, Jet!" He reared back. "I didn't mean for you to cry! I meant for you to tell me what happened." He pushed the hair off his forehead.

"I'm sorry. I'm really okay. I'm just so mad I need to hit something, and I can't so I cry."

His shoulders relaxed. "What did she say to you?"

"She told me I was only up here for a few kicks, completely out of touch with real people's problems, and that it was all an act." She swallowed the remainder of her tears. "Basically, I have no hope to accomplish anything of value and clearly I don't care because I haven't made any progress in her class." She pursed her lips then said, "She's right about that. There isn't any excuse, I know. But everything else she said was so unfair."

"Ruecroft has always been wacko, but this is over the limit. I'm not sure it would work but you could try to report her."

She stiffened at the suggestion. "I wouldn't give her the satisfaction."

"You're tougher than you look, you know?"

"Thanks. And Ruecroft isn't scaring me off my goal. I will succeed." She clenched her jaw.

He bit his lip. "Jet, what does that mean? There isn't another Movement professor here at Quadrivium. No one else would dare try to teach it. She has tenure. That means unless she actually kills a student, we're stuck with her."

Jet laughed.

"I'm serious. People complain about her all the time, but nothing sticks. You have to get by her to get in to SWW. She's not going to give you the marks." His shook his head. "I don't understand why she hates you so much. You're a likable sort."

"Thanks, Will. I needed this. I feel better." She stood and brushed the sand from her clothes.

"Hold it a minute," he said. "How exactly are you planning to accomplish your big goal? I've been paying attention these past weeks. I know you want Wave and Wing more than anything. You have something to prove to all Pelagiana and you think earning Wave and Wing will do it. So what do you have in that head of yours?"

Suddenly she felt lighter, more positive. She could do this, but she'd need help. "Will, stop worrying. I've got a plan." She smiled.

"I was afraid of that."

~ * ~

The very next day in her Movement class, Jet remained quiet while Professor Ruecroft passed out worksheets with new defensive positions for review. When Jet received hers, there was a note in the corner in angry, red ink: *For your outburst yesterday in my office, you receive another rip.*

Her shoulders dropped. She nudged Charlie next to her and showed her the paper. Her friend's wince was all the evidence Jet needed to know another rip was terrible.

Morwenna, Will, Charlie, and Jet gathered outside the classroom in the hallway. Jet dropped her bag in front of Morwenna. "I know a rip is a punishment, but I haven't reached that part in the handbook. How do they work?"

Charlie's eyes widened. "A punishment? The rip is the penal code for all Quadrivium. You only get ten chances for your entire four years, and you've already got two. Professors don't just hand them out for little infractions either, because they know how serious they are. If you get three in one school year, your final grade's reduced. A rip affects everything—like whether you can compete in the extracurriculars or even pledge a society." She gulped. "You're skating by, Jet, just barely."

"That isn't fair. I was late to class once, and I voiced my disagreement over something a professor said. Those are 'little infractions' to me."

"They are usually," Morwenna agreed. "But Ruecroft seriously hates you, and the reason doesn't matter. Rips are subjective. Just because most professors don't hand them out for little things doesn't mean it doesn't happen." She patted Jet's arm. "Listen, Will told me he talked you down yesterday after your run-in with Ruecroft. He also told me he mentioned how crazy Ruecroft is."

Jet couldn't explain why she was hurt that he would share their moment on the beach with Morwenna, but she was. Telling herself it didn't matter, she said, "Well, I won't give her a reason to punish me."

He jumped in. "Good luck with that, Jet. The lady is nuttier than a dopefish. There isn't a shot of you getting out of her class without another rip. Ruecroft has it out for you. You should find out why and confront her with it or transfer to another class and skip Movement."

"That isn't going to happen." Jet lifted her chin. "Zephania Ruecroft is not stopping me from getting into Wave and Wing, I can promise you that."

Charlie chuckled. "Easy there, warrior Princess." She patted Jet's shoulder. "What are you going to do, then?"

"That's easy. I'm going to get help from the best."

Every eye gazed in Morwenna's direction. "Oh, no," she said. "I'm not comfortable being responsible for you."

"As usual, Morwenna, you are brutally honest. But I have no other choice. You have to help me."

"Is that a royal command, Your Highness?" Morwenna's eyes narrowed.

"Don't be difficult, Morwenna," Will said. "It's a nice thing to do, and frankly, you're Jet's best hope."

She melted under his gaze. He was the only one she'd bend for. "All right, but if you fail, it is not on me."

"Don't worry," Jet said. "I won't."

"Hmmm," was the uncertain response from Morwenna. "We'll see about that. I don't think I can start anything until after rush. I'm too busy. But after that, we'll meet three times a week for two-hour sessions." She paused for a moment, and then fixed her intense stare into Jet's eyes. "I'm not a pushover. Dealing with me will be the hardest thing you've ever done in your life. Don't expect a free pass because we're friends. And I won't make this easy on you because you're the princess."

"I'm counting on that, Morwenna."

~ * ~

Later that night, alone with Peppercorn in her room, determined as she practiced the new movement stances from the worksheet Ruecroft assigned that week, Jet tried to clear her mind. Peppercorn interrupted her focus.

"We need to talk."

Her legs wobbled as she lowered herself to the new stance. She blew out a breath. *"I agree. Now that you've found a way to get to the Sagesse Chambers, we need to find a way for me to get there undetected."* She settled into the next stance.

"This entire place is riddled with tunnels and passages. Some even lead to below the lake bed and then back up into Aurealia."

"You can get home from here?" She jumped out of the stance.

"It's fascinating how they tunneled under the rock of the earth and then back up into the village below the Shield. But that isn't important right now." His voice was brisk. *"Do you have any ideas?"*

"Timing is important. Too many people are still watching my every move, and I need to find a way around that. My father said the opening session of the Sagesse is next Tuesday night. Maybe I could go then."

"I'll keep scouting for alternate routes," Peppercorn said.

"I'll pay attention to timing. I have to sneak away when I won't be missed by anyone."

He nodded. *"One more thing, Jet."*

"Yes?"

"If I go missing, promise me you'll find me." His black eyes watered, and she was ashamed her pet would think so little of her. But

she deserved it—she hadn't spent much time with him since she started at Quad. She tried to assure him. *"Oh, Peppercorn! Of course. I wouldn't rest until I found you. You're my best friend."*

"There are people who've lost their animals, and they can't do anything about it."

"I understand. I'm sorry for not spending more time with you. I'll try harder."

"You should know that I've spoken to some animals here at Quad. There is another sable called Norman. He told me the animals believe the disappearances aren't random. Many animals are considering leaving their Pelagi partners. I don't have to tell you how devastating that would be to the future of this island. The Pelagi are losing the trust of their animals. You need to do something about it, Jet. And fast."

Fifteen

A week had passed since Jet and Peppercorn formulated their plan. They spent the time since, honing and practicing. Fortunately, the opening of the Sagesse session coincided with one of the busiest nights of the year: Tap Night. This offered her a huge opportunity. She had plans for Tap Night and needed to use the chaos to disappear without notice.

She didn't pledge any societies, even though Charlie asked her to join the Appollonian Octet. She wasn't into performing in public, and Jet couldn't commit herself to any other activities. Doing the job her father had assigned and practicing Movement with Morwenna would be intense enough.

Tap Night was raucous as the members of the societies barged into the pledges' rooms. If a pledge accepted the tap, he or she was whisked away. What happened after that remained a mystery, and no one would give Jet any more information, no matter how many times she asked.

Even more intriguing were the secret societies like Cloak and Veil. These members wore capes and hoods. The desire for secrecy was so great that even their shoes were the same size, so you couldn't tell a male member from a female. The hooded figures marched the hallways of the residential colleges, stalking their new pledges. No one said anything, since voices could be recognized. It was crazy, this obsession with secrecy and keeping membership private. Morwenna had tried to explain, but it all seemed silly.

She didn't know how you pledge a secret society without knowing who the current members were. Morwenna told her that all you had to do was say, in a crowd, that you were interested, and if the society chose you for a pledge, they would contact you. She didn't believe it, but according to Will, it happened all the time.

She asked Morwenna if she had been contacted, and Morwenna claimed, "I have no idea what you're talking about." If the Society of Cloak and Veil needed a new pledge to keep a secret, Morwenna was their girl.

Jet put it out of her mind as she listened to the eerie quiet of Arctic Hall. She could just make out noises from distant celebrations and knew the noise would be a good distraction.

She peeked outside her room to check it out. As pledges trudged along the corridors that led to the Ordinary, she finally realized why Tap

Night was such a big deal. Every staff member lined the corridors, standing or sitting in chairs they had pulled from their classrooms. They chatted companionably or cheered when a new pledge and his or her club went by. Some groups carried their new pledges over their heads, screaming down the hallways, some marched along in dignified processions. The only similarity she noticed was the smiles on everyone's faces. Then she saw the hoods.

She had no idea if the sixteen hooded and caped figures were members of the Society of Cloak and Veil, but this group definitely valued their secrecy. Each member of the group paced in precise synchronization, left foot, and then right with the same slight swing of the arms. Perfect formation, and she couldn't tell any one of the members apart as she searched for even the slightest differences. Peppercorn's voice in her mind interrupted her thoughts.

"Okay. All you have to do is open the third door on the south wall of the Ordinary. Follow the stairs down and go past four doors and stay put," he instructed and then dove into his own exit next to the fireplace.

She made her way to the Ordinary, which was deserted, since most of the action of Tap Night happened in the residential halls. Getting across campus unnoticed was tricky though, since the students would end up in the tunnels. She and Peppercorn had worked for days on the plan. The Sagesse meeting schedule was posted to Eelfare, so everyone could access it.

She scanned the Ordinary and luckily it was empty. She and Peppercorn had agreed if anyone was there, she would abort the plan for another time. They had timed it so she would catch the Sagesse in session and get out of the main building without notice.

She took the stairway down to the passage beneath the building. It was dark, and she used a small light to guide her. It didn't stop her from stumbling on her own feet, though, and she blew out a frustrated breath. She passed the three doors and stopped.

"Now take the fork to the right and follow it to the end. You are underground the entire way and will arrive underneath the Sagesse chambers. When the tunnel reaches a dead end, go up the stairway and stop. I will let you know if you can get in undetected."

While she heard him, she had no idea where he was because the tunnel was so dark.

"Got it." She inched her way through the passage.

It was clean and there were doors along the way, because the student clubs used them. Charlie rehearsed for Apollonian Octet down here. Soon, however, the passage grew smaller and less well kept. There were no longer doors or even old torches lining the walls. Jet assumed she was now under the grassy areas between the main building and the Sagesse chambers.

"Hide! Quick! Someone is coming!" Peppercorn startled her with his shout.

She clicked off her light and pressed her body against the stone wall. Darkness shrouded her as she tried to make herself smaller. She kneeled, knowing most people wouldn't look down. The figure panted as it hurried by. She smelled a noxious scent, like rotting fish. She held back the gag and waited, her heart hammering in her throat.

Jet couldn't make out the figure as it passed. The only thing she could tell was that whoever it was wore a hood. She wished she could follow and find out where the cloaked person was going, but she had to stick to the plan. Jet would do some searching on her own another time. Peppercorn gave her the directions again and the all clear.

When she reached the stairs, she ascended and stood before a huge, wooden door. She stared at the doorway and shuffled her feet, growing impatient. *"Where are you?"*

"I'm where I should be. You've already missed the beginning," he said. *"Open the door slowly and come out to the right. Move immediately to the wall opposite and hide in the drapes."*

Opening the door at a glacial pace, she peered into a long corridor. Tiptoeing onto the crimson carpet, she zipped across the hall and hid against the cold, stone wall behind matching crimson drapes. Voices echoed from the chamber and the door to her left. A large, bronze handle was within her reach. She eased it down, and the door released, opening just a crack. It was enough to overhear the Sagesse, and she squeezed herself against the wall again, checking to make sure her shoes weren't visible from below the drapes. The Sagesse had one hundred and two members, and for a moment, it was as if they were all talking at once. There was a sharp interruption from a rapping gavel, and the room quieted.

"Now moving on to new business…it has been brought to the attention of this body that another animal has gone missing." She recognized the voice of Declan Newcastle.

"King Magnus received another request from an Aurealian down below that we investigate this matter. The animal in question is a schipperke by the name of Cinnsy, and the owner said it is odd that she would leave with no notice. The king has requested we discuss initiating an inquiry."

"Preposterous. This is a waste of our time. The animals will return when they feel like it and not a moment sooner. I understand your desire to investigate this matter, Declan, as it looks quite bad for you. These animals are supposed to be protected by your family, but surely you have to agree we have more important things to discuss."

Jet had no problem recognizing Roger Saberton's voice.

"I believe we should do as the king asks and discuss this matter." Mr. Newcastle's voice remained calm.

The murmur of several voices rose.

"I will tell the king myself that this is a waste of time, just as I have in the past. Can we move on to something else? I'm sure you'll find most here agree with me." Saberton's smooth voice rang out over the crowd.

The voices grew loud again, making discussion impossible.

"Very well. What is it you would like to discuss?" Newcastle asked.

"I would like to discuss the princess and how she has progressed at Quadrivium," Saberton said, and another murmur spread in the chamber.

Jet heard "hear, hear" and "such an embarrassment" from other members, and her ears tingled. Why were they talking about her?

Saberton cleared his throat. "Calm yourselves. This experiment by the royal family will reveal whether young Jaiette is fit to lead us. I know there are many among you who question whether we even need the monarchy any longer. I feel—"

"Member Saberton, this does not fall under new business," Declan interrupted. "The idea of Pelagiana without a monarchy is preposterous. There are protection mechanisms in place that only those in the direct line are privy to. Neptune knew what was best for our world."

She clutched the necklace at her throat. This small pearl was one of the protections meant only for those in the royal line. Would its powers work for anyone else?

"We have already decided that we shall see how the princess progresses throughout the year before we evaluate anything," Newcastle said.

"I disagree with Member Newcastle. These protections only the royal family knows of can't be that important, as we haven't needed them in over two thousand years. However, that is neither here nor there. I would never question Neptune's wisdom. I was only mentioning that some people here believe the monarchy to be obsolete. I didn't say I agreed," Saberton said.

At these words, rumbling moved through the crowd.

What did Saberton believe? His words were so smooth it was difficult to tell which side he was on, and Jet figured that was how he had become so powerful.

"Soon we will have her midterms to evaluate. I have it on good authority she isn't doing well. I only wish to offer the members of Sagesse the full story."

"Then I suggest you keep what can only be counted as gossip from your teenage daughter to yourself, Member Saberton. As we all agreed, the scholarch will keep us apprised with full reports," Newcastle said.

It's about time. She was mortified. The entire chamber of the Sagesse was discussing her grades? And, of course, Morwenna would tell her father about Jet's abysmal performance in Movement. She could think of nothing worse than being the topic of discussion of a hundred people. Yet, if she was going to be queen, she'd deal with that all the time. Maybe she wasn't fit for the job. The idea of them checking on her like this just didn't seem right. She forced herself to listen to the rest.

"Of course, Declan. We will wait. I want only what is best for Pelagiana. It is my fervent wish the young princess doesn't disappoint us."

She couldn't tell if Saberton meant it or not, but from the echoes in the chamber most agreed with almost everything he said. Her father should hear this.

"Peppercorn! Get me out of here."

"You have mere seconds to cross the hall before they exit the chamber. Move!"

She lunged for the door and rushed through the passage. She got to the Ordinary in half the time it took her to get to the Sagesse's chambers. When Peppercorn gave her the all clear, she dashed through the Ordinary to her room in full darkness. She used her Elver at once.

Her father's face appeared on the screen. "Jaiette, it's late."

"Dad, we don't have time for that. Now listen." Jet told him everything.

He didn't interrupt. At last he said, "Well, that doesn't provide us any new information."

"What does that mean?"

"It means I was already worried, and I expected they would track your progress at school. It's the nature of the job, and I can't stop them. It would appear I am hiding something, if I did. I trust you are doing well?"

"Of course," she lied then said in rush, "But what about what Saberton said about the monarchy?"

"Roger's interests are worthy. He is a good friend to me. He has not lied, and I am sure he would like to see you do well. You don't understand how much he loves Pelagiana. If he believes you aren't right for the job, he will not hesitate to tell me. Of that, I can be sure. But don't worry. He is my friend first, so I'll hear of any failures on your part before anyone else does. Still, it does make me curious. Why the grumblings about the monarchy? Is he behind them? Did you hear him say that specifically?"

"No. He said only that some of the Sagesse members had those concerns."

"Very well then. We shall see what else you find out. They meet again next week. Try to make time."

"I will."

"This is a heavy burden you carry, Jaiette. Not only must you be flawless as a student, you must also prove your mettle during this crisis of politics that has nothing to do with you. How I hate this subterfuge!"

"Relax. I can handle this. Since I'm going to be queen one day, I'll have to get used to it." She shrugged. "Speaking of which, what exactly did Declan Newcastle mean about the protection mechanisms only we royals know about?"

"That would fall under need-to-know information, Jaiette, and right now you don't need to know."

"Is it my pearl?" She touched her necklace again.

"In part," the king said. "But Neptune never put all his fish in one basket, so of course there is more. Patience, Jet."

"Okay. I'll have to live with that for now. Tell Mother I'll call later. I've got to get to work. Those guards you have trailing me won't have anything to do if I don't leave my room." Jet winked.

"It was not my idea, young lady," her father teased. "But it is a safe one, so I don't complain. Now get out there and remember who you are."

She swiped the conversation closed. Remembering her father's last words, she vowed she'd never forget who she was again. It was time to prove she was worthy.

Sixteen

"Good, good. Now let's move to something less easy."

Morwenna's voice broke through the haze of pain in Jet's body. It had been six days since Tap Night. She and Peppercorn were planning another trip to the Sagesse the following day. A sliver of fear snaked through her at the idea of sneaking out in the middle of the day instead of the cover of night. Right now, however, after three practice sessions, her sole focus was pain as she panted out her reply.

"That was *easy*?" She giggled at Morwenna's glower. "You know you sure can be intense."

"I am serious when it comes to being the best."

"I can't believe I'm saying this, because it is so unlike me, but…lighten up."

"This isn't a game, Princess."

She hated when Morwenna called her that, but before she could remind her, Morwenna crouched into a striking stance.

"Everyone in this school knows I am tutoring you in Movement—simply because you can't sneeze without someone gossiping about it. I will not have my reputation tarnished and prospects destroyed because you decided you could coast by at Quadrivium by talking to weird animals."

"That's unfair." Jet grunted as she struck her shoulder. "I am making an effort at every aspect of my life here."

"Say what you will, but that is how people would see it," Morwenna said. "Now let's move on to trapping and sensitivity practice. Try to anticipate and block my attack. Focus and remember bamboo—strong but flexible."

"Why do you care so much what people think?" She gulped as Morwenna's foot landed hard on her already throbbing shin.

"Why don't you?" Morwenna snarled. "Focus, Jet."

"You're focused enough for the two of us," she huffed. Her leg was killing her.

"I do know that, but not everyone has the same choices you do."

It was all Morwenna was willing to give. No matter how hard she tried, she couldn't breach her wall. The more she got to know her, the more mysterious she became.

Morwenna's bark broke Jet's concentration. "Hey! We only have two weeks until our first exam. Let's do this."

The one unwavering fact Jet knew about Morwenna was she never lacked enthusiasm. Jet lowered into hippocampus stance, her legs shaking with fatigue.

"Enough. Now back to synchronized Fight Flow," Morwenna said.

But was this enthusiasm a good thing?

They worked the positions in quarter time, each movement a work of art—or, in Jet's case, a work in progress. She still had difficulty relaxing her mind and body.

Morwenna keyed in on this fact as she said, "Jet, have you been working on your meditation?"

"Every night." Jet clenched her jaw.

"I don't understand this. You're able to talk to a tiger shark but you can't hold a passable hippocampus stance. The concentration required is the same." Morwenna melted into encroaching warrior position.

"Ruecroft's face pops into my head, and every muscle tenses."

"That isn't going to earn you high marks."

She rolled her eyes. "No kidding."

"I don't believe in failure."

Jet raised her arm to block the blow. "Please stop implying that I do believe in failure, Morwenna. You're no better than Ruecroft."

Her friend exhaled. "You're right. I'm sorry. I know I can come on too strong. Let's call it a day, and I'll consider possible solutions to your Ruecroft block."

Jet lowered her arms. "Okay. I do appreciate you giving up your time like this—especially if you've been chosen for Cloak and Veil." She batted her eyes.

"Nice try, Jet. I'm a vault," Morwenna said as both girls toweled off.

She chuckled. "Of that I have no doubt."

~ * ~

As Jet headed to meet Charlie after her Apollonian Octet practice, she thought about Morwenna. Why didn't she let her guard down with anyone but Will? Jet had even tried to get several animals, including Peppercorn, to talk to Morwenna. But Peppercorn said he wasn't ready to trust outsiders.

Perhaps she could breach the emotional wall Morwenna put up and also get her to talk about Cloak and Veil. Jet needed any information she could get to help with the animal disappearances. Charlie had said something about Roger Saberton being tough on Morwenna, so maybe that was the reason she didn't get close to people. She might be too busy trying to make him happy.

Jet strolled into the Apollonian Octet practice room below the Ordinary and immediately forgot all of her problems. A girl named Lilly was alone with a huge, black dog.

"Who is this handsome boy?" Jet slowly approached.

"That's Onyx. He's my keep."

"May I talk to him?"

"Sure. He's not much into enComm, but that might have something to do with me not caring about it too much either."

"Hi, Onyx. It's nice to meet you," Jet tried.

When the dog tilted his head from his mat by the fireplace but said nothing, she tried again. *"Won't you at least say hello?"* Again nothing. She was about to try again, when Charlie came out from a room in the back.

"You ready for lunch?" Charlie asked.

Jet nodded to her friend, and then stared back at Onyx. *"Maybe you'll feel like talking next time we see each other?"*

He didn't answer.

Jet and Charlie made their way to the Ordinary. Jet couldn't understand Onyx's hesitation. Could it have something to do with the missing animals?

"Jet, aren't you listening to me? I was telling you that Lilly likes Samuel."

Oops. She hadn't been paying attention. "I didn't know."

Charlie sniffed. "How could you not? It's so obvious."

"I guess I was too wrapped up in my own stuff."

"Of course you were, and I know Lilly from last year, so that's my fault for not realizing all of us are still new to you." She bumped Jet as they moved. "Don't worry, another few weeks, and you'll be able to tell who's interested in whom."

She wasn't sure she'd ever be able to pick up on details like that.

"Listen. You're doing great, and I'm sorry I made you feel bad."

"You didn't. I'm fine. I just need to pay attention to more things around me," Jet said.

Before either girl could say another word, the scholarch approached them. "Good afternoon, ladies. A moment, Miss Lennox? We won't be long, Miss Houndswood, if you'd like to wait."

Charlie stepped back, and Jet followed the scholarch a few feet away to a table in the Ordinary.

"Yes, Madame?" Why would the scholarch need to talk to her? She heard that Scholarch Wolverhampton prided herself on letting the students do their own thing with little interference from administration. Could she be in trouble? Ruecroft popped into her mind.

"I was just checking to see how you were doing, Miss Lennox," the scholarch asked.

"I'm fine, thank you."

"Specifically, I was inquiring if you've found your adjustment to Quadrivium a smooth one?"

"Yes." She had no idea if this was normal or if the scholarch was asking because she was a princess.

"I like to check in with our new students. I hear reports that you are doing quite well, except for a misunderstanding in Movement?"

Her stomach dropped. How much did she know? "I'm working on it."

"I'm sure you are, dear. Professor Ruecroft is known for her intensity. She expects the best, and gets results. The committee from the Sagesse that oversees Quadrivium holds her in high regard. I just thought you should know. I'm expected to update the Sagesse on your progress after midterms."

The scholarch winked and walked away. Definitely the weirdest conversation she had since coming to school.

Charlie came to stand beside her. "What was that about?"

"I believe Madame Scholarch wanted me to know that even though Ruecroft is batty, she can't get rid of her because the Sagesse loves her." Jet scratched her head. "Really weird. Madame Wolverhampton knows all."

"At least you know where you stand," Charlie said.

"I wasn't going to try to get rid of her or anything. I wouldn't use my parents to do me any favors like that."

"I didn't think you would. But it would have been nice."

"Getting rid of Ruecroft would be like graduation, my birthday, and Springtide ball every day."

"I'm not sure anyone, even the king himself, could get rid of Ruecroft."

"I won't try, but I have no intention of letting her chase me off either."

"She'd be crazy to attempt."

"I'm not so sure. One thing I do know is that Ruecroft isn't finished torturing me yet." Jet frowned. "I have to figure out a way to deal with her."

"Good luck with that."

She nodded. She'd need it.

Seventeen

"Where is Morwenna?" Excitement pulsed through Jet.

After several weeks of school, today was the first day students were permitted to leave campus. This was the beginning of Family Faire. There were festivities planned in the city and at Quad. Some students met their families in Indigo City and brought them back to Quad to see their rooms and meet the professors.

The Family Faire Welcome party, hosted by the Newcastles, was happening the next night at their mansion. She had never seen Indigo City without her parents in tow, and then it was only for official visits. Now she stood with her classmates, ready to leave on the Hippio Strata. This was far different from riding with her family. Charlie kept Jet company while they waited for Will and Morwenna.

An older woman with graying auburn hair approached them. The woman wore a shapeless, smoke-colored dress that hung like a bag. She also wore a harsh expression.

Charlie's spine straightened, and her smile slipped into more of a twisted expression. "Hello, Grandmother."

"Charlotte." The woman inclined her head. "Where do you think you are going?"

Already, Jet did not like Charlie's grandmother.

Charlie tugged at her collar. "Grandmother, this is Her Royal Highness, Princess Jaiette."

"You neglected to introduce *me* to her, Charlotte. How will she know how to address me?"

"I wasn't finished," Charlie said, but it was lost on her grandmother.

"Please excuse my granddaughter's appalling manners, Princess. I am Eveleen Houndswood."

Jet hated to lie but saw no way around it. "A pleasure to meet you."

"I had heard you were attempting to finish your education here, but I must say I don't agree with changing traditions on a lark."

"Grandmother, please," Charlie begged. Her grandmother rounded on her, hatred glowing in her green eyes. "I am permitted to voice my opinion, girl."

Charlie jerked back from her grandmother.

"Thank you for letting me know how your thoughts," Jet replied in her formal, court tone. "We always welcome differing opinions."

"Ah, the royal 'we'. How amusing." The woman smirked.

She might be crazier than Professor Ruecroft, and Jet reached for Charlie's arm. "Your granddaughter has offered to show me Indigo City. Will you be joining us?" She prayed the answer was no.

"I shall not. Neither will Charlotte," Eveleen Houndswood snapped. "Charlotte, your dorm room at once." She sniffed and spared Jet a glance. "You may say goodbye. I will wait for you in the atrium." Charlie's grandmother spun on her heel without saying another word.

Charlie stood frozen, her mouth hanging open. "I'm sorry. She is difficult."

That description was a huge understatement, but Jet said nothing. Instead, she tried to focus on the positive. "Well, I'll see you later at the Newcastles' maybe?"

Will trotted up to the girls. "Morwenna isn't coming with us. Her parents summoned her for lunch. She'll meet us later at the Cocoa Cup."

Jet tilted her head. "That's strange. I thought she was looking forward to showing me Indigo City. It's all she's been talking about in practice."

He shrugged. "Morwenna had no choice."

"I hope everything is all right."

Charlie, still pale from her grandmother's visit, said, "I'm sure everything is fine. Her father just expects her to show up when he calls. And she absolutely adores her father. She wouldn't consider a change in plans a problem at all if he's the one doing the changing."

"Are you two ready to go?" Before they could answer, he continued, "We're supposed to meet the king and queen at my place for tea in a few hours. That doesn't leave us a lot of time to explore."

Charlie's shoulders sagged. "No. You two are on your own. I'll try to see you at Will's for tea. I am going to have my grandmother sit with Madame Scholarch, because I should get some things straightened before she gets to the disaster that is my and Morwenna's room. The girl is like a tsunami when she packs. There will be total destruction left in her wake. My grandmother will think it's me, and it's easier to clean it than listen to her complaints about me being a slob." She rubbed her forehead. "Just another part of the glamour of living with Morwenna." She patted Jet's shoulder. "Have a great time."

After Charlie's departure, Jet followed Will through the station. "Too bad Charlie couldn't come, but I get it. I just met her grandmother." They stopped at the line of students assembling on the platform to board.

He winced. "She's horrible, isn't she? She expects Charlie to be perfect. I think living with Morwenna is a day at the beach for Charlie in comparison."

"Speaking of Morwenna, it's weird she isn't here. Is her father as hard on her as Charlie's grandmother is on Charlie?"

"No. Not the same. I've never seen anyone get along with their parents as well as Morwenna does. She's an only child, and I think she feels responsible for their happiness. I think she actually likes them, though."

"But you don't get why she likes them?"

His brows drew together. "Her father is a demanding blowhard, and his wife is more interested in their furniture than in Morwenna."

"Well, that was direct."

"Sorry. It's a long argument between Morwenna and me, so I stopped pointing out all the times her parents have ignored her or when their expectations are ridiculous. She always defends them, so we don't fight about it anymore. We just agree to disagree."

"You're a good friend, Will."

He shoved his hands into his pockets. "Thanks. She needs one, even if she doesn't admit she needs anything. Ever."

"I can totally see that side of her personality."

"Yeah, well. Enough about the Sabertons." As they approached the platform, he stopped. "You okay with me giving you the grand tour of our fair city?" He held out a hand to help her up.

"How can I refuse such a kind invitation?" She took his hand.

"First thing we need is a ticket for you," he said. "How's your shellback situation?"

His innocent inquiry sent a wave of embarrassment through her. Money. She had none. She and her parents hadn't thought of everything before she came to Quad. She hadn't needed any pocket money before this. Everything she needed she charged to her school account. Royals didn't handle money, but she wasn't going to point that out. Sounded stupid.

"No problem. I'll float you until we see your parents. I mean, since your ancestor's pictures are on it, I imagine I can trust you." He said.

"Thanks. Sorry. I didn't even think about that."

"Hey, relax. Don't be so hard on yourself. You don't have to have everything figured out all the time." He led her to the AutoVend machine in the wall of the Strata station. He inserted several jaspers, and the machine spat out a ticket. "Besides, I really think you ought to be focusing on my problems, not yours, right now."

"What problem?" Jet asked.

"I'm seeing the king and queen today, and I don't know what to wear."

"My mother is fond of puce. Do you have anything in puce?"

He shuddered. "I'm not sure it goes with my eyes, but for royalty, I am but a slave." He motioned her toward the line of passengers.

"Enough of your problems now," she said. "I have my own. I still haven't met the rest of your family besides your dad." A thought struck her. "What about your parents? Is your relationship with them good?" She really did want to know.

"The same as everyone, I guess."

"That isn't actually an answer."

He sighed. "Well, my mom is terrific. I can talk to her when I need, and she doesn't turn everything into a lesson."

"I get that. It's like they have this need to use every conversation as a lecture." She thought of her father.

"Exactly." Will rubbed the back of his neck. "You just described my relationship with my dad. I'm okay with him most of the time, but the lectures on responsibility tend to get old. I'm supposed to take over as guardian of the animals—follow in my father's footsteps." He gestured to the city outside the windows of the station. "I'm well aware of my duty to my family and Pelagiana I was born into, and I believe in continuing the traditions. It's just the only thing we talk about." He gazed across the platform. "Don't get me wrong, my dad is amazing. Seriously. His politics, his inventions. I agree with all of it in theory, but I'd like him to trust me to make some decisions on my own. Before I do anything I have to do, I need to do some things I *want* to do."

"Such as?"

"I'd like to explore the globe like my dad has. I'd like to see it for myself and form my own opinions about the humans. My dad loves them. Morwenna's dad hates them. I've been living with the back and forth forever, and I should make my own choice."

"I can understand that."

Will cocked his head. "I bet you can. Here I am going on about my future…"

"Right? Our futures may be mapped out for us, but there's always more than one route to a destination."

"I know I've said it before, but you are something else, you know that? How about this? I'll consider your suggestion." He nudged her arm.

"Sounds fair. When you talked about your dad's politics, what did you mean?"

"Oh, no, we're not ruining this day with debates on progressive versus traditional Pelagiana politics. Let's have some fun." He took her hand in his, and Jet couldn't find any reason to argue.

~ * ~

Jet's first glimpse of Indigo City on a student pass was awesome. She peered through the oval windows of the train into a cloudless blue sky as the skyline grew in front of her. Never before had she been allowed to roam so freely, and her heart drummed in her chest. The fact security followed her and blended into the crowd didn't even bother her. She just soaked in the moment.

Unlike most cities in the modern world, Indigo City planners had learned from and capitalized on lessons of human and Pelagian history. Each building, structure, park, and street had been thoughtfully planned. The architecture utilized the natural environment from start to finish, from building materials to temperature controls once the building was occupied.

Sustainable and ecologically inclined, Indigo City was a beacon of cooperation between the Pelagi and the natural world. They used reclaimed materials and sustainable food sources, and continued to educate themselves on better ways to interact with nature. Pollution was kept to a minimum with strict laws forbidding transport that wasn't solar powered.

He showed her his father's offices and the enormous complex where the Sagesse assembled when in the city. Stopping in front of a bakery, Jet was captivated by the colorful display of confections and the people lined up to buy them.

As they slowed, Will asked, "Have you ridden a MotoPearl before?" He led her to a Pearl Strand station with thirty or so MotoPearls. He reached into his pocket for money.

She gulped. "No, I haven't," she answered, hoping he wasn't going to suggest she try now. Her clumsiness was epic when it involved her own two feet. She couldn't imagine introducing motorized transport.

"That's okay. You can ride with me, and we'll practice before you get one of your own." They crossed the avenue, and Will found the AutoVend and inserted several jaspers. The MotoPearl's double metal lock unhinged, and he pulled it from the bay. "You just stand behind me on the platform here and hold on."

"Hold on to what? You have the handlebars." She swallowed the panic in her throat.

"Put your arms around me, and you'll be fine."

This might not be so bad. She'd always wanted to ride a MotoPearl. She stepped onto the iridescent platform, which was shaped like a huge, elongated clamshell, and wrapped her arms around his waist. They took off down the avenue, joining hundreds of others riding Pearls, and passing bikers and walkers on the promenade. As they went, he pointed out shops and buildings again.

She interrupted him to ask, "How did your dad ever come up with the idea for a MotoPearl?"

"Pretty great, aren't they? My dad modeled them after the noble pen shell. He figured two or three people could stand in a shell that size, laid on its side, and boom—the idea popped. I have no idea where he gets most of his ideas. He's one of those people who have ideas pop into their heads fully formed, and they are almost always genius ideas."

She doubted he realized the pride came through as he talked of his dad.

"Dad said he figured the people of Indigo City needed a compact, efficient way to travel around the city, and the laws state they have to be powered by the sun or the Array. The hippocampi are okay, but not everyone has your ability with animals, and the Pearls are better suited to the city. The Hippio Strata is great too, but since it's mass transit, that's limiting in terms of schedules. Now people can come and go as they please, on their own timetable."

They zoomed along the street, stopping for pedestrians and other MotoPearls, Will navigating the pearl with ease. "In my father's line of work, he interacts with humans outside our world a lot. He visits and works with them on biomimicry projects and other global environmental concerns. He believes it's a benefit to cultures, theirs and ours. He said they have finally gotten around to adding something like this in their own cities, but they use bicycles instead."

Will brought the MotoPearl to a stop in front of a salmon-colored building. They hopped off the little vehicle, and he docked it at the stand.

"What's this place?" Jet asked.

"That's a bank," he said. "When your parents give you some shellbacks, they'll probably get them from one of these."

She slapped his shoulder. "Ha, ha. I'm not a complete idiot."

"Well, I'm giving you a pass this time, but next trip into the city, you're buying."

Sounded amazing. "You got it. But why are we here?"

"I thought you might want to do a little exploring on foot before we reached the Cocoa Cup. Have you been to the one on campus?"

"Haven't had a chance yet. Still getting my bearings."

"Yeah, I get that. It was tough last year to get used to Quad and weird not living at home, so the freedom was brand new."

"I've never been able to do what I want when I want. I guess I'm still getting used to that too." Jet remembered the guards posing as students and thought that she wasn't as free as everyone else.

She didn't recognize anyone on the street, but there were too many people everywhere for her to really see well. She considered saying something to Will but didn't want him to be uncomfortable.

They set off down the street. He pointed ahead. "This section of the city is the old town. It was here where the idea of Indigo City was born. I'm sure you know the history of our people, but I wasn't sure if you had seen it."

"Not like this," she said. "I've seen it from carriages in parades mostly. This is completely different."

"I like to get out into the world and see what I've read about. It's important to appreciate the place and the people." He cleared his throat. "That's just my opinion, anyway."

"I completely agree."

"Your parents must be out of their mind to see you."

"I think so. I miss them too. It will be good to catch up."

"You'll have enough to tell them to last three weekends, let alone one, when we've finished our tour. Between your adventures at school and the city, you've pretty much done it all," he teased.

"Not even close, but I plan to try."

"Why does that answer scare me so much?"

She giggled. They strolled along the busy street, stopping so she could look in every shop window. He seemed content to wander along at the glacial pace. By the time they reached the Cocoa Cup, she counted sixteen separate times she wanted to buy something. She vowed to visit the city soon. She wished she had been able to buy the little periwinkle earrings for her mother. Next time, she promised herself.

The Cocoa Cup, as Will explained it, was where all Quadrivium students met up at some point or another on campus. The Cocoa Cup in the city was bigger and offered more variety than the one on campus.

They specialized in hot beverages and snacks. The café was decorated with brown and blue overstuffed chairs as well as couches and low conversation tables.

She loved it. The smell of warm chocolate wafting from behind the counter was reason enough. But the spot itself was cozy and welcoming. As she and Will made their way through the queue, he angled his body to her, his eyebrow raised. "What's your choice, Jet?"

"I have no idea what to order other than the Original Cocoa Cup."

"You need a triple layer *pôt á crème* to go with it, then," he suggested. "You won't be hungry for snacks at my house, but it's worth it."

"Everything smells so good. I'll try anything."

As they took their snacks to a sofa facing the large window looking out onto the street, she couldn't think of another day when she had so much fun. They talked for a few minutes before she remembered to ask, "Where do you think Morwenna and Charlie are?"

He shrugged. "No idea. Haven't given either of them a thought since we left Quad."

His answer pleased Jet so much she bobbled her cup. His chuckle erased her clumsy discomfort, leaving only warmth in its place.

Eighteen

When Jet and her parents arrived at the Newcastles' grotto, her foot bounced on the carriage floor. The mansion appeared magical, much altered from her visit yesterday. She hadn't appreciated the house, as she was too excited at seeing her parents to notice of the details. She needed to tell her father about the last Sagesse meeting, and they had retreated to the royal apartments after the tea party yesterday so they could strategize. The view was breathtaking. Fox-fire garland illuminated the trees, which lined the extensive drive leading up to the estate and twinkled in the purple light of dusk.

Her mission hadn't changed, but now she needed to focus on the keeps. Peppercorn could help with this part in case some animals didn't trust her. For now, though, her father told to enjoy herself. She planned on doing just that.

Descending from the coach, she followed her parents up the long, marble staircase to massive entry doors. Will's home, she learned, had begun as a simple stone grotto, but had grown into a sprawling waterfront estate with gardens and an indoor stream.

Just inside the doors, the grand foyer's brilliant chandeliers cast an elegant glow on the partygoers. Declan and Sabrina Newcastle stood with Will between them, greeting arriving guests.

"Hiya, Princess." Will winked.

Sabrina Newcastle reached for Jet's hand. "William Newcastle, will you please greet our guests more formally?"

"Good evening, Mrs. Newcastle, it's a pleasure to see you and Mr. Newcastle again."

After formal introductions, Mrs. Newcastle suggested Will show Jet around, and they jumped at the opportunity to leave the foyer and receiving line.

Jet meandered along with Will. "I can't get over this gallery. It's gorgeous." The Newcastles were known for their art collection comprising some of the best examples of Pelagi art in various mediums.

"Sometimes I forget how amazing it is," he said. "I guess because I can see it any time. My parents are so committed to the cause, especially my mother. Our goal is to provide young Pelagi artists a place to display their works without having to bend to current politics." He focused on a marble sculpture of Neptune and Salacia. "It's actually quite beautiful, isn't it?"

"It's impressive." Jet moved in for a closer look.

He clasped her hand. "Hey, let's go and see what Charlie and Morwenna are up to."

He drew Jet toward a dim, stone hall. If possible, the hall was larger than the one they just left. At the far end, they entered a room in the center of which bubbled a huge pool with a splashing fountain. The pool of water opposite the entrance flowed out of the room. This was part of the Newcastles' famous indoor stream.

She drank in the view. "It's stunning."

"Yep. Never gets old." He peered into her eyes, then swallowed hard. "I wanted you to see this. It's my favorite spot in the house." He brought his hand up to her cheek and brushed aside a whisper of her hair. They stared into each other's eyes for a long minute. His head bent closer to hers.

Harsh voices in an adjoining room broke the spell. She whirled around at the same time as Will, hitting him with her elbow. "Sorry," she muttered.

It was Charlie and Morwenna, and the two were arguing. Charlie's words were clipped. "I won't do it. It isn't right."

"I don't care if it's right or not. It's happening," Morwenna said.

Jet's wanted to hear more but Will's cough interrupted the escalating argument before she could hear Charlie's answer.

"Hellooo, ladies? Uh, you have an audience here. The bickering is offending my tender ears."

Morwenna and Charlie came around the corner and joined them by the fountain. Both girls scowled.

"You know this is supposed to be a party, right?" he asked.

Morwenna flipped her hair over her shoulder. "Of course. We were just arguing over who would get first dance with you, Will." She batted her lashes.

"Hilarious, Morwenna. You know I'm not a big dancer. Besides, I brought Jet down here to meet Svashi."

"Of course. I'd love to talk to Svashi. You said she stopped speaking to you altogether?" Jet asked.

Morwenna answered before he could respond. "That stupid sea mink is stubborn and spoiled. Will lets her have run of the estate."

"Morrie's just jealous," he said.

Why would Morwenna be jealous of his animal unless she thought he paid too much attention to it?

"I can't bring Svashi or Viktor to Quadrivium as my keeps," he said. "They are too rare and are safest here in our stream. Since Atlas has gone missing, Svashi and Viktor are the last pair of sea minks anywhere. As far as the humans are concerned, the entire species is extinct." He frowned. "Viktor isn't a big talker, so Svashi is my only communication with the two. She used to talk to me all the time, and now she just ignores me. She isn't behaving like herself, and she isn't eating."

He led them through twisting corridors and rooms, following the stream through the estate.

"This is all just to get attention, Will, and you are playing in to Svashi's game."

"Stop judging Svashi on your actions, Morwenna. I hardly believe Svashi would pretend to be sick," said Charlie.

Morwenna pushed between Will and Jet and took his arm. "You know I'm just as worried as you are, but you'll make yourself sick if you keep up like this."

"I've known you a long time, Morrie. You might be worried about me, but you certainly don't worry much for Svashi's well-being," he said.

"You worry enough for all of us. Of course, my major concern is for you. I believe the animals can care for themselves." Morwenna didn't give up her position next to him.

They rounded another corner and entered the original, ancient estate—a stone grotto decorated in marine motifs. The bioluminarias along the walls illuminated the water. The bouncing reflections danced along every ripple, bathing the entire sea cave in flickering light.

Jet sucked in a breath. "This is one of the most beautiful places I have ever seen."

He straightened his shoulders. "We aim to please here at the Newcastle estate."

Morwenna and Charlie moved to a stone bench carved into one of the walls. Morwenna crossed her arms. "Where is she, Will? Now we have to miss the party to search for her?"

A black snout surfaced. Sleek and fat, Svashi made her way to the rocks bordering the edge of the pool. Following close behind was another mink, her mate, Viktor.

The minks shook off the water beading on their coats. Svashi was as beautiful as Peppercorn, though Jet would never share that observation with her pet. She let the minks settle themselves upon the rocky shore of the pool, tiny skeletons of mice and fish scattered nearby. There were also empty oyster and clamshells. At least Viktor must still be eating.

As the minks dried, the coloring of their coats became more of a dark russet than black. They ignored the four students in the grotto. Soon Will, Charlie, and Morwenna stared at Jet.

"I know you're expecting a miracle, and I hate to disappoint you. This will be a bit."

Morwenna groaned. "I don't have the patience to wait here. Come on, Charlie. Let's get something to eat. This could take all night." Before leaving the grotto, she turned back to Will and stroked his arm. "Save some time for me later?"

"You know I will."

He deserved a better friend than Morwenna. Jet pursed her lips.

"Morwenna isn't really capable of feeling when things don't directly affect her," he said after she and Charlie had left. "One of these days she is going to realize the entire world does not revolve around her."

She couldn't disagree.

He shrugged. "Thirteen years is a long time to know someone, and she deserves some slack. She's been a great friend. Growing up the son of Declan Newcastle—scientist, inventor, and advisor to the king— wasn't always easy. It got lonely. Morrie always could tell when I needed her."

"So of course you're loyal to her. That only makes sense."

"That's true. Maybe I'm too loyal. But one of these days, she is going to need a true friend, and right now, I'm that guy." He shook his head. "Besides, the entertainment factor alone is reason to keep her around. When she gets pissed, it's hysterical and frightening."

Jet pretended to shudder. "I'll stay on her good side then."

"I can't imagine anyone being mad at you. You're too nice. Not everyone could easily accept Morwenna's dramatics." He reached for her hand. "You make it so easy to tell you what I'm thinking. We're all lucky you decided to ditch your tutors and enroll at Quad."

Jet considered his slate-blue eyes and swallowed.

"Speaking of luck," he said. "Are you feeling it with Svashi?"

"Um, yes. I'll just need a minute."

"Why, Princess, something got you flustered?"

She opted for the direct answer. "Not something—someone. But I think you already know that." She lowered her head. "I'm not used to your games."

"I'd never play a game with you, Jet."

When she glanced at him, she believed him. He cleared his throat, face reddened.

"Thank you for that. And now stop. I have to concentrate."

He chuckled but said nothing.

Just as she had with Jax the tiger shark, Jet stared at Svashi. Svashi stared back. Svashi had intelligent, brownish-black eyes with a fringe of fine lashes. With no expectations, animals usually talked to her in the end, she would sit with her as long as it took.

"Hello, Svashi. My name is Jet. How are you feeling?" She kept it simple.

Svashi flicked her tail. Several minutes passed before she spoke. Jet asked her questions and eventually wrapped up the conversation by asking, *"Can I tell him? He is so worried about you."*

"Please tell him not to worry. What I am going through is natural. I just don't feel up to long conversations. Thank you for caring about him enough. I must be careful of whom I trust. The other wouldn't have tried so hard."

Did Svashi mean Morwenna when she said "the other." Jet wasn't sure but didn't want to press her.

After telling him what Svashi said, he let out an ear-splitting whoop of excitement. Picking Jet up off the floor and swinging her around, he repeated, "Thank you, thank you, thank you!" As he put her down, he lowered his head and kissed her soundly. "Thank you," he whispered.

Heart pounding in her ears, she brought shaking hands to her hot cheeks. Her stomach fluttered. He didn't seem to need her to do or say anything. This was good, because she had no words.

Nineteen

Before she could react to the kiss, Will grabbed Jet's hand and pulled her from the grotto. "Come on. I have to tell my parents!"

They rounded the corner and ran smack into Morwenna. He didn't bother to pause. He just grabbed her hand with his other and dragged both through the twists and turns of the vast estate. Once they reached the grand foyer, he arrowed in on his parents at once. Almost at a full trot now, he didn't stop until they landed at his parent's side.

"Will! Where have you been?"

"I'm sorry, Dad, but could I speak to you and Mom a moment?"

"Of course, son." Mr. Newcastle took his wife's hand and bowed to the couple they were speaking to before Will's interruption. "If you'll all excuse us a moment?" At their nods, the group moved to a more private area.

He pulled Jet with him and left Morwenna behind with the couple. "Svashi isn't sick," Will rushed out the words. "She told Jet she's pregnant."

Mrs. Newcastle gasped, and her eyes filled with tears. Mr. Newcastle let out a breath. "Are you sure?" He looked at Jet.

"Yes," she said. "You all love her so much, don't you?"

Will's mother answered, "Not only is this news a blessing, but it also offers us relief in knowing Svashi isn't sick. Our animals are part of our family."

"I feel the same way."

Mr. Newcastle pivoted to the crowd, clapped his hands and shouted above the din of the party. "Ladies and gentlemen, please, may I have your attention?"

As the crowd's conversations dulled, she was swept into the fold of the family. Queen Phoebe and King Magnus appeared, and Declan acknowledged them.

"Ah, Your Majesties, please join us as we celebrate some joyous news. Our keeps, Svashi and Viktor, are expecting."

The crowd burst into applause. As the people began chatting and mingling again, Jet was bombarded with questions about her ability with reluctant animals. Most people were polite but some, like Eric, grated on her nerves.

"How do we know you're telling the truth, Princess?"

"I guess you could ask Svashi to submit to a physical exam, but be careful, Eric. She bites."

He just strode away. Professor Miles joined the group surrounding her and shared the story of her classroom interactions with the juvenile tiger shark.

A petite woman she had never met said, "I find this terribly hard to believe. Sharks do not speak to us."

Jet forced a smile and answered, "It is true sharks have difficulty trusting us. But Jax is young, and he has been more open than most."

Morwenna stood to the right of the woman. "Mother, the princess isn't lying."

"Of course she isn't. It's just all so unusual."

"Yes, Mother. Princess Jaiette, may I present my mother, Judith Saberton."

"A pleasure to meet you, Mrs. Saberton," Jet said.

Finally, the newness of the princess talking to Svashi wore off, and the partygoers dispersed until only the Newcastles, the king and queen, the Sabertons, and Jet and Charlie were alone.

Mr. Saberton spoke to Jet for the first time since his arrival. "Princess Jaiette, such wonderful news you were able to extract from the beast."

Jet bit back her first reaction and instead said, "Svashi is a proud animal and doesn't trust lightly. I am honored she chose to share her joy with me. She and all the animals are important members of Pelagiana."

He clenched his jaw. "Yes, well. It is lovely to see a royal embracing the old ways and practicing encephalic communication." He grunted. "Isn't that right, Morwenna, darling?" Morwenna's icy-blue eyes glared for a moment.

"As I was saying, Your Highness," Roger directed this to King Magnus, "we need more traditional values celebrated among our youth. Your daughter is a great credit to you."

"Thank you, Roger. Of course, I believe my daughter is a great credit to all of Pelagiana."

"None of this interacting with humans for you is there, Princess Jaiette? Your practice of enComm speaks to the traditions of our people. Though I believe the animals are fine on their own, this doesn't look too good with the animals disappearing on your watch, Declan—"

"Miss Lennox, forgive us," Mr. Newcastle said. "We are just revisiting an old political discussion. Roger believes I am crazy for interacting with the other world out there, and I think him antiquated in his belief that all humans mean to cause us harm. We certainly didn't intend to pull you into the argument." He raised his eyebrows toward Mr. Saberton.

"Quite right you are, Declan. This is no time for a debate." He patted Morwenna's shoulder. "Why not let these kids enjoy the party? Morwenna tells us you and she are best friends, Princess?"

This was news to Jet, but Morwenna's sudden, desperate expression begged for her agreement. She'd get to the bottom of it later. "Morwenna has made my transition to Quadrivium quite easy."

"That's my girl. She's something else, isn't she?"

Morwenna stood taller under his praise.

Charlie interrupted and asked if Jet was hungry.

"Excellent idea. You young people go and get your fill. The Newcastles know how to put on a party."

The rest of the party passed so fast, Jet's head whirled with the excitement. She spent most of the night dancing. Morwenna reverted to her usual confident character, and for some reason, Jet found it a welcome return.

She wished the night wouldn't end, yet she was excited to get back to school. An overwhelming sense of belonging washed over her. Will was a huge part of that. Throughout the evening, he had introduced her to everyone he knew. He clasped her hand as he walked her to the door, her parents a discreet distance ahead.

She stopped on the path. "I had a wonderful time. Thank you. Not just at the party but yesterday in the city too."

"How about we call it even since I had just as much fun, and you got Svashi to talk to you. I can't repay you for that." His eyes shone in the moonlight as he lowered his head to hers.

"Jet, dear, the carriage is here." Her father's voice broke the spell.

"Another time," she murmured.

Will squeezed her hand. "Definitely."

She floated to the carriage on his promise. As it rolled along and she smelled the last of the summer flowers in the air, she had a thought. She should really thank Roger Saberton one day. If it weren't for him, she wouldn't even be at Quad.

Twenty

Midterm marked important milestones for all the students at Quadrivium. In most classes, this would be the first examination on what they had learned up to this point. Jet had been too busy to see much of anyone since Family Faire two weeks ago, and she and Will never got a moment alone.

The one person she saw plenty of was Morwenna. Practice for the Movement midterm had picked up, and Jet had the bruises to prove it. Professor Ruecroft hadn't relented in her apparent hatred, and she found herself faced with it again one week before her big exam.

"Since some of you are unfamiliar with last year's examination structure," Ruecroft eyed Jet, "I will go over the expectations for the entire class." Professor Ruecroft assumed her normal pattern of pacing the front of the classroom. "A quick overview before I lay out exam expectations." She snapped her fingers. "This would be an excellent time to take notes."

Every student lowered their heads to their Elvers.

"Movement is based on *Dunamaii*, which requires traditional dress. This consists of uniform, mouth guard, and fist pads. The uniform is the sarabara and banded short robe. Even though we haven't competed against each other formally yet, from here on you will be expected in traditional dress for the examinations and competitions in this class."

Jet's palms dampened. She didn't mind the traditional dress, but the exam was fast becoming a reality. If she failed this midterm, she had virtually no chance of being chosen for Wave and Wing. For some reason, she couldn't let go of that goal. She had to get it.

"Everyone in this class, except Her Highness, has demonstrated proficiency by a three-arbiter panel to move to Beta Level. Since I was not asked to evaluate your proficiency, Princess, you might find your examination has additional requirements of the remedial sort. The scholarch is in complete agreement with this additional requirement. It's only fair to the other students."

Jet's cheeks burned hot with anger. Charlie squeezed her wrist to stop Jet from doing anything stupid. Charlie's hushed words cut through the haze of rage. "Don't let her bait you. It's what she wants."

Acknowledging Professor Ruecroft with a short nod, Jet forced a smile.

"As you are all aware by now, this year is devoted to drills and reinforcing knowledge to progress to self-defense next year." Ruecroft clasped her bony hands in front of her. "I am reviewing this brief history not only for our very special student. This information may find its way onto your written or oral examination.

"Tournaments and examinations are judged by three arbiters. Thirty is a perfect score and eighteen is the minimum needed to pass. You will all keep this in mind as you choose your partners for the flow sequence portion of the examination."

Jet and Charlie had decided on being partners because, next to Morwenna, no one looked good, and they needed all the help they could get. She and Charlie had practiced their routine in front of Morwenna, and even she admitted it was coming along.

Class ended, and as they began to shuffle their way to the door, Ruecroft stopped Jet. "Ah, Princess, I have a little surprise for you during your examination. I do hope you're ready."

She had been expecting something like this. "I look forward to it, Professor."

Charlie, Will, and Morwenna expressed their sympathy, but other than helping her study and practice, there was nothing anyone could do. Jet didn't want to give the professor the satisfaction of asking for special consideration. That's exactly what she had been accusing her of from the beginning.

She focused on her other midterm examinations and counted herself lucky they were fair. In BioEcology, the midterm exam was oral. Professor Alexander presented each student with one question, and he or she had to stand in front of the class and answer. It was a terrifying form of pop quiz. When it came time for her question the following day, her nerves were at the fraying point. She stood, bumped her knee on the table and limped to the front of the class. No one snickered, but she caught Morwenna's eye roll. She couldn't help but smile at Morwenna's expression. It reminded her of how often she bemoaned Jet's awkwardness during Movement practice.

Professor Alexander asked his question as Jet gripped the lectern. "Miss Lennox, please describe in detail the relationship between the Divine Shield and the Heliopons."

She let out pent up breath. *I've got this.*

"The Divine Shield, also known as the Paragon, is a perfect, single, lattice crystal of pure diamond. The absence of grain boundaries renders it impenetrable by any other substance other than itself and the Baroque—the pearl Neptune gave us as a portal to the surface. The Paragon wall ends at the Heliopons, the bridge unifying Aurealia and the surface of Indigo Lake. This graduated helix to the surface has undergone much renovation over the centuries, including the draining of several of the passageways and the atrium for the building of the Hippio Strata platform, and the Emporium. There remain underwater pathways to the surface, which serve recreational and athletic purposes. Several of the passages are closed or under excavation." She released her hands from the lectern.

"Excellent, Miss Lennox. You receive the mark of Optimum for your answer."

Whew! Thrilled with the grade, she returned to her seat. All grades at Quadrivium were given using the same scale—except in Movement. In Movement, her numbered score from Ruecroft would be translated into Quad's acceptable grading scale. Jet's mark of Optimum or best in BioEcology earned her the highest point value of five.

After that each grade was given in descending order: Second Optimum; Bonum, which meant good; then Inferiorem, which meant the student needed remedial work on the topic. The last grade available to students was Defectus, meaning failing, and earned the student only one point.

She had now passed the midterms of BioEcology and enComm with Optimum grades. Before her Movement midterm, she had Human Studies and World Lit to get through. The prospect of Movement terrified her, but she had to focus on everything else too.

As she sat studying in her room for what was sure to be a very dry exam on *As You Like It*, Peppercorn appeared from his hole.

He snorted and settled himself on the chair. *"When you finish midterms, I want you to meet someone."*

"Okay. Anything that you think might help us. And by the way, Eelfare just posted notice of another special session of the Sagesse next Wednesday. I'll have to find a way to get there after my Movement midterm."

"We'll figure it out," he promised.

She hoped he was right.

~ * ~

Jet received Optimum grades in Human Studies and World Lit. Her relief was short-lived. The Movement midterm loomed.

Upon entering the Movement classroom, the chairs and tables repositioned around the perimeter allowed a vast open space in the center. This would serve as the square where the pairs of students would perform their physical portion of the exam.

Ruecroft had structured the exam so everyone would be surprised. No one knew whether they would be asked to perform a solo routine or partnered one.

Jet had seen other physical exams already. Having over forty students in one class meant the exams had to be broken up over several days for each student to get the allotted twenty minutes. Will and Morwenna had already been tested. Both passed with distinction. She received the highest marks in class so far.

Jet and Charlie were last. Ruecroft called Jet to the center of the room. "Princess, please take your position."

Jet glanced at the professor and the two other arbiters. The judges were students in their Omega year. So far, they had been demanding but fair. Panic snaked through her as she edged to the square. Her hands were damp against the palm pads she was required to wear, and she fisted her shaking fingers. Fighting for some control, she scanned the room, frantic to see her friends. Will and Morwenna sat side-by-side in the improvised gallery, offering smiles.

Jet sucked down a huge breath. *I can do this.*

She reached the center of the square. The cold mat beneath her bare feet crackled. Her toes dug into the hard sponge, and it gave very little. She faced the table where Ruecroft and the arbiters sat. Following Morwenna's instructions from their study sessions to excruciating exactness, Jet nodded and waited for acknowledgement.

Ruecroft didn't waste time. "Princess Jaiette, I know you planned on sparring with Miss Houndswood, but I have selected someone else."

Her heart sank. Ruecroft reserved the right to change anyone's partner without notice. Only she hadn't exercised this right…until now.

"Miss Saberton, please take your position."

Jet's shoulders slumped. *Oh, no, not Morwenna.* Next to her, Jet would look as inept as an Alpha on her first day.

She glanced at Will. His eyes widened, and he shrugged. So Morwenna hadn't told him about this, but had she known ahead of time? Why wouldn't she have told her? Jet couldn't worry about that right now. She needed every ounce of focus she had. Morwenna met her in the center of the room and stilled.

The other girl didn't acknowledge Jet in any way. Her friend took her studies and competition seriously, but why was she behaving like this? Jet had to force her worry about this unusual behavior aside as Ruecroft stood at the judges' table.

"Ladies, please perform the Thirty-Form Fluidity Flow in half-time, mirroring each other. No contact, please." The professor sat and nodded at them to begin.

Jet let out a breath. This was difficult but not impossible. She was surprised that her midterm comprised of last year's Movement curriculum with only the added challenge of half-time. This was not in character. Focusing now, she bowed to Morwenna and assumed neutral position.

Beginning the flow, Jet moved with fluid effort from one stance to the next. It was easier to focus now because she had trained for this. Inside she celebrated as she and Morwenna ended in thanksgiving stance. It might not have been perfect but it was close.

Jet caught Will's smile and fist pump of triumph. At least he thought she had done well. Ruecroft and the judges conferred.

The professor stood. "We have judged Princess Jaiette's form flow as above average. She receives a twenty-four out of possible thirty points."

It wasn't perfect, but she could work with it and make up points over the remainder of the year.

Ruecroft cleared her throat. "As we have ten minutes left of your exam time, Princess Jaiette, the judges and I would like to see this semester's curriculum, Fight Flow. Any points you earn additionally will go to extra credit toward your final exam."

It would be stupid to turn down the opportunity for more points. With Ruecroft as her instructor, Jet would need all the extra points she could get. She nodded.

Both girls squared off, once again in neutral position. Morwenna's expression was still unreadable and stony. Jet raised her eyebrow.

With the barest of whispers, Morwenna said, "You shouldn't have kissed Will."

She blinked, confused. Certain she had misheard Morwenna, she bobbed her head in question. Her friend said nothing. Why would she bring up the kiss now—weeks after it happened? She and Jet had spent more time together in the past few weeks than before Family Faire, and she could have asked her about it any time. What did she mean?

Ruecroft raised her voice to issue additional instructions. Jet couldn't focus because of the head-pounding confusion Morwenna's words caused. Finally Ruecroft's words got through, and with them came the sickening realization that she had been set up.

"Princess Jaiette and Miss Saberton, you will perform the full-contact fight simulation." Ruecroft had just issued Morwenna full rights to pulverize Jet in hand-to-hand combat. Even if she was diminutive in stature, she was far more experienced and prepared. She also had excellent floor technique, which was quite useful for disabling a taller opponent.

Jet steeled herself. She hoped her eyes showed just as much determination as Morwenna's icy gaze. Now, she understood. Morwenna was not her friend. She must have believed she and Will had something more than friendship, and Jet had encroached on that. Now she just had to get through the next ten minutes with some sort of dignity.

Morwenna's first brutal blow landed across Jet's cheekbone. Bright pain exploded with the connection, and she fought to shake it off. She responded with a forearm strike against Morwenna's jaw, which surprised her. Yet, with each movement, the other girl was quicker to recover.

Scant minutes had passed, but it felt like hours as she landed constant punches, and Jet could only struggle to remember her defensive moves. Morwenna's violent kick to her midsection landed her on her hands and knees on the mat. Behind the ringing in her ears, Jet heard Will's voice along with the murmur of the class protesting the fight.

Dizzy and sick, she pushed herself to her knees. A bit of blood dripped from a cut over her brow, and she wiped it away before it could blur her vision. Morwenna hovered as Jet struggled to her feet. Her chest heaved, and each breath was agony. Could she have a cracked rib? As she saw Morwenna's faint smile, Jet drew herself up straight. She would not quit.

With a clap of her hands, Ruecroft put a stop to the examination. "My, that did get out of hand. Excellent work, Miss Saberton." She glanced at Jet and sniffed. "I can see we have some work to do this year, Princess." Clapping again to calm the still murmuring class, she said, "Ladies, please take your seats."

Fury pulsed through Jet. Without a thought to the consequences, she limped to the judges' table.

"I want my points first." She at least earned something from this set-up, and she wanted those points in front of witnesses. In the last five minutes, she had learned a great deal about the people she could trust— Morwenna wasn't one of them.

The professor shrugged. "Very well, Princess Jaiette." She turned to confer with the other arbiters. "We award three additional points."

Jet must have looked insane, blood dripping from her brow, likely bruises already forming. But she didn't care. Every muscle and joint screamed in pain, but she refused to acknowledge it in front of the class.

As she limped back to her seat, Ruecroft tapped the table with knuckles. "A reminder to anyone who did not receive a perfect score on the physical portion of the exam, your ineptitude has created quite a challenge for you for the rest of the school year. The deficit in points will be difficult to overcome. If induction into the Society of Wave and Wing is your goal, a point deficit all but guarantees exclusion."

Seething, Jet lowered herself into her chair. Charlie's Movement midterm blurred by, and Jet didn't even realize it was over until Charlie nudged her. "Hey, let's get you to the Eripium. You need to get patched up."

Her whispered words and comfort did little to calm Jet. Between the pain and anger, she was ready for another confrontation with Morwenna. As Jet exited the Movement classroom with Charlie, Will yelled at Morwenna.

"That was out of bounds, Morrie!" He slashed hand through the air. "How could you be a party to that? I thought I knew you, but now I wonder. Does your need to win know no limits? Jet hasn't had any true combat training, and you and Ruecroft knew that. Why would you do this to one of your friends?"

Morwenna stood motionless. "I never said *Princess* Jaiette was my friend." Her lips twisted into a sneer. "You assumed I would accept her because you and Charlie did. Well, I don't. She thinks she can get whatever she wants with no consequences for her actions. Besides, what was I supposed to do? Ruecroft wanted to evaluate Jet and told me my grade depended on it."

He shot her a disgusted look. "That isn't an excuse. We're done now, Morwenna. I can't even look at you, and I won't forget you did this."

Jet could barely stand. The adrenaline rush over, every sting and throb in her body screamed. Leaning on Charlie, she staggered past the curious students watching the hallway altercation. At this point, she didn't care. She needed to be alone to heal. She would never forget this betrayal.

She promised Charlie she'd go to the Eripium later, then shut herself in her dorm room, grateful for the solitude.

Twenty-One

"You should have had that looked at," Peppercorn said for at least the hundredth time.

"It's fine. I'm fine," Jet insisted and pulled a bit more of her bangs forward to hide the healing gash on her brow bone.

She and Peppercorn had been at it for several days following the Movement exam. She refused to go to the Eripium, and he refused to stop suggesting it. At least he finally agreed to bring his animal friend to meet her.

"Let him in, Peppercorn," she said.

He went into his hidey-hole near the fireplace. He returned with Norman, the other sable on campus. Both sables were beautiful, but Peppercorn had a bit more spring in his step as they moved to the center of the room. Jet sat on the cobalt area rug to get closer to both animals.

"Princess Jaiette, this is Norman. His Pelagi partner is a Gamma year female. Her name is Chelsea Brooke. Her family doesn't really enComm, but he is here to help Chelsea do well in that subject." Peppercorn snorted.

"Your Highness, I don't understand what you need. It wouldn't be right for me to tell you what my family speaks about," Norman said.

"I would never ask you or any animal to betray such a confidence. Breaking the partnership with your Pelagi family would go against our duty," Jet said. *"I was wondering if you could help gather some information for me along with Peppercorn. It wouldn't betray your duty to Neptune or to your family."*

"I will do whatever it I can to help get Atlas, my sea mink friend, back. He was an excellent hunting friend. He wouldn't just leave."

"Okay, Norman. All I need you to do is reach out to all the keeps you can at Quad and see what they know about the missing animals. I am trying to compile a list of keeps living here without asking for it from the scholarch. It would seem strange to people, I think, if I asked for something that isn't my business." She cleared her throat. *"If your family wonders what you are doing, please don't lie to them. I won't ask you to do that."*

"Princess Jaiette, my family rarely enComms with me. I doubt this would register with them. I will do as you ask and help my new friend Peppercorn as well. Good luck in what you are trying to do."

"Thank you, Norman." She patted him and was surprised when he snuggled closer to her, inviting her without words to stroke his fur.

Did Norman receive any affection from his Pelagi family? She didn't ask. The two sables made their way back to Peppercorn's exit. As Norman slipped through and out of sight, Peppercorn twisted back to her.

"This was very well done, Jet, quite befitting a future queen who cares about her subjects."

She could only nod her thanks. After her Movement defeat, it felt nice to be good at something.

~ * ~

Avoiding Will and Charlie for the next few weeks proved quite easy. Jet hadn't talked to anyone during her classes and ate meals in her room. She had to figure out how to balance everything she was doing, and she needed the time away from them to do that.

She realized she allowed herself to be swept up in the moment and the excitement of a new place. A future queen couldn't get carried away like that or trust so easily, otherwise she'd make a terrible leader. She had trusted everyone—and that had been a mistake.

Looking back, she didn't understand Morwenna's response to the kiss because up to the day before the Movement exam, she was still helping her. How could Jet know Morwenna was hiding her true feelings so well? And how did Charlie figure into all this? How could Charlie not know what her roommate planned? Could that be what they were arguing about the night of the Welcome party at the Newcastles'? There was nothing she could do about that right now. She needed to focus on something she could control.

It was up to her to make herself into a good queen, and with Peppercorn's praise still fresh in her mind, she decided to work harder. She wasn't going to let things happen *to* her anymore. She was going to play a more active role. Her family needed to keep the monarchy alive, and she could do more to help save it. She would start now.

~ * ~

The week after meeting Norman, she devoted a lot of her free time to researching the missing animals. Information from Peppercorn and Norman trickled in, and her list of keeps kept growing. So far, all the stories from them were the same—none of the missing animals would have left for good without saying goodbye to their partners. She would also have to again try to talk to fellow classmates about their loyalties— Sagesse or monarchy—but for now, she let herself heal.

As far as her social life, she continued to eat her meals alone in her room. Occasionally Bertie Cox would offer a wave in the hallway or

Chace Traven would mock salute as she passed. They were being nice, but she still needed time.

The real problem was she wanted to make friends and fit in too much, so she got distracted from her mission. She promised herself that wouldn't happen again. Even Will and his sweet attempts to get her to open to him wouldn't sway her.

To her surprise, there was no fallout from Ruecroft's nasty exam. No one had dared report it to the scholarch, and daily Quadrivium routines resumed. Morwenna waited for Will after every class and tried to get his attention. He pivoted and picked up his pace when she tried to follow him. Jet believed he would soon forgive Morwenna, because it was her experience that the other girl was relentless in the pursuit of her goals.

After everything that happened, Jet still planned on getting into Wave and Wing if she made up the three points she needed in Movement by the end of the school year. She just had to outsmart Ruecroft. Finally, as the close of first term approached, she was cornered by Will and Charlie in the Ordinary.

"Jet, this has got to stop," he said.

"Yes, we've let you pout long enough. But that's over." Charlie stood in Jet's path.

She lifted her chin. "I don't know what you two are talking about."

"Don't play princess with us." He flanked Charlie. "We know how devastating that sham of a midterm was for you. You deserved the time to get over it. But Charlie and I have discussed it, and you need us more than you need solitude."

"You aren't going to succeed here if you let Morwenna beat you down," Charlie added. "You have to fight back."

Her shoulders dropped. "I agree, and I'm working on it, but I can't handle the distractions of other people right now."

His brows lowered. "That's ridiculous. Like I said, you need us. You aren't going to pass Movement without help."

She shook her head, but he put his hand on her shoulder. "Save it. I know you need to beat Ruecroft for what she pulled, and Charlie and I have come up with a way for you to do it."

The Ordinary began to fill with students in search of lunch. Activity buzzed, and Jet relented. She could use all the help she could get. "Okay, what's the plan?" It warmed her heart that they were on her side. "I'll use any help I can get—as long as it isn't from Morwenna."

"Don't worry," Charlie said. "Morwenna has nothing to do with this." She nudged Will. "Explain."

"I'm not sure if you know, but the tournaments in the second term offer students the chance to earn extra points toward their final year totals. Whatever points you earn in each category you can apply to any point deficit you have."

Jet jumped in. "I don't want to use other points if I can help it. I should have Movement points for Movement class. There has to be some other option for help with Movement besides Morwenna."

"I've heard Professor Stemp is decent," Charlie said. "But that isn't the plan."

Will pushed the hair off his forehead. "We figured how you'd feel about the full points. We think you should enter at least three events. Movement, of course, but then pick two others you're excellent at. We already know enComm is a given, because no one else can get that shark to talk to them, and rumor has it that Professor Miles is picking something just as crazy for the enComm event, so we don't have to worry about that. You should have extra points no problem there."

"Okay," Jet said. "That sounds reasonable. What's the rest of the plan?"

"Well, that's up to you," Charlie said.

"Exactly. The rest is up to you. We can coach you in Movement. You aren't half-bad. But *Morwenna*," his eyes darkened, "tied you up in knots, and you haven't been able to recover. Charlie and I think we have that covered if you are willing to give it a go?"

"Of course. I'll do anything."

"Good, then the last thing we have to figure out is your other tournament event."

This was better than sulking and trying to do everything on her own. "Thank you both for the help. I should have trusted you two."

Charlie blushed a bright red.

"Now how do we decide which tournament event I should go for?"

Will patted Jet's shoulder. "That part's easy," he said. "Unless, of course, you have no talent other than enComm?" He grinned.

She crossed her arms. "Oh, I think I can come up with something I'm pretty good at."

Twenty-Two

"I don't care if *everyone* in this chamber disagrees with me!"

Jet and Peppercorn listened to Roger Saberton shout as they hid in their usual spot outside the Sagesse chambers. Under discussion was an idea to post more animals outside the island as information gatherers.

"We don't need more information about the human world. The more Pelagi and animals we send out, the more danger there is for us!" shouted Mr. Saberton.

"Member Saberton, it is just a suggestion from Fin and Feather that we should utilize our assets while we still have them," said Mr. Newcastle.

"I don't like it. The animals can't always be trusted."

"Perhaps they feel the same way about us." Mr. Newcastle's tone was placating. Peppercorn snorted his agreement.

"I am not concerned with what the animals think, nor am I interested in finding out about the human world. We know enough from what happened two thousand years ago. I am only interested in preserving our safety and way of life."

A buzz grew from the members. Jet couldn't tell if they agreed with Saberton or not. Mr. Newcastle said, "If we don't come up with a way to have contacts in the human world, we cannot succeed in the duty Neptune left us."

Another round of muttering echoed from the members.

"I would prefer to discuss the issues we have here on our island rather than worry about outsiders," Saberton said.

"Then Member Saberton agrees we should investigate the animals disappearing?" Mr. Newcastle asked.

"That was smoothly done," Jet said to Peppercorn.

Saberton cleared his throat. "I will compromise. We can revisit this subject in the upcoming Springtide session. I would still not condone an outright investigation. It wastes resources for animals better suited to care for themselves than we could ever hope to. For now, we have earned a respite from our duties as elected officials. Unless there is other business, let us close this session and look forward to Wintertide break."

Jet glanced at Peppercorn. *"Both of them won a battle but not the war."*

"I think you're right. You should speak to your father."

"Get me out of here, so I can do that."

~ * ~

Between her classes, training, and the additional practices on her own for Movement, Jet had very little time to spare. Wintertide recess approached, but before that, written exams loomed.

These written exams were rigorous, with hundreds of questions on each. She devoted most of her time to studying for the Movement exam knowing it would be the most difficult test she would have, and it didn't disappoint. After the exam, Charlie and Will met in the corridor. Jet rubbed her eyes, gritty from reading. Chace and Eric passed them then stopped.

"I can't believe there were four hundred questions on that exam." Eric dropped his bag.

"She didn't miss one opportunity to stick it to us," Chace said. He looked at Charlie. "What about you, Houndswood? How do you think you did?"

Charlie stumbled a moment then recovered. "Held my own. How about you?"

"All right."

Morwenna neared the group with her usual band of girls surrounding her. Angela snickered at Jet, but she ignored it. As had become her habit, Morwenna tried to get Will alone to talk to him. Charlie, Chace, and Eric made themselves scarce.

Will turned away. "We've been over this, Morwenna. I have nothing to say to you."

Jet picked up her bag and started down the hall toward enComm.

Morwenna huffed away with her friends as Will caught up with Jet. "She catches me once a day. I keep refusing, but I don't think she's getting the message."

Secretly pleased with this information, Jet said nothing. She couldn't help being angry with Morwenna. He told her that Morwenna was just a friend. And he kissed Jet. If Morwenna had a problem with anybody it should be with him. If she told Jet she had feelings for Will, Jet would have respected that. It wasn't fair that Morwenna attacked after pretending to be her friend. It didn't make sense. Had he lied to Jet or was Morwenna seeing something that wasn't really between them?

By the end of exam week, Jet had passed every test, including Movement, with Optimum marks. Since a proctor graded the multiple-choice exams, Ruecroft didn't have a say in her final grade. This was a relief. The first term over, Quadrivium students received a one-week break for Wintertide recess. Most went back to their family homes for much-needed rest. She took the Strata to the Heliopons and returned to Aurea Regia below the water with Bevan covering her security.

Jet rested and enjoyed the solitude, and when it was time to go back to Quad for second term, things were better. She and her father discussed the last Sagesse session again during her time at home, and he agreed she could do little more than she already was, given her limitations as a student. Jet promised to contact more keeps and students, but she had little luck so far. It was time to sneak into the tunnels. Just because the animals wouldn't report on what was being said behind closed doors of Quadrivium, didn't mean she couldn't. She was ready to do whatever it took to find out what was going on.

Back at Quadrivium, she jumped into the term. Five classes were the requirement for first term, but students had to add an additional class to their second term curriculum. On their way to their new class, Hydroderm, she, Will, and Charlie strolled through the Ordinary. As they traced the perimeter of the huge room, raised voices in one of the chambers off the main hall caught Jet's attention. Everyone stopped.

"I think that's my dad yelling," Will said. "Wonder what he's doing here."

"Is that Mr. Saberton's voice?" Charlie asked. "Why is *he* here? I mean, your dad has a reason, Will, with his Wave and Wing duties, but Morwenna's dad never visits the main building."

Leading the way, Jet and the others moved to the entrance and leaned closer to the oak door to listen. King Magnus's voice rose above the group. "I don't care that there doesn't seem to be an explanation. We've now lost a honey bear and a schipperke. These animals don't just walk off Pelagiana. Someone must have smuggled them out."

"I'm sure Declan realizes the implication this matter has for his political future. These missing animals are happening on his watch, and we should know what he plans to do about it," said Saberton.

She could tell Newcastle was answering but couldn't make out his words.

Will clenched his fists. "That isn't fair. My dad is doing everything in his power to solve this problem. Up until now, Saberton has been sidelining my dad's request for an investigation."

"I'm sure every member of Sagesse knows your father cares, Will," Jet said.

"Saberton thinks the animals can take of themselves. He's always said this. Questioning my father's competence works to

Saberton's advantage. He only cares about what's going on in Pelagiana and how it affects the people."

"I thought your dad and Saberton were friendly?"

"Friendly enough, but they don't agree on how to govern Pelagiana. Both care a lot, just in different ways." Will shrugged. "I think Saberton secretly resents that my dad holds higher office."

The door to the conference chamber opened. She and her friends froze. Holding her breath, she waited for one of the adults to say something.

"Jet, dear, I am so glad to run into you like this." The glint in Queen Phoebe's eyes told Jet her mother knew they had been eavesdropping.

"Hello, Mother. What a pleasant surprise to see you," Jet said.

Queen Phoebe hugged her and acknowledged Charlie and Will as each made their bow. "Before you all run off to class, I'd like to invite Charlotte and Will to the Aurea Regia for the Springtide gala. I have cleared this with the scholarch. If you wish to invite anyone else or bring an escort, just be sure to advise Scholarch Wolverhampton, and she will get their names to me at the Regia. Jet, I will need the name of your escort."

Quickly, she kissed her mother's cheek. "We'll be late for class. It was wonderful to see you."

She pushed Will and Charlie out of the Ordinary and headed down the steps of Quad and onto the Proprietary grounds. Their new class was scheduled to meet at the beach.

Chuckling, Will asked, "What's the rush, Jet?" He slung an arm around her shoulders to slow her down. "You aren't embarrassed about your mother's obvious good taste in escorts for the ball? You can't blame her really. While I'm not the best dancer, my conversation skills are sparkling. Some might even say I'm one of Indigo City's most eligible escorts."

His lopsided grin made her knees tremble, but Jet decided he had enough fun at her expense. "I think you misunderstood my mother, Will. Obviously, she would like you and Charlie to be our guests at the ball, but she knows I already planned to ask Chace as my escort."

Charlie giggled.

Will stopped on the shell pathway to the beach and held Jet's hand. "As much as I hate to disappoint the queen, I'm afraid that solution isn't going to work for me. You're going with me because any other option simply won't do. You want to go with me, right?"

For all his confidence, she heard a hint of nerves in his question. After heaving a mock sigh, she said, "If I must."

He beamed. "Well then, that settles it. Charlie will go with Chace, and you and I will go together."

"Hey," Charlie said. "Who says I'd like to go with Chace?"

Jet winked. "You do. It shows every time you stare at him in class or stumble over your words when you talk to him."

Charlie stared at the shell path. "All right, but who says Chace wants to go with me?"

"Chace does," Will said. "He thinks you have intelligent eyes."

"Glad we figured that out," Jet said. "Now let's get to class. We have work to do this term, and I need all the help I can get."

Twenty-Three

They broke through the frangipani hedge and made their way barefoot on the pink, sugar-sand beach. A few other students joined the class from behind. Eric and Morwenna had chosen this class as well. Wishing she had chosen something else was stupid. Determined to ignore the situation altogether, Jet stood with the rest of the group waiting for the instructor to show.

A cheerful shout broke through the murmur of the class. She glanced around the beach to see where the shout originated. Suddenly there was another, then a splash drew her attention to the surface of Indigo Lake. A graceful female form surged from the lake and executed a flip and dive so quick, Jet had to blink to make sure she hadn't imagined it.

She clapped and cheered with the class. Morwenna didn't partake in the applause, and her face scrunched. Ignore her, Jet reminded herself.

She stood at rapt attention, watching the lake for the mystery woman to surface again. Finally, a head popped up, and she stared as the woman glided out of the water. The woman was dressed in a swim suit the color of plums, her feet bare and her toenails tinged pink. Flaming auburn hair, still wet, glinted under the sunlight. Her green eyes shone bright, and her lean body emanated strength from every muscle.

Grabbing a robe that matched her suit, she tied it tight and stood before the class.

Charlie's whisper reached Jet. "I know what she is! She's a mermaid! I heard about her from some older students, but I thought they were making fun of me."

"Charlie," Will said, "we're all descendants of Mer. She isn't any different than us."

"Did you just see that jump and dive?" she asked, eyes wide. "She clearly is a bit different than us."

"Shush, you two," Jet said. "I don't care what you call her, she's amazing. I need to know how to do what she just did."

The woman paused until the entire class settled and hushed. "Ladies and gentlemen, welcome to Hydroderm. My name is Rosamund Hyde. As your professor, it is my duty and honor to teach you the art and skill of Hydroderm. Before we commence, I will offer a brief lecture. I will require answers to questions when I ask them, and this can affect your mark at term's end. For the most part, this class shall be judged on practical application."

Unlike most of Jet's other professors, Professor Hyde stood still as she lectured the class.

"Another ancient ability Pelagians are born with, Hydroderm requires intense training and focus because of its inherent danger. Students need practice, stamina, commitment, and, of course, talent to transmute. Despite being born with them, most modern Pelagians do not develop these natural abilities. Hydroderm is a precious natural gift from Neptune himself. Do not allow yourselves to ignore your natural abilities. Hydroderm is far more dangerous than Movement or enComm, as it involves a complete surrender to the water. As with all talents, some of you will excel, while others will struggle. Therefore, you will be assessed for your *efforts* in my class."

A sigh rocked through the class.

"If you seem to have a special talent for Hydroderm, I will, of course, guide you in the direction of tournament entry and help in any way I can. If you do not show a proclivity for the art, I will guide you elsewhere. Not because you aren't welcome to learn, but because I don't need a record of careless injuries in my file."

Some students giggled.

"That isn't a joke," she continued. "There is a high probability of injury to yourselves and others, more so if you refuse to take my class seriously. Also, the intense speed of Hydroderm is a particular concern when first learning. I caution you against carelessness and taking unnecessary risks. Learning to harness and control power at such a great speed is an integral part of the process. As I am sure you know, Hydroderm is like flying underwater, if done correctly, and awesome speed is needed to accomplish this feat." Finally, she moved, but only to push a stray lock of hair from her forehead. "Any questions?"

Eric's hand shot up. "I've heard there are some Pelagi who learned to breathe underwater."

"That is correct. This is very difficult and requires intense training for many years. It isn't impossible, because remember, this is a gift inherited from Neptune. This is something we have often dismissed as obsolete, but should be valued."

Bertie Cox extended a tentative hand, and Professor Hyde acknowledged him.

"What about the tail?" he asked.

"Ah, yes. The tail. I was wondering when someone would ask. When we begin hydroshifting or transmutation in the water, it can be very scary. That is why we delay our study of Hydroderm until you've had some Movement training, because it requires great strength in mind and body. The same type of focus is required for success in Hydroderm but even more so, because most of us will panic when we shift the first time. Most of you will never surrender to the water enough to transmute to full form. This includes the tail."

Why couldn't she focus in Movement when she had been hydroshifting for years? Everything about Movement was difficult, but Jet had never experienced anything but pure relaxation in the water. She supposed it was just another thing that made her different.

"Just like underwater breathing, shifting requires years of intensive training," the professor explained.

"What about us? What will our skin do?" Angela Lorente, Morwenna's friend, asked.

"Your skin will become a better form of itself. It becomes waterproof, tougher, but also smoother. Most of you will feel a natural pull in your body to shift, but you might have ignored it. Some may have already accomplished transmutation on their own. In my opinion, full skin shifting is our most beautiful form. We belong in the water." Professor Hyde clapped her hands together once.

"Now, everyone please use the changing rooms and get suited up. From now on, please come in suits and robes for class. You do not need anything else," she called out over the sound of students scrambling to get to the changing rooms first.

The changing rooms were housed in two separate stone buildings. Jet was surprised to find a wooden locker with her name on it. Inside she found a black suit, which matched everyone else's. She wasn't sure what she should do with her pearl necklace. She remembered her father said not to take it off, so she decided he would know best, and she left it on.

Jet and Charlie came face-to-face with Morwenna as they exited the changing rooms. Hoping to avoid a confrontation, Jet increased her pace; however, Morwenna blocked her path.

"I can't imagine why you'd pick a class that required coordination of any kind, Princess." She sneered. "I'm sure you haven't forgotten the lesson I taught you in Movement?"

Jet stood her ground. "Morwenna, any lesson you think you taught me had the opposite effect. You must be too self-involved to have noticed."

A group of girls gathered to watch.

"Now please get out of my way, Morwenna. I have a class to get to."

Eyes flashing with fury, she snarled, "I'm telling you now to leave Will alone. He's too good for you."

"I'm not pursuing Will, so you should direct your rant to him. He's the one who needs to hear you staked a claim on him, because he doesn't seem to be interested in you. Stay out of my way. I have a lot more important things to worry about than your boy problems." She pushed past Morwenna toward the beach and left the group of girls behind.

Twenty-Four

When Professor Hyde returned to the center of the group, Jet stood composed, focusing on her.

"Now, as I mentioned before, to achieve proficiency in Hydroderm, one must learn to control the natural powers within. You would not have been permitted to attend my class if you had not been judged ready to tackle the rigors of this course. I would like to see where you all are in terms of skill level before we go out into the deep water, so I will now conduct a quick individual assessment of your hydroshifting abilities. All of you enter the water now. Go ahead and observe your classmates. I'll call on you one at a time." She looked in Jet's direction. "Miss Lennox, please," the professor called, "I first need to see your shift from terra to hydro and back. I am here if there are any issues."

"Thank you, Professor." Jet entered the water a few feet away from the professor.

The familiar rush of warmth welcomed her, and she arched into the water. She surrendered herself to her water world as she had so many times back in Aurealia. Her mind was strong, and her breathing slow and even. As her body broke the surface, in an instant she hydroshifted, summoning the gifts of mighty Neptune. Flying just beneath the water, she sailed past the professor and the class. The pearl glowed warm against her hydroskin, and Jet sensed power there. What did it mean? She would have to explore when she was alone.

Then, just as fast as she hydroshifted, she terrashifted. Emerging from the waves, she strode toward Professor Hyde. As she approached, the entire class stared at her like she was a freak again.

"Excellent," Professor Hyde said. "Miss Lennox, that was tournament worthy."

"Thank you, Professor." Jet's cheeks flared hot.

Professor Hyde clasped her hands in front of her. "As I told you all, some of you would be better suited to Hydroderm than others. As usual, I was right." She chuckled. "Your classmate, Miss Lennox, is a natural."

Jet surveyed the class again, while her face burned even hotter. She needed a win after the Movement exam last term.

"All right then, next student, please," the professor asked.

Will waded in next to Jet as they floated near the shore then nudged her shoulder. "Show off," he teased. "I guess we know the third event you're entering this spring tournament."

She peered at him through lowered lashes. "I thought you might be impressed. I warned you I'd keep a few secrets up my sleeve." He gave her a strange look. "Come on. Let's see how you do."

His easy grin back in place, he winked. "Oh, I think you might be a little impressed yourself after this class is over. I'm going to crush it, of course."

"You're arrogant."

"Yep," he said. "But in my defense, it isn't arrogance if it's true."

Jet rolled her eyes and watched as the professor called on the other students.

Professor Hyde methodically swam to each student and worked with him or her. Sure enough, Will proved just as much a natural as Jet. When it came time for Charlie, her friend had some trouble.

"That is all right, Miss Houndswood," the professor said. "You'll come along with practice. No need for concern."

Morwenna shifted with little effort. Jet wasn't shocked by this at all. Her ex-friend proved quite adept at almost everything.

After finishing with each student, Professor Hyde once again addressed the entire class. "We are, and shall continue to be, water warriors. We do not seek trouble, but we don't shy away from it either. To call us any form of servant is an insult to our ancestors. Remember and honor our history."

Her father would approve of Professor Hyde's characterization of their people. No matter what happened in the past or what the future held, the Pelagi endured. Professor Hyde shifted the lecture back to Hydroderm.

"Now, only four of you have shown the natural ability that would safely allow me to let you hydroshift without my close supervision. Lennox, Saberton, Newcastle, and Traven, I've a mind to throw caution to the wind and let you all have a go of it. Starting with Mr. Traven here, just do what you're comfortable doing. Everyone else, please submerge and watch your classmates. I will remain here to monitor your efforts. When we have progressed further, you will monitor each other and serve as spotters." She gestured them underwater. "Go ahead, Mr. Traven."

Jet followed Chace and Professor Hyde farther out into the welcoming Indigo Lake. Once submerged, Jet ached to speed off into the distance and leave everything behind. Chace executed a few very well done three-sixties and rolls, then plunged quickly to the lake's murky depths. Not half-bad, she thought.

Next up came Morwenna, who proved far more adventurous than Traven. Again, this was not shocking in the least. She, at first, just glided with ease, and then she sped up and performed a leap and backward flip so well done, Professor Hyde applauded underwater. Morwenna embraced the high speeds. As she twisted, she came within inches of colliding with Jet at a chilling velocity. She flashed a small, hateful smile as she passed. The water bubbles rushed over Jet from the swift kick of Morwenna's last-minute rotation.

Professor Hyde's jaw clenched when Morwenna kicked at Jet. She didn't care either way. Morwenna threatening her out in the open proved a welcome relief to the first term, when she pretended to be her friend. Now she was on guard.

Professor Hyde motioned to Jet. She took off like a shot, reveling in the sensation of water racing over her body as she ate up the meters of water. Plunging to the rocky depths of Indigo Lake, she launched her body upright, back toward the sparkling surface. She cut the water, thrusting into the air, and then dove back into the water, landing in front of Professor Hyde.

The students remained beneath the water until Professor Hyde gestured them upward. As they all broke the surface, Professor Hyde said, "Mr. Traven, excellent start. I sensed your reticence, but I don't mind a bit of caution in the beginning. Miss Saberton, your technique is almost flawless. If, however, you pull a dangerous stunt like you did and put another student in your path, you will receive a rip."

Jet couldn't believe it. No one dared discipline Morwenna. This shocked her as well, if the vile expression aimed at Professor Hyde was any indication. Professor Hyde ignored her and pivoted to Jet.

"Miss Lennox, your technique is outstanding and fundamentals are in place. I congratulate you on what must be both natural ability and many years of intense practice. I would like to recommend you for entry into Hydroderm Competition in the spring tournament."

Jet took her place next to Will. His furious expression darkened his features. He shook his head to her questioning look. Professor Hyde motioned to him, and the group descended.

At first, his performance rivaled Jet's. He'd be fun to race in open water. After a bit of observation, however, something was wrong with his form. Too tense, his muscles bunched and jerked while executing his dive. Unlike his normal manner, he was ill at ease. She would need to breathe soon but she had to see what he did next. He needed to regulate his powers, or something could go wrong.

As he overcompensated in his plunge, the class chased after him when his descent became too swift. If he swam any wilder, he would spin out and collide with the rocks below. It was clear he hadn't been taught to channel his body's reaction to the high speeds. Suddenly his body jetted out of view. Jet trailed him. The jerking of his body from side-to-side turned her stomach. Will smacked into a rocky crag, the side of his head and left shoulder sharing the brunt of the impact. A light pink mist of blood flowed up from his temple and dissipated in the water.

Jet overcame even Professor Hyde to reach his side first. She thrust her arms under his body and lifted his dead weight. Shooting straight for the surface, she pulled them both above water.

"Miss Lennox, let us help you, please." Professor Hyde's shrill voice rose over the waves.

The burden lessened as she and the others carried him to the sand. The other students raced from the water and gathered around them.

Professor Hyde and Jet leaned over him. The professor examined him, searching for any other injuries besides his bleeding shoulder and temple. She lifted the lids of his eyes and rolled his body a bit.

"He'll be okay, Miss Lennox. We'll get him to the Eripium straight away. You'll see." She touched Jet on the hand, then looked to the remaining students. "You may all change and head off now. Nothing to worry about. Just a bit of a bump."

Incredulous at her cheerful disposition, Jet's heart hammered in her chest. Tears streamed down Morwenna's cheeks. She couldn't help but feel sorry for the other girl.

Will stirred, hacking and coughing as he woke.

"Mr. Newcastle, are you all right?" Professor Hyde asked.

"Sure." He rubbed his injured shoulder.

Jet let out a breath.

"We'll get you off to the Eripium to be sure, of course. You owe Miss Lennox a debt, Mr. Newcastle. She saved your backside."

"That's the princess for ya. Such a show-off." He groaned as he tried to rise.

"Yup. That's me, Newcastle. You know me so well," she said.

He got to his feet on his own, wobbling a bit. He slung his arm around Jet. "The thing is, Lennox, I do know you so well. You were worried."

"You're an idiot. You have no idea what worries me or not."

"Whatever you say, Princess," he said. "But I'm betting one of the things that has you worried is me."

"Worried you're going to kill yourself." She took some of his weight as they hobbled along the path. "Now let's get to the Eripium, and you can explain what you thought you were doing down there."

He stumbled and for a moment, she worried he was hurting.

"Such a nag. It's shocking how much you care, Your Highness."

The smile was in his voice, but Jet said nothing. What he said was true.

Twenty-Five

Will was diagnosed with a slight concussion and a surly attitude. Jet stopped listening to his complaints about being forced to sit out Hydroderm for the next few days. She decided he could brood on his own.

Her classes kept her busy enough. What bothered her most, of course, was Movement and Morwenna.

The double *M*s, as she had begun to call them, had become the bane of her existence. She had no problems ignoring Morwenna, but for some reason she showed up wherever Jet went. Charlie told her she was imagining it, but she didn't think so. It became more difficult to ignore someone when that person was everywhere you were.

And Morwenna, never at a loss for friends, was always surrounded by a group of admirers. Piper and Angela were a constant presence, and they never lost an opportunity to mock Jet. She didn't retaliate. She couldn't afford another rip. Knowing Morwenna's true personality now, the real reason she stalked Jet was because of Will, who pretended his childhood friend didn't exist.

The other *M*—Movement—proved more challenging, but she reconciled the fact that Zephania Ruecroft was just a bad teacher in general, with a specific hatred for Jet. Even with a student she favored, Professor Ruecroft never showed support or encouragement.

A few mornings after Will's injury in Hydroderm, he, Charlie, and Jet entered Movement together. Morwenna and Professor Ruecroft were in the corner of the room, heads bent together and whispering.

Will lifted his eyebrow at Jet and said, "What do you think that's about?"

"With those two, we could have a hundred guesses and still not come up with the answer. Although whatever they're talking about, I am inclined to think it's bad."

He let out a bark of laughter, which alerted Ruecroft and Morwenna to their presence. They jerked apart, and Ruecroft peered around the room, her glare resting on Jet who met her gaze.

The professor strode to her desk at the front of the room, as Jet and the others settled themselves at their tables. "Excellent timing, Princess."

Jet almost groaned but reminded herself to stay calm. "Yes, Professor Ruecroft?"

"In evaluating each of you for Aquaticup, I can recommend just a few of you for entry into the Movement category."

The familiar drone of angry blood pumped in Jet's ears. Morwenna aimed a triumphant sneer at her as Professor Ruecroft paced.

"Many of you just haven't shown the proficiency required to score well in the spring tournament. While I can't stop you from entering the category, I can discourage you. As you compete, you are doing so under my tutelage, and I wish not to be judged based on your poor performance.".

Jet thought maybe she would leave it at that, as it was insulting enough, but she found out Ruecroft had other plans.

"So, the following students have my blessing to compete—Saberton, Newcastle, Houndswood, Traven, and Furax. The rest of you, please do not embarrass yourselves and most importantly me, by trying to compete. It is my recommendation that remedial study continue for the rest of you before you attempt public competition. This extends, in particular, for our princess."

Even half-expecting it, she couldn't help the heat that crept up her neck at the public humiliation. Angry with herself for not controlling her reaction, she plastered a sugary smile to her lips and raised her hand.

"Yes, Princess?" Ruecroft asked.

"I'd like to thank you for your obvious concern for your students' academic success, most especially mine. While I so value your opinion of my classwork to date, with respect I would like to submit my application for the Movement category in Aquaticup."

Ruecroft folded her arms. "If that is your wish, Princess, or anyone else here, as I mentioned, I cannot stop you. Princess Jaiette, I do suggest getting help somewhere. You're going to need it."

Probably best to let Professor Ruecroft have the last word.

~ * ~

"You better watch yourself, Jet," Charlie warned in the corridor outside of Movement class. "Ruecroft has final say in the requirements for the competition. She may not be the only judge for the tournament, but she sets the standard for what competitors are expected to perform." She shuddered. "You've made her so mad now, she'll throw everything she can think of at you. And it will be in front of the entire school and our parents."

"You and Will won't let me make a fool of myself in front of all of Pelagiana. Besides, Ruecroft can't make it any more difficult on me than she would for any other Beta in the competition. There'll be too many people there."

Charlie nodded although her expression still showed concern. "Including the king and queen, and I can't think she'd be brazen enough to break the rules with your parents in the audience."

Chace drew her attention. "I'll tell you, Jet, I wouldn't poke at Ruecroft too much. As amazing as that was back there, she doesn't care if you're a member of the royal family."

"I have to think that has something to do with why she hates me. She sure made it clear from the beginning she wasn't impressed with 'the princess'," Jet muttered. "Unless I'm missing something…"

"Well, I heard there are rumors that Ruecroft applied for a full-time tutor position in Aurea Regia, and your mother deemed her personality unfit for teaching her daughter. No one ever mentioned it before now, because it didn't come up until you got here." He shook his head. "Why Ruecroft would sentence herself to a life at the Aurea Regia is beyond me." Will elbowed Chace, and he had the decency to look chagrined. "No offense, Jet, but life down in Aurealia strikes me as a little boring."

She shrugged. "None taken. It's not for everyone, I suppose."

Chace let out a breath. "Either way, the way I figure it, Ruecroft has a major grudge against your mother, and is aiming it at you. It doesn't help that the lady is certifiably insane, so all bets are off anyway."

Will nudged Jet. "Chace and I were talking about the Springtide ball down at the Regia. He's going to bring Charlie on the Strata because they are supposed to be meeting his parents at the Emporium." He bent his head toward Jet. "I have a surprise for you, if you're up for it?"

"Sounds intriguing and mysterious."

He wagged his eyebrows.

Morwenna approached Will, and his face hardened. "I need to get to class. See you all at the Ordinary."

~ * ~

The following day, Jet decided to broach the topic of Morwenna with Will. "You know, you're going to have to speak to her again at some point."

"See, that's where you and I disagree."

"Will, come on. You've known her most of your life, and when I first got here, you called her your best friend. You've got to be missing her."

"Why are you saying this?" He pushed the hair off his forehead.

"Because I can't be the cause of breaking up a relationship that lasted almost thirteen years. Whatever feelings I have toward Morwenna, I don't need you to take them on for us to be friends. I think you should talk to her. Hear her side of things, that's all. What can it hurt?"

His expression tightened. "Jet, that's a nice thing to say, but seriously, come on. What could she possibly say to defend what she's done? What makes you think I want to hear it?"

"I don't know, but it's obvious she has *something* to say to you. You're being unreasonable."

He frowned. "I suppose you're not going to let this go until I talk to Morwenna?"

"I won't mention it again. I know this must be difficult."

"Let's just leave it."

When they arrived at the doorway for enComm, they found a note indicating the class needed to make their way to the Eripium. Maybe this meant Jax had been reunited with his mother and they were going to visit him there.

Professor Miles ushered them in with the other stragglers. "Find your seats. Today we are going to practice something very special. But before we get to work, we can stop a moment to see how well Jax and his mother are getting along." He beamed.

The huge glass panels that formed the walls of the Eripium allowed the sun to shine in and warm the aquarium. Several other huge rooms, with tanks and displays in each, encompassed the entire building. The Eripium also served as the primary animal hospital for Pelagiana.

The main hall, where the students were seated, held the largest tank and had water access to Indigo Lake. Jax and his mother swam before them. Jax's fin parted the water as he circled the tank. His mother's fin had healed from the jagged butchering. She had been fitted with a prosthesis, which the experts at Eripium provided, to swim well and survive in the open water.

Unable to hold herself back, Jet leaned her forehead against the cold glass. Jax stopped his circular route and met her eyes. *"How are things going?"*

"Fine. I am pleased to see my mother is doing so well, and I am even happier to be with her."

"But?"

"I hate to be fed. I would like to hunt, and no one has told us when we will be allowed to return to open water."

"Have you asked the scholarch?"

"We prefer communicating with you. She is kind, but she is overly cautious. My mother is healed. We just need to go home."

"I'll see what I can do."

Jax began to swim again.

Jet made her way to Professor Miles. "They want to know when they can leave."

"Well, that isn't surprising." His brow furrowed. "I'll talk to the scholarch and see if she would do something about their release date. I am not privy to those decisions." He patted Jet's shoulder. "Take your seat, Miss Lennox, and thank you for the update on Jax."

As she sat beside Bertie Cox on amphitheater-like stairs in the hall of the Eripium, Professor Miles spoke to the entire class.

"Before we begin class, I would encourage you to later explore the Eripium and all they do here. There are specialists here for both the Pelagi and the animals. Some of you may have already had the occasion to visit, as I hear injuries are not uncommon in a lot of your classes. But serving as a hospital and clinic is not all they do. The Eripium houses rescued animals and, in all cases, do their best to get the animals back to their environment. If rehab isn't possible, the animals are given a home here." He cleared his throat. "Today we shall begin a very special type of enComm. It was my belief that by showing you that communication with one of the most reticent animals in our waters is possible, you might open your minds to the idea that any communication is possible."

"What could be harder than that shark you made us practice on?" Eric asked.

"Well, Mr. Furax, I'm sure it hasn't escaped even your attention that everyone in this room is an animal too?"

A buzz erupted throughout the class.

"I heard from an Omega student that he might try this on us," Eric said

Professor Miles clapped his hands to silence the class. "I knew you'd all be as excited as I am. As you know, it is beyond difficult to achieve success using enComm with one another. It is because of our human side, of course. We must have the ability to trust the person with whom we are sharing our thoughts, and this type of trust can take years to develop. Indeed, Mrs. Miles and I often use enComm when one of us needs to duck out of a party early."

The class laughed a bit at this admission.

"Let me be clear about our purpose. This is not an exercise in mind reading. Just as with our animal partners, we must allow someone to share our thoughts. Not even the best or most practiced enCommer can walk into someone's mind uninvited."

"That's a relief," Will said.

"Now, I am sure you have many questions, but before we get to them, you must partner off. I have chosen your partners for you." At the loud groan from the class, Professor Miles raised his hand. "I know you would have preferred to pick a friend, but it isn't advisable." He strode to the lectern in front of Jax's tank and reached for a folder. He drew a sheet from it and began reading names. At last he said, "And since we are odd numbered, I will serve as your partner, Mr. Furax."

Jet was partnered with Elliot Bennett, a boy she had never met before. Gangly, tall, and awkward, with flaming-red hair and freckles, he was tongue-tied. "I'm Jet."

He swallowed hard. She could just make out his raspy, "Hello."

"Shall we go find a quiet spot to start working?"

They made their way to an open spot next to one of the floor-to-ceiling glass panels along the perimeter of the huge room. They sat on the floor, facing one another. Both drew out their Elvers. Jet asked him where he was from.

"I live in the city, but we have a place in Aurealia as well," he murmured.

"Do you have a keep here?"

"No, my keep stays at home with my mother. He's a warrah named Storm. He's very special. There aren't many wolves like him left in the world, and he helps my mom at home because her eyes are failing."

"So you think enComm with animals is important?"

"Very. My mom also thinks that bringing the endangered animals here to Pelagiana is one of our greatest duties...and she thinks the Sagesse is shirking their responsibility. We love Storm."

She was about to question Elliott further but Professor Miles drew their attention.

"Okay. Now I've sent instructions to your Elvers. Begin the exercise on the first page," he said.

Jet and Elliott did as they were told. Will had been paired with a girl Jet didn't know either. Mousy and petite, the girl and Will made an interesting pair. He was at least a foot taller than her. He glanced sideways in her direction.

He winked and mouthed, *get back to work.*

She tried but she couldn't stop thinking about what Elliott said about the endangered animals. If Pelagi didn't go out into the world, how would they keep the animals safe? And why didn't Roger Saberton care? She needed to find out.

Twenty-Six

It was on the way to Aurea Regia for the Springtide ball two weeks later when Jet and Will were alone again. He had arranged a hike of one of the old passages into the palace compound. They waved off Charlie and Chace and made their way to Indigo Beach and the ancient ruins there.

As they strolled along, he asked, "Why don't you have any guards?"

She swallowed. Even now someone was following them, and she had no idea where or who they were. She had to notify Bevan ahead of time of what she was doing. She didn't always tell him everything, yet he always found her. She knew her friends would be uncomfortable with the idea of being spied on. It was weird even for her, and she had someone watching for her entire life. Bevan was just doing his job, but she still wasn't going to volunteer that she had hidden guards.

She chose her words with care as she said, "There hasn't been a threat against the royal family in thousands of years. Humans don't know we exist, and even though I'm the heir, I'm not threatening anyone's way of life, so why would anyone bother?" She shrugged.

"So it's been discussed, then. And here I'm thinking I just brought it up."

"My security has been discussed, believe me. They have me covered. Plus, my parents wanted me to try and have somewhat of a normal existence here. Why do you ask?"

"It just seemed weird to me the next in line for the throne would be allowed to wander free. I didn't think to ask about it until this point because we haven't been off grounds except that once in Indigo City." He took her hand in his warm grip. "I just need to make sure you're safe."

"That's sweet, Will. But the worry isn't necessary. I'm not really allowed to 'wander free,' as you say. I made my parents a deal when they allowed me to come to Quadrivium. I promised I wouldn't do anything stupid." The shell path leading to the ruins of the old passage crunched under their sandals.

"I have to wonder, though, if taking the ancient passage down alone with you could be labeled as 'stupid.'" She raised an eyebrow. "You do know what you're doing, don't you?"

"Trust me. I've got this."

They strolled along the path in companionable silence until a thought occurred to her. "I've got a question."

"I'm all yours, Princess." He said the words without his usual joking tone.

For a moment it flustered Jet. She tripped a bit on the path, but he held her steady.

"What's the question?" he asked.

"You told me you chose this way for a reason. I just wondered what the reason was."

He lowered his head for a moment. "I had a couple of reasons really, but the main one was to get you alone. We haven't had a chance to talk about anything important since Family Faire." He shrugged. "Are you doing okay?"

"I'm great, Will. I appreciate you looking out for me."

"I'm serious. Morrie likes to win, and she isn't finished with you yet. Are you sure you can handle this? Because she is really good. I know you think you have it under control—"

She cut him off. "I do have it under control." She fisted her hands by her sides.

"It isn't a crime to care about what happens to you."

"No crime at all, as long as you don't patronize me. Would you treat Charlie this way, or Chace?"

His slate eyes grew stormy, and he stopped and spun her toward him "What is that supposed to mean? You know it isn't the same. We're more than friends."

"How can we be more than friends when you don't respect me or believe in me? I don't get what you're trying to warn me about here. I was the one Morwenna pulverized last term. Did you think I'd forget? And now you're telling me I don't have a shot against her?"

"That isn't what I'm saying. I believe in you, but I'm worried too." His jaw clenched. "I'm allowed to worry."

"Would you worry about Chace if he were the one Morwenna singled out?"

"It isn't the same," he bit out.

"It is to me," Jet poked him in the chest. "If we really are friends, or even more than friends, you'll respect the fact that when I say I can handle it, I can." She took a breath to calm herself. "Listen, I had an off day or I trusted the wrong person, or whatever. It doesn't make me weak or stupid. It makes me just like everyone else, including you. Or have you forgotten that Morwenna was your 'best friend' before all of this happened?"

"I haven't forgotten anything!" Will shouted. "I blame myself for what she did to you. I pushed you into being friends with her!"

She snorted. "Oh, please. Whatever would I have done before I met you? So in your mind I never made a decision on my own or even made a mistake before we met? That's insulting and makes me seem stupid." She shook her head. "You didn't push me into anything. I chose to ask Morwenna to help me with Movement. I chose to be her friend. You aren't responsible for me, or my decisions."

"I never said you couldn't beat Morwenna. I know you can, and if I hadn't you've made it perfectly clear now. You can take care of yourself. I got it." He stomped off.

She rolled her eyes behind his back. "This is shaping up to be a lovely afternoon. Whatever will we do on our third date to top this one?"

His large muscular frame shook with amusement, and he stopped on the path. "I've got to hand it to you. You sure don't need lessons in diplomacy. Your witty comebacks will have them lying at your feet."

"I'll take the compliment and suggest a subject change."

"I'll grab that subject change like a lifeline," he said, his frown relaxing into a smile.

"You said you had a few reasons for asking me today. What was another?"

He stared at the ground. "Um, I just really hoped to be alone with you when I first asked."

"And now?"

"Now I could use some help with enComm."

"What seems to be the trouble?"

"I didn't have that much trouble getting Jax to flick his tail for me, but getting my partner, Sarah, to communicate is like having a kidney removed. Actually, I think kidney surgery would be less painful."

"Oh, poor Will. You're good at almost everything. This must be a terrible blow to your ego," Jet purred.

"Don't push it, Princess. How about some of that famous diplomacy right about now? Tell me what I'm doing wrong."

She patted his shoulder. "You aren't doing anything wrong. enComm between people is extremely hard. I can't get Elliott to tell me if he likes an apple or a pomegranate with lunch."

"Well, that's somewhat of a relief. But it isn't going to help me earn Optimum in enComm, and I can't accept less."

"I think I've almost figured you out. You act so nonchalant, but you want Wave and Wing and everything that goes with it as much as I do. You're even more competitive than Morwenna."

He crossed his arms. "We all have pressure and expectations to live up to, so I get the comparison, but even I have my limits. There isn't much I wouldn't do to win, but I would never go as far as Morwenna. I won't lie and say Wave and Wing doesn't mean something to me, but I'm not about sharing my deepest wishes to the masses either." He reached for her hand. "I will say this—I'm sure glad we don't have to compete against each other, because I wouldn't stand a chance. I mean it. I'm not just saying it because you are the best enCommer I've ever seen or because you're amazing at everything else."

"Except Movement," Jet said.

"Except Movement." He nudged her. "But you'll get there, and I mean that, Jet. You'll be amazing at Movement because you won't accept anything less from yourself. This might surprise you, but you and Morwenna have a lot in common."

She narrowed her eyes.

He held up his hands. "You just compared me to her too, so hear me out. You're both beyond talented, exceptionally intelligent, and super stubborn."

"Gee, thanks."

"The main difference is how you approach things and your attitude. If Morwenna can't force something to go her way, she's ruthless in her methods to win, no matter who it hurts. You, on the other hand, are kind and hardworking. If you aim for something, you just keep at it without looking for shortcuts or blaming someone else. You just don't give up." He coughed.

She placed her hand on his forearm. "Thanks. That means a lot, but I could work harder." She thought of the fact that she was no further in helping with the animal disappearances. She said nothing to him about her concerns. Today was supposed to be fun.

"Well, don't let it go to your head, Princess," he said. "Now enough of this nonsense. Let's get you to the ball."

They made their way through the low-hanging branches of sabal palm. The scent of the honeysuckle that dotted the path perfumed the air. He led the way, and she followed. Birds called, and she sensed a very strong animal presence, which wasn't unusual at all given where they were.

The path widened, and he stopped to show her the ruins at the opening of the cave. "Rumor has it that Neptune himself used this passage. These stones were an altar honoring Neptune for his gift of Pelagiana." He tilted his head. "Have you ever traveled this way before?"

"This is my first time in one of the tombs."

He guided her into the cave. "Tomb is a pretty good description. When we enter, we make a slow descent until we are, in fact, under the lakebed of Indigo Lake. The ancients were geniuses for their construction knowledge alone."

As they made their way through the dampness, it became darker.

He produced a lantern from his pack. "With a lantern, we'll see the entire tunnel, not just straight ahead."

"Okay, let's get going," she said. "I'm ready for this."

Twenty-Seven

Will took her hand and led the way farther into the cave. Soon the rocky ground began to slope, and the cave narrowed into a tunnel. Ahead of the light from the lantern was a black nothingness. Nerves tightened in her stomach for a moment, and then Jet laughed.

"What are you laughing at?" he asked.

"I started to scare myself, considering the blackness ahead. I was being silly…although this cave is pretty much the definition of creepy."

They forged ahead. As the tunnel revealed itself to them under the glowing, lantern light, Jet couldn't believe the sophistication of the construction. The entire tunnel, had been built with adamantine, the same stone used in the construction of Quadrivium. As they descended, a familiar pressure built in her ears, and she forced yawns to pop them.

Will stopped, reached into his pack, then offered her a piece of mint stick. "This should help with the pressure."

"Thanks." She chewed with relief.

When they'd first begun, there had been occasional evidence of animals and Pelagi. Pictures and little messages carved by both ancient and modern Pelagi scarred the stone walls. Animals had brought smaller prey in to eat and left behind the bones.

Now, heading into a new segment even lower in the tunnel, there seemed little proof that anyone at all came this way, except an occasional set of footprints. Dust coated the symmetrical stones of the walls, and spider webs hung from the ceiling. Will's tall frame proved a hindrance, and his sandy-brown hair became coated with the silken snares.

They hiked a bit farther, and Jet caught his hand. "Hey, let's practice enComm."

"Now?"

"Yes. We can stop for a second. This is a perfect place to practice because there are no outside influences to distract us."

"Okay. I'm game if you are. I need the help." He placed the lantern between them in the narrow tunnel. His back faced the direction they were heading. Jet stood opposite him.

"Tell me what to do," he said.

"Clear your mind and try to relax your muscles."

"Jet, I'm always relaxed."

"Not always, but we'll let that go for now." She held his hands and quirked her lips at him. "Now, allow your breathing to slow—inhale, exhale—even breaths. Don't expect. Don't convey. Just be here in this moment. Breathe."

"That sounds easy."

"Now open your mind to my voice. We'll start with something simple. I'll send you a color. When you hear it in your mind, answer me if you can. Don't break focus. You may be surprised at first, hearing my voice this way, but I'm only there because you invited me. Remember you control who you let in."

With their hands still joined, they continued to stare into one another's eyes. Just inches apart, she forced herself to focus. It was harder than it ever had been with Elliott. That was the pull she felt whenever she neared Will. His eyes glowed in the lantern light. His angular jaw was even more pronounced with the shadows of the tunnel.

He whispered as he lowered his head. "I can't concentrate when you stare at me like that."

She leaned toward him as his lips met hers. Unlike the last time, he didn't rush the kiss, brushing her lips softly until she kissed him back. His grip on her hands tightened as he moved closer. Finally, when they broke apart, he lifted his head and gazed into her eyes.

"There was no way I could have enCommed with you when I couldn't think of anything other than doing that." He swallowed.

At last, when her heartbeat slowed, she asked, "Can you concentrate now?"

He let out a sigh. "I'm not sure if that helped or hurt my chances of concentration, because now all I can think about is doing it again." He tugged at his collar. "The real reason I asked you on this hike is just so we could be alone. Like this. But I still do need help with enComm so I promise to try and concentrate." He shook the hand he held. "Let's do this."

She slowed her breathing, inhaling, then exhaling. With that exhale, she released her distractions, her tension. The steady rhythm of Will's heartbeat echoed in her brain, and she knew he had let her in. It didn't take any longer than thirty seconds.

"My favorite color is red too."

"It shouldn't be this easy."

"Why does everything have to be hard? Just accept that we have this."

"This could come in handy," she said, trying to recover but still reeling from the implications. No two Pelagi she knew of had been this successful their first time trying. What could it mean?

"Stop thinking so much, Jet. I can hear every thought. Just accept. And you're right—this will come in handy. I'm thinking Ruecroft's class is about to get a whole lot more interesting."

Needing to get to the palace, they broke their bond. Neither said anything for a while. Jet was too wrapped up in what the enComm connection with Will could mean.

A putrid smell radiated from deeper in the tunnel. She wrinkled her nose. "I smell death."

"Me too. Watch yourself."

"You too."

He jumped in front of her. "What the…?"

"What is it?"

"A dolphin. Someone left a damn dolphin down here." His harsh voice was absorbed into the tunnel walls. "This is against our laws. No animal could have brought this here except for one of us." He kneeled to examine it. "We don't kill animals."

Jet bent and studied the animal.

"Someone murdered it. There are slash marks." She struggled to hold back tears. "How he must have suffered."

"I know."

"What I don't get is how they did it. Dolphins travel with their families and they enComm. How could anyone get away with this without the other dolphins interfering?"

"There is one way, but it's been outlawed. We learned about it in Alpha Year BioEcology. There's a plant derivative that can cause paralysis in animals. Humans have converted it to chemical form and use it to paralyze large schools of fish to catch them. It wouldn't be impossible to incapacitate a family of dolphins."

Jet shuddered. "Let's look around and see if we find anything else. Maybe we can figure out who did it."

They explored the small area. Neither said anything, and all she could hear was an occasional scrape of their footsteps. "Doesn't it seem strange to you that we're this deep inside the passage and the whole area is clean?"

"What do you mean?" He scratched his head.

"There are no webs or dust or anything. It's as if someone…cleaned it up."

"You're right. Except for the floor. And I don't think it's one person either," he said. "I think it's a group. There are shoe prints."

"So they clean the walls and ceiling but not the floor? Why?" She studied the marks. "There are animal prints here too. There's a raccoon and a capybara—that I can tell." She shook her head. "This is weird. What are people and animals doing down here when you said yourself no one uses this tunnel?"

"I have a theory, and it isn't good."

"Let's have it."

"I think it's one of the secret societies," he said. "Rumor has it that Cloak and Veil makes their new pledges bring a sacrifice."

Jet gasped. "That's terrible! You mean they have to kill an animal?" She couldn't believe it. "I know there are Pelagi who still eat animals, but it's so rare. My father has talked of outlawing hunting for good, but most Pelagi wouldn't do it in the first place. The idea that someone would kill an animal just for fun or ritual makes me sick."

"Yeah, but no one has been able to prove Cloak and Veil is behind it, and supposedly it's been going on for centuries. One of the rumors is that they have a trophy room somewhere in the tombs, but no one has been able to find it."

"A trophy room? Do you mean a room full of bodies or bones like this?"

"Or some other trophy from an animal—like horns, feet, teeth, or hides."

"So Cloak and Veil could be behind the recent animal disappearances?" Jet couldn't keep the rage from her voice, or the excitement. This was real information she could share with her father. Maybe it could help.

"It might be, but like I said, no one has been able to prove it." Will pulled himself up from his crouched position. "Whoever is doing it is pretty sick. Dolphins are our greatest allies in the waters."

"And why, if they have a trophy room somewhere, did they leave the body here?"

"I hate to say it, but I'm so angry right now I'd rather try to answer these questions than go to your Springtide ball. But we have to go."

"Let's get going then. I should fill Peppercorn in on this. He might have some information or ideas."

Jet and Will made their way farther down the tunnel which began to ascend gradually. At the end, ladder rungs made of iron buried into the rock wall showed the next part of their journey. He took the lead.

Once they cleared the stairs, they were in another little passage constructed like the one they just exited.

"We must be under the lakebed still but making our way back up under the village," Jet said.

They inched upward into another cave. Sunlight beamed into the darkness.

"I don't care how normal this is for you. It's still weird that the sun shines under Indigo Lake."

"Neptune provided the sun, moon, and stars. We need those gifts to survive. We country folk even have weather," she gave him a sassy smile. "You should visit down here more often, city dweller, and then it wouldn't seem so weird for you."

He hugged her. "Seems I have a reason to visit now. But let's get out of this cave. I know the king and queen would like to see their daughter, and I'm not going to be responsible for her tardiness. After you, Princess." He gestured for Jet to lead.

She tried to keep up the conversation with him the rest of the way, but her heart wasn't in it. All she could think of was Cloak and Veil and that poor dolphin. She had to speak to her father as soon as possible.

Twenty-Eight

Thousands of fairy lights twinkled above as five hundred guests twirled about in their finery. Candles flickered and buffet tables groaned under the weight of the banquet. Jet had experienced Springtide before, of course. When she turned twelve, the annual celebration had become part of her royal duties to attend, as well as any other formal event.

She always loved to watch the guests mingle and dance, or even shuffle around the perimeter of the mirrored ballroom. Tonight, for the first time, she was a real part of the festivities. As she shook hands with smiling guests in the receiving line, she realized that, in the time from Family Faire to now, most of the members of Sagesse and other Pelagi society had warmed to the idea of Jet attending Quadrivium. Her mother had let slip that the scholarch "accidentally" revealed Jet's excellent performance at end of term, leaving out the point deficit in Movement. This satisfied anyone who might have had misgivings over her enrollment. Now that she loved Quadrivium, she wanted to return next year.

Her mother had also informed her, as they were getting ready for the ball earlier, most of the members of Sagesse were walking around as if the idea of Jet enrolling had been their own. Queen Phoebe found this quite amusing and kept giggling about "pompous politicians" while Jet dressed.

She had chosen to wear red. It was her favorite color, after all. The iridescent pearl at her throat glowed against her skin. Charlie and Jet sat gossiping on the bed in Jet's room before the ball. She held Peppercorn close as she revealed the information about the dolphin. She stroked her beloved pet as she and Charlie talked.

"Oh, how romantic!" Charlie said. "You and Will in the passages and stumbling upon a mystery that needs solving!"

"You wouldn't call it romantic if you had seen it," Jet said. "Nor would you think Will's reaction romantic at all. He's in shock, and I can't blame him."

"I bet he is, and I know what the animals mean to him and his family."

"He is always in protection mode, whether for animals or people."

"I think his protective tendencies are one of the reasons he and Morwenna stayed friends as long as they did."

Jet didn't need to get drawn into the drama again but couldn't help asking, "What do you mean?"

"The thing is, Morwenna can be an amazing friend at times. She makes you believe you are the only person in the room, but this more often than not turns out to be to her benefit. Other times she has the ability to make you feel smaller than a minnow." Charlie shrugged. "Will saw through the façade of her huge personality and understood she had something to prove to her father. He kind of adopted her because she wasn't accepted for herself at home. He hasn't been the same since she clobbered you in Movement. I think it was a betrayal to him." She cocked her head. "Are you ready to go?"

"Not yet. I should ask Peppercorn what he thinks about the dolphin."

Peppercorn leaped from her arms, circled exactly three times, and settled himself on a satin pillow. *"I think the animals of Pelagiana are nervous, and they should be. I've spoken to a lot of species, and none of us know why the others have disappeared. Sacrifice should be considered."*

"You have nothing to worry about, Peppercorn. I won't let anything happen to you."

"I should hope not."

Jet stifled her giggle, and he spoke to her again. *"It wouldn't be wise to share what you know with too many people, Jet. There is danger in Pelagiana right now. I know you must solve this mystery, but be careful and don't go anywhere alone."*

"I'm never alone, remember? Somebody is always watching me. Besides, I wouldn't dream of it." Jet stroked his fur one last time.

"Now let's make our grand entrances." She lifted a brow at Charlie.

As they descended the grand staircase, Charlie put her hand on Jet's arm. "I have a great idea about your Movement practice. I'll mention something to Will."

"I'm so lucky to have you, Charlie. You're a great friend."

Charlie's eyes shined.

"I didn't mean to embarrass you."

"You didn't. I'm just overtired, I guess, and it was a nice thing to say. I'm lucky to have you as well."

Now Jet shook hands in the receiving line alongside her parents. Soon she would be free to see Charlie and Will, who were already enjoying the party with Chace, Bertie, and even a smiling Eric. After the receiving line, her father would make a speech. Then at last, she could dance. The minutes stretched far too long, until she came face-to-face with Morwenna.

"Lovely to see you again, Princess Jaiette," Mr. Sabertons said.

Jet couldn't lie, so she only said, "It's a great evening for a ball."

"Indeed. We hoped to see you around our chateau this term, but Morwenna tells us you have stretched yourself a bit and might not have the time."

She almost disabused him of the notion but held back at the pained and embarrassed expression on Morwenna's face. *How did that girl get people to feel bad for her so easily?* "Enjoy the evening." This ended the conversation, and Jet was glad when the Sabertons moved on.

Lilly Parmenter appeared in the receiving line with her parents. Jet reached for her hand. "Hi, Lilly. I've heard the Octet is performing. I can't wait to hear you all."

But Lilly leaned forward and whispered, "I'm so scared. Onyx is missing!" She squeezed Jet's hand. "Charlie said I should tell you."

This was terrible. Another animal missing, and it happened at Quadrivium? Jet's heart sank. "Let me finish up here and we can talk. We can all try to find Onyx together." She gestured to their group of friends across the room. Lilly sniffled, and her eyes watered. She shuffled along.

At last, the final guest's hand was shaken and small talk made. Her father took his place on the stage in the ballroom. Jet listened as the king welcomed them. His welcome speech was short, and then Jet was swept into Will's arms.

"How 'bout a dance, Princess?"

"Sounds perfect."

They spun around the room. She pulled Will to the side of the dance floor. "Lilly's dog is missing."

He frowned. "We have to do something."

"I know. I wish we could get back down into the tunnels."

"We can't tonight, but could you use some help when you figure your next move? I'd like to know what's going on too. Two heads are better…"

She thought about this and about Peppercorn's warning not to share what she knew. It couldn't hurt. She trusted Will, and he might be able to help.

"You're right. No one is getting anywhere." She stopped herself. "No offense."

"It's okay. My dad is just as frustrated too. He's doing what he can, but this is beyond all of us. The more people working on it the better."

"Let's keep it between us for the time being."

"You got it, Princess. Now let's try to enjoy what's left of the night." He led her back onto the dance floor. "Listen, Charlie shared her idea for your Movement training. We're going to start tomorrow, if it's okay with you? We still have to pass our classes, even if we are taking on an investigation…"

"I have no idea what Charlie's idea is."

"No problem. We're going to meet tomorrow and use another passage to my house. Let's check in on Svashi and Viktor, and then you and I are going to the beach."

"Oh, you think so, do you?"

"I do. And I also know you well enough to know you'd want to check on Svashi with me. So are you in?"

"I think I can fit you in."

~ * ~

Jet had to do something. Later that night, while everyone slept, armed with a small knife and flashlight, she slipped out of the palace. Peppercorn was on a nightly hunt, and she wouldn't know who might be lurking in the tunnels so she needed the weapon. She wasn't seeking out trouble, but she had to go back to see the dolphin for herself. Someone had killed that poor animal. She hoped whoever did it wasn't down in the tunnels tonight.

She traced the same route she and Will had come earlier. Bevan already knew about the body but Jet didn't know if there had been time to remove it. Fully grown dolphins were not easy to move, especially in the tunnels. Bevan had told her they would wait until the guests had gone home. No one wanted this news to get out.

When she lowered herself down the ladder rungs, the flashlight tight between her teeth, she smelled the damp and death. Sweat trickled down her back, but she wouldn't let fear stop her. She stuck close to the cave walls and lowered her light as she approached the corpse, its outline still visible under the soft light. She kneeled at the tail of the tortured animal and examined the body.

Her mouth filled with saliva as she fought back gagging. Her eyes watered, and her nose ran from the smell. It permeated the entire tunnel. She flashed her light over grotesque gashes, large and small, that riddled the corpse. Several different weapons had been used. It would have taken hours for it to die.

Jet laid the flashlight on the cold floor and searched around the animal for anything that someone might have dropped or lost. Several people had to be involved and someone could have made a mistake and left something behind. She tried to be methodical as she worked around the corpse. Finally, she made her way to the head, studied its face. Someone had removed its teeth and eyes. Jet did gag then. How could anyone do this? She didn't know if they'd done it while the dolphin was alive or dead. She couldn't bear it; she let the tears flow.

"Miss Lennox, you better have a very good explanation." It was the scholarch.

Jet dropped the flashlight as she stood. How would she explain this to her father?

~ * ~

"Your majesty, I will have to report this," the scholarch said.

Jet flanked her father as the three of them stood in the foyer of the palace. Jet tried to explain herself on the way back to the palace but the scholarch told her to save it.

The king rubbed his temples. "I understand Madame Scholarch. What exactly will you report? I'd like to know the charges and consequences in store for my daughter."

Jet stared at her feet. This wasn't good. She couldn't get another rip.

"Technically, your daughter was on weekend leave, so the consequences should be up to you, but the portion of the tunnel I found her in is on school property." Madame Wolverhampton clasped her hands in front of her. "It is a quandary on how to deal with this. What were you thinking, Miss Lennox?"

Jet caught her father's eye. She knew she couldn't tell the scholarch everything. "I just couldn't bear to think of him alone in the tunnel. I know he's dead, but I thought I'd stay with him until his body was recovered. We don't even know if his family knows he's dead. There is no one to mourn him." She swallowed, holding back her tears.

The scholarch sniffed. "Yes, well, that is a lovely idea Miss Lennox, but also a dangerous one. We can't have students wandering tunnels in the middle of the night. I told you I would trust you until you gave me a reason not to. This is it. You're sidelined for the remainder of term. You'll send me your schedule on the network and be on your guard.

I may not be able to follow you day and night, but I will check up on you. You won't have the freedom you had."

The king inclined his head. "And your report, Madame?"

"I only report to one body, and that is the Sagesse. They will hear about this at the end of term." She stared at Jet. "Unless you give me a reason to act sooner, Miss Lennox." The scholarch bowed to the king. "Good evening, Your Highness."

The king rounded on Jet. "What were you thinking?"

"I was trying to do what you asked me to do." She crossed her arms. She'd have to figure a way around the scholarch, but right now, she needed to convince her father. "I'm not stopping either. This is too important. A lot of people are involved in this. No one can lift a five-hundred-pound dolphin on their own."

"Jet, you can't believe I would let you continue. It's too dangerous and now the scholarch is on to you."

"No, she isn't. She doesn't know the whole reason I was there. Why was she?"

"It's a good question and one you can't answer now that you've been caught." He cleared his throat. "I'm not sorry about that. I need you safe."

Jet kissed his cheek. "I know but don't ask me to stop. Let me tell you why."

She filled him in on the dolphin corpse, and for the first time in her life, tears welled in his eyes.

After taking a deep breath, he asked, "Will Newcastle thinks it's Cloak and Veil?"

"Yes. It seems there have been rumors for years."

"I'm aware of the speculation. It hasn't been proven, and we've tried to infiltrate its ranks."

"Who is 'we'?"

"Not something I'm sharing with you at this point," her father said. "You know I must ask you to stop. If you get caught again, it would be a disaster. If my daughter is hurt, I wouldn't be able to go on."

"I'll be careful. I know the scholarch could be a problem, but I'll figure something out. But I can't stop. Someone is killing animals we are bound by duty to protect and partner with. I have to do something. It's my job."

"It is not your job yet, young lady!"

"It was several months ago when you gave it to me with little choice. Now you try to take it away? You need to trust me."

"I do, but the situation has changed."

"Father, I won't do anything stupid. Until tonight, I've never been the reckless sort. But I'm not quitting while animals are being killed. And we still don't know why someone is threatening the monarchy. They are related. They must be. Quad is where I need to be to find out more. out. Let me do this. I won't fail."

Twenty-Nine

In the end, all the king could do was agree. Jet didn't give him a choice. He told her he believed in her, but warned her to be vigilant about the scholarch. Neither she nor her father knew who they could trust. She collected Charlie and Will in the grand foyer of the Aurea Regia the next morning, and the trio made their way back to Quadrivium. The way they went back to Indigo City was more traveled and far less disturbing than the one she and Will had taken the day before.

As they ascended, he pointed out different pathways off the main tunnel. "These are passages Indigo City elite built into the main line so they could easily access their mansions. They had to get royal permission. Some are centuries old and aren't used that much anymore, but my family still uses ours now and then. Once we had the MotoPearl and the Hippio Strata, most city people choose those forms of transportation. The tombs are down this way." He pointed to another tunnel on the east side of the main route. "When we were kids, we'd dare each other to see who could go farthest. It's creepy because none of the offshoots are lit, so unless you bring a light, it gets dark fast."

Charlie shuddered. "Those are *the* tombs? The tombs where the secret societies bring their pledges and where Pelagiana's secrets are held? I heard there are vaults and hidden rooms down there."

"Yep," he said. "I have no idea if any of that is true, though. Once you get into them, it's too easy to get turned around. The tombs are so deep under the lakebed, the pressure in your chest as you descend is awful, and most of us would submit to the natural panic. As far as the secret rooms, I believe they are there, but very well hidden. No one has been able to catch Cloak and Veil. And after that dolphin corpse, I wish something could be done."

Jet bit her lip. "Um, about that…" She hadn't been sure if she should tell Will and Charlie what happened last night, but if they hung around her, they'd know something was up when the scholarch checked on her so she filled them in.

"I can't believe you went there alone, without Peppercorn," Charlie said.

"I couldn't let it go. If Will and I weren't going to be late for the ball we both would have stayed. I only had a few hours between us finding it and Bevan and his team coming to get it. I wanted to see if anyone left anything."

"And?" Will asked.

"They took its teeth and eyes."

Charlie's gasp echoed in the cave. "That's disgusting. Who could do this?"

"This has something to do with the other animals disappearing, and Will believes Cloak and Veil could be responsible."

He rubbed the back of his neck. "I do, but it's just based on rumors. Now the scholarch is on to you, so we can't go looking for anything either."

"I can lay low for a while. She likes me, I think. I won't do anything crazy, but we have to research this more." Charlie shook her head. "Jet, I want to help, but you're not going to convince the scholarch you're on the straight and narrow if you aren't ready for the tournament. The Aquaticup is in two weeks. That isn't a lot of time."

"I know. I have to do both." Jet sighed. "I just have to figure out how."

"You won't be able to investigate anything if you flunk out," Will said.

She knew they cared what happened to her, so she let the matter drop. She took the lead toward Will's house. "For now, let's visit Svashi and stick to the plan. The scholarch knows my schedule, and I'm not giving her a reason to doubt me."

~ * ~

Svashi was in excellent spirits. Will wasn't sure if he should hold his pet, and Jet told him to go ahead. "It won't hurt her. She's having babies. She's not broken."

When he locked into Svashi's gaze, Jet was glad the sea mink talked to him this time. Jet, Will, and Charlie were about to leave when Morwenna appeared. Too surprised to do anything but gape, Jet froze.

At last, Morwenna said, "Will, can I have a word?"

He cocked his head at Jet and sighed. He looked back at Morwenna. "Okay, but we don't have a lot of time." He gestured to Charlie and Jet. "We have to get back to Quad." His voice took on a hard glint when he talked to her. He turned to Jet and Charlie. "We'll be gone for just a minute."

Morwenna's eyes hardened when she passed Jet. She forced herself to shrug it off. "Take your time, Will. I wanted to talk to Svashi anyway."

Charlie, who up to this point had been seated on the stone bench built into the wall, popped up. "I need to get going. I'll see you at Quad." She hurried out of the grotto.

That was strange. They had all agreed to go back together, but she didn't blame Charlie who wasn't great with confrontation. Even Jet wished she could disappear when Morwenna showed. She and Will left, and Jet talked to Svashi.

"Hi, Svashi." She told the mink about the dolphin. *"I wondered if you had any ideas."*

"I don't. I'm sorry. My mind is consumed with staying healthy for my unborn. The responsibility of being the last in a species is great. My only focus can be the safe delivery of the next hope for our continuation on earth."

"Of course. I understand. It's insensitive of me to burden you with this."

"Do not concern yourself. I am aware of the problems happening outside my grotto. But the Newcastles keep Viktor and me well protected here. I do not fear for our safety. The disappearances disturb me, but I have faith the Newcastles will succeed in finding the cause before it becomes too out of hand. My belief is that to solve something like this, one should investigate close to home."

She didn't know what to make of that, and when she questioned Svashi, the sea mink had nothing further to say. Jet thanked her, wished her good health, and thought the mink more stubborn than Peppercorn.

Intent on sharing Svashi's interesting words on the animal disappearances with Will, Jet hurried, but she'd forgotten about Morwenna. It was lucky she heard their voices before she burst in on them. Jet tried not to eavesdrop but couldn't help herself when she heard her own name.

"You've known her for approximately five minutes, Will, and now what? You two are inseparable? Poor little Princess Jaiette, no friends and no talent, and you being you must offer her pity friendship? We've meant more to each other for years than she could ever understand. What happened to your loyalty? You forced me to teach Her Highness that lesson in Movement. You needed to see how weak and unworthy she really is."

The venom in Morwenna's voice shocked Jet. More shocking, though, was the realization that he didn't disagree.

Morwenna raged on. "We had plans. We were a team. Your one great shortcoming is feeling sorry for the weakling, and now what? You've got that girl believing you care, when in fact you only became her friend because our parents made us." She snorted. "I'll give you that she's beautiful, but she's also a bore. Were you ever planning on telling her the truth? That you became her friend because our parents wanted to stay in the king and queen's good graces, and we were their pawns? Not even my father or you could force me to stay friends with that joke of a princess. Princess Jet, the laughingstock of Pelagiana, so naïve and innocent, completely unaware of what it takes to make it. What a supreme fool she is."

Shaking from the hate she spewed, Jet couldn't help the silent tears. In her heart, she hoped he would deny her allegations.

But the denial never came. Instead, he murmured, "You're right, and I'm sorry, Morrie."

Jet gasped. After all the nasty things she said, and after all the special moments Jet believed she and Will had shared... Morwenna was right. She was a fool, and she needed to get out of there.

Jet stumbled back into the grotto. Crying and not thinking straight, she had to escape. She jumped into the pool. Hydroshifting at once, she submerged. The grotto and its pool led to either Indigo Lake or the sea beyond. At this point, she didn't care where she ended up, as long as she didn't have to face Will and Morwenna. She could only imagine the laugh they were sharing over her innocent belief they were her friends. How could she have been so stupid?

Becoming friends with Will had been too easy, too comfortable. It wasn't because she had learned to talk to people and gotten past her own shyness. He had been her friend because he had been forced to ignore her awkwardness and befriend her no matter if he liked her or not. She remembered the kiss in the passage before the ball. How difficult it must have been for him to pretend to care.

She wound her way under the water, dodging rocky walls and unknown terrain. The water offered a balm to her aching heart. Trusting her instincts on which direction to go, she swam out of the little underwater caves and into the river that led to Indigo Lake. Taking her time, she did not surface until she'd reached the quiet center of the lake. She needed more time to even out, so she once again dove. Reaching top speeds, she swam until she exhausted herself. Then, at Aurealia, she stared below at her home before returning to the surface. A pang of despair hit her so hard she shuddered underwater. She missed home. All she could think about was leaving Quadrivium forever and leaving all the pain behind.

She didn't need Will, or anyone else for that matter, to succeed. She could do it. She didn't look below again; she emerged close to shore.

She waded to the beach and collapsed onto the pink sand. Sunlight baked the sand where she lay. She closed her eyes to the awful brightness of the sun. As her breath evened and her heartbeat slowed, she allowed the warmth to lull her into fitful sleep.

~ * ~

A shadow eclipsed the sun waking her up. Jet opened her eyes. Will stood above her, the sun forming a corona around his head. She leapt to her feet.

"What are you doing here?" Her words came out thick with emotion.

"What am I doing here? You and I were supposed to come together. What the hell, Jet? Why did you leave without telling me?"

A red haze of fury clouded her vision. "I didn't realize I was under obligation to share my schedule with you and account for every moment of every day. Or was that another order from your parents? In addition to pretending to be my friend, were you also supposed to spy on me?"

He had the decency to cringe. "I thought you might have overheard."

"Then I guess we understand where each other stands. I must thank Morwenna someday for enlightening me. Imagine how embarrassing it would have been for you if this had gone on."

He pushed a hand through his hair. "You evidently didn't hear everything, because it's clear you don't know where I stand."

"I know right where you stand. Your need to prove yourself to your father was motivation to pretend to be my friend. Did it work? Is he thrilled with your inside information?"

"Leave my father out of this. You need to hear my side." His voice broke.

"As wonderful as that chat might be, I actually don't have the time. The scholarch will be checking for me. I am not your responsibility, and I have way too much pride to be your pet project."

"Jet, that isn't what you are to me. Let me explain."

"I wouldn't believe what you had to say."

His cheeks mottled red. "You know me better than this."

He moved closer to her, and she backed away. "I don't know anything right now, except I have to get out of here."

Thirty

Several days later, Charlie was still trying to convince Jet to listen to Will. She ignored her pleas. Both girls were in Jet's room, studying for Ruecroft's class.

"Jet, you can bury your head about this, but you know better. Maybe Will started out being your friend because his parents suggested it, but he wouldn't have stayed your friend for that reason."

Humiliation bubbled to the surface and with it shame. "I don't care. And if you keep this up, you can leave me alone too."

Charlie drew back, hurt etched on her face. "I'm sorry. You're right. I'll let it go." Seated in one of the chairs by the window, she stretched her long legs out in front of her and leaned her arms on her thighs. "One thing I can't let go is the Movement issue. We need Will for this."

She shook her head. "No. If I can't do it with your help or by myself, I don't want it badly enough. I know I can do this. I'm sorry for being stubborn." It was all she could give right now; she was just too hurt. "You never told me about Movement. What's the big idea?"

"Well, I noticed how amazing you are in water in our first Hydroderm class. It seems strange, because you're so clumsy." She winced. "Sorry. No offense."

"None taken. I'm practically a ballerina in water compared to my navigation on land. You won't offend me by speaking the truth."

"Well, I thought that since you're so comfortable in water and you have no fear, it would stand to reason that you should practice Movement in the water."

"How will that help once I am back on land in front of hundreds of people and about to be brutalized for sport?"

"It's muscle memory, Jet, and you use it all the time in all your other classes. You just have a block now about Movement, and that's what's holding you back."

"You're right. But you already knew that. So tell me what to do."

"Let's go to the beach," Charlie said.

~ * ~

Jet and Charlie made their way onto the beach.

"Okay, what we should do is get into the water to the point where we can still stand but most of our bodies are submerged and our heads are still above water," Charlie said. "We can't hydroshift, but try to release your fears about Movement. We need to keep this practice as close to a Movement simulation as possible."

Both waded into the water past the rolling waves along shore until they were standing at neck level.

"I need you to use the water for two purposes." Charlie rolled her neck for a stretch. "The first is to find the groundedness you feel in water and apply it to Movement. Also, since the water flows around us with some current, use the outside force to develop your balance." She tilted her head. "I think we'll start with the Thirty-Form Fluidity Flow. Just face me and concentrate on the water. I'll look at the shore, and that way you won't be distracted."

"Charlie, I haven't told you enough how much this means to me. You're the one person I call a friend."

Her eyes widened. "I don't deserve all that." As she opened her mouth, Charlie hurriedly said, "All I can say is that you're a pretty amazing person, and it's easy to be your friend. There aren't a lot of people who would have given me a second chance after what Morwenna did to you. I mean, I'm still her roommate."

"One has nothing to do with the other."

"Still, you aren't like anyone else. And I know you don't like to talk about this, but let me get it out, please. I know you feel stupid about what you heard. But you should let him explain. One of your best qualities is that you believe in people. Don't lose that because of one bad experience. Not everyone is like Morwenna." She shrugged.

"I'll think about it," Jet said.

"That's all I can ask. But right now, let's focus We have practically no time until the tournament."

"I know. I just can't stop worrying about another animal getting hurt. I've been trying to figure out a way around the scholarch so I can go searching again."

"Jet, you can't yet. It's too soon. The scholarch might relax a little after the tournament, especially if you do well."

"I know you're right; the tournament is something I have to get through first."

"You can only control so much."

"Okay. I'll try to stay out of trouble before the tournament. Thanks for looking out for me, Charlie."

She splashed her. "Good, now that's settled, get to work."

They faced each other, ready to practice.

"Assume neutral position. Now begin the breathing. Act as if you are about to talk to Peppercorn."

She did as Charlie instructed, sweeping all distractions from her mind. With the water surrounding her, she felt altogether different than she did when practicing on the mats in Ruecroft's class.

Charlie exhaled. "Now begin the fluid form."

Something took over Jet at that moment. Her pearl glowed warm again, and she calmed her racing heart. Her thoughts inextricably bound to her movements, she melted and glided from stance to stance through the fluid form. She was at one with the ebb and flow of the current. She felt graceful in her Movement routine for the very first time. It was heady. She finished, bowed with hands clasped in the stance of gratitude.

Charlie gaped at her. "I can't believe how well that worked. I mean, Will said this would work, but I don't think even he could have predicted…"

"Gee, you make it sound like I was beyond repair."

"I don't think you realize how amazing that was. You were flawless."

"Thanks. It wasn't bad. But, we need to make sure this will translate to land. That's the scary part."

"I agree. Let's do that again, and this time we'll up the tempo. Next time, we'll move to Fight Flow and simulation."

Jet took a breath, and Charlie lifted a hand out of the water. "We don't know what Ruecroft has planned for you. You have to assume she'll come at you with everything allowed in tournament regulation—that includes hand-to-hand."

"I know we have to practice it, but I really don't like the idea of punching you."

"It's not my dream either," she said, "but we do what we have to." She inclined her head. "Unless you'd like to reconsider having Will here? He'd make an excellent punching bag."

"Ha. Ha. I think you and I are doing just fine. But I'll give the matter some serious thought." She circled her neck and stretched her arms in front of her in the water. "Now let's do this."

By the time she and Charlie pulled themselves out of Indigo Lake, only a small group of students remained on the beach, and Jet didn't mind collapsing her exhausted body onto the pink sand. Labored breathing and quivering muscles needed quieting. Lost in a companionable silence, she ignored the stares from those students still on the beach.

Charlie said, "You've got a bloody nose."

"You have a gash on your cheek, so don't get cocky, Houndswood. I gave as good as I got."

"And here I thought my new best friend would spare me the full force of her fist. Instead, the princess gets ugly and lands a few lucky ones. I'll be scarred for life."

The minor aches and bruising meant nothing when she could almost taste success. "Let's train tomorrow after you get out of AO practice," Jet suggested. "I'll need to speak to Lilly first. I want to tell her I have Peppercorn asking around about Onyx. I wish I had answers. After that, let's to go to the training room and practice on the mats."

Charlie bit her lip. "Don't you think we should solidify the work before you head back to the torture room?"

"I need to know if it worked. We don't have the luxury of time, and if the water workout didn't help, we'll need to regroup and try something else."

"That does make sense." Charlie said. "Still, I wish we had a few more days' practice out here before bringing it inside. There are too many people in the training room, and they could tip off Ruecroft that you might be improving." She shrugged. "I guess we don't have any control over what other people will do anyway, so you're right. We need to just focus on the training."

"Speaking of having no control over other people, do you have any idea why that group seems to be staring at us today?"

"I'd venture to say they're staring at you and not me, Jet. It might have something to do with the fact you're a gorgeous princess at the beach, but I could be wrong," Charlie said.

"You're hilarious," Jet said. "People got over the princess thing last term. This is different."

"You know I am always willing to help out a friend, so what I am about to do, I do for you. It has nothing to do with the fact that I find him absolutely adorable and I haven't heard from him since the ball."

Jet raised her eyebrow. Charlie waved across the beach to the group and whistled for their attention. This time both of Jet's eyebrows rose in surprise, and she bent closer to Charlie. "What are you doing?"

"Solving two problems with one question," Charlie explained. "I want to talk to Chace again, and we need to know why people are staring at you." She lifted a shoulder. "I told you, Jet. I'm always willing to help a friend."

Chace jogged over and plopped himself down in front them. "What's up, Houndswood? You miss me or something?"

"Or something. Any idea why people are staring at Jet today?"

Chace rubbed the back of his neck and winced. "Yeah."

"Want to clue us in?"

"Not particularly."

"Listen, Chace, whatever it is, I won't kill the messenger. Okay? I understand it could be stupid gossip," Jet said.

"Yeah, okay. Just so you know, though, none of us believe it."

"Believe what?" She swallowed.

"The Newcastle sea minks are missing."

She gasped. "Oh, that's terrible! Will must be frantic." He loved Svashi and Viktor. She would have to go see him now.

Charlie nudged Chace. "But what does that have to do with everyone staring at Jet?"

Chace winced again. "There is some speculation that since Jet was the last person seen with Svashi and Viktor...that she had something to do with the disappearance."

Thirty-One

Jet found Will in the Ordinary, slumped over an untouched plate of curry. Her first reaction came fast—she wanted to give him a hug. She sat next to him.

When he lifted his head, his slate-blue eyes were bloodshot and angry. "I knew you'd come." His voice was ragged.

"Of course I came." She patted his shoulder.

"Yeah, you would. You're the only one who would."

"What do you mean I'm the only one?"

"I'm kind of considered *persona non-grata* right now. From what I can tell, there isn't a Newcastle welcome anywhere in Pelagiana." He closed his hands into tight fists. "It's funny. No one seems to care at all that we are missing two members of our family. With Atlas gone, then Svashi and Viktor missing, there is no hope for the species. No one is bothered about the missing animals or the death of an entire species. All anyone can talk about is that Declan Newcastle failed Pelagiana." His head fell forward into his hands, elbows propped on the table. "Of course, Fin and Feather are investigating the disappearance, and there is to be a formal inquiry from the Sagesse. My father may be censured and stripped of his duties in Fin and Feather."

"That isn't fair!" Her throat burned. "There isn't anything you could have done if someone wanted to steal Svashi and Viktor. I could have done it myself." She could have bitten off her tongue. "I didn't. You know I didn't. I could never…"

Will shook his head. "After this experience, I've learned I don't know people as well as I thought I did. But one thing I do know is, no matter what, you would never hurt an animal, Jet."

"Thanks, Will."

"According to my dad, it's only a matter of time until the Sagesse does something." He shook his head. "My father feels personally responsible. I guess I can't blame him. We should have used more security, but we pride ourselves on giving our animals free rein. Confining Svashi and Viktor contradicts our mission to honor and respect them. We're guardians, not jailors."

"That's right," Jet said. "And that's what your dad's counsel should say in the inquiry. When is the inquiry taking place?"

"They are waiting until the school term is up. They won't replace my father in his other duties until then. The rumor is they'd like me to withdraw from Quad over the break, before next year begins. They have no right to ask me to do that. I should still be allowed as a student, but I think they want the scandal as far away from here as possible. This is another way to hurt my father."

"That isn't happening," she snapped.

"Not even you can make this go away. The king and queen can offer support to my dad and, in the past, that would have swayed the Sagesse. I'm not sure it would work now. The rumor is that the Sagesse is having a special session to discuss how this could happen under the king's watch. People are saying he doesn't care. I'm sorry. You know how rumors are."

Her stomach dropped. She needed to get to that special session and find out what was going on. She didn't dare tell Will of her plans. "I'm not running to my mom and dad to fix this. We need a better solution than that. If my father stepped in, the Newcastle name would still be tainted, even if your family did retain their title and position. That isn't acceptable."

"You're right." He slapped a hand on the table.

"I'm also not letting some mystery person destroy thousands of years of tradition on a whim. My family serves Pelagiana as Neptune decreed. We can accomplish two goals with my plan. We can save our families and the animals."

"Okay, but how?"

"Instead of trying to win at the inquiry, we make the inquiry unnecessary."

"I'm not following."

"We find Svashi and Viktor."

"Of course, but how? You can't go anywhere right now, and they'll be watching me too."

"We still have to try."

"I agree with you, but that doesn't mean we'll be able to find out any more than anyone else. We reported the dolphin, and there is nothing new from anyone."

"I disagree. No one knows I could use Svashi and Viktor's pool in your grotto to swim out to Indigo Lake. We can use that information."

"How?"

"I think whoever took Svashi and Viktor did it through the tunnels or that pool," Jet said. "I'll go through them again. The last time, I was too upset to notice anything, and I could have missed something."

He shifted, and his brow furrowed. "About that... We have to clear the air."

"Let's leave it," she said. "I'm just not ready to talk about it."

"You don't have to say anything, but please let me explain. If you hear me out now, then we can move on. Believe me when I tell you I will get this out sooner or later."

Jet relented. "Say what you need to."

He took her hand. "I'm not sure what you overheard. But I know you didn't hear all of it. Morwenna isn't who I thought she was. Something has changed her, and I couldn't believe the things she was saying that day. It took me aback, and I didn't defend how I felt about you until the end. You didn't stay around to hear that part, I guess?"

"No." Jet's eyes watered. Should she believe him?

He cleared his throat. "Yeah, well, once I told Morwenna the truth, things didn't go well from there. I really do care about you, more than you know. It infuriated Morrie, though."

"I imagine it did."

"I'm not pleading innocence in this. I did talk to you at first because my parents encouraged it, but not in the way Morrie made it sound. Mom and Dad suggested that you might be a little lonely and overwhelmed when you first started here. It made sense to me, so I told Charlie and Morwenna I was going to get to know you." He shook his head. "It appears that Morrie's father had the same idea but for political reasons. He wanted the princess to be best friends with his daughter. Roger Saberton will do just about anything to get ahead or advance his interests, and he doesn't mind using anyone to do it, and that includes Morwenna."

"She can make her own choices."

"I told her the same thing, but she doesn't think she did anything wrong, which is crazy."

"Okay. I understand. Thanks for telling me."

"Not so fast, please." He took her arm as she started to stand. "Where does this leave us?"

"It leaves us as friends and right now partners in this investigation."

"I thought we were becoming more than friends," he murmured.

"Me too. I think that was a mistake. Listen, I've given this a lot of thought. Everything between us happened so fast, and I wasn't thinking." She lifted a shoulder. "Your parents were right. I was lonely and overwhelmed, and you offered an anchor when I needed one. You also offered me a security blanket I could hide under. I didn't bother to try to get to know anyone else other than you, Charlie, and Morwenna. That was wrong, for a lot of reasons." She swallowed hard.

"That day I overheard Morwenna, something happened to me. I realized I wasn't doing what I set out to do here at Quadrivium. I came to Quad hoping to show people we cared. Instead, I buried myself in the comfort of three friends, two of whom weren't there for me to begin with. I kind of coasted on that and stopped trying to find my own way. I succeeded academically, but I didn't do anything more. That's not who I want to be."

"You're too hard on yourself." He clenched his fists. "And what you think about me isn't fair either. Morwenna may have only been your friend because of her dad, but that isn't true for me."

"I know that now. But it doesn't change facts. I think we should be friends. But I can't think about anything more than that. My emotions can't factor so much into my decisions anymore."

"That's stupid." He glared at her. "Your personal feelings should always be a factor. It's what's going to make you a great queen someday. Don't close off because of one bad experience."

"That isn't what I'm doing," she said. "I am just taking a break from letting it run my life. I've said it before—I'm not comfortable with the drama Morwenna seems to thrive on."

"I understand."

"You do? Because three minutes ago you called me stupid."

"I didn't call you stupid. I said your idea was stupid. There's a difference."

"So now you understand?"

"I understand I messed up by not telling you the truth. I understand you need time to trust me again. I understand you need to kick Morwenna's ass in the tournament next week, and I understand we need to help clear my family name and save the monarchy. It's a lot to handle, and…you definitely don't need any additional complications, so I understand. For now."

"That's a lot of understanding for one person. I am curious as to what 'for now' means, though."

"It means my feelings haven't changed. I'll wait." He squeezed her hand.

She shook her head, about to argue.

"Save it. I told you I understand, and I respect your feelings…but I know feelings change, and I'm counting on the fact that yours will one day." He shrugged. "Now, as you are fond of saying, Princess, 'we have work to do.'"

Thirty-Two

Dawn came too fast the morning of Aquaticup. Jet hadn't slept. Throughout the night, she could think only of the coming challenges. Trying to keep her mind off the Movement matches ahead by reviewing her training didn't help. The same thought kept running through her mind. If she did well and progressed to the final, she would no doubt face Morwenna at the end. And even with all the practice, Jet still wasn't certain she could beat her.

Jet got ready for the day. She dressed fast so she could stretch away her tension, forcing herself to remain positive. She'd worked hard for this moment. The best way to train for all the tournament events she entered was in the water, and she'd done just that. Even after Charlie and Will left to practice for their own events, she trained for hours. In return for their support, she assisted them with enComm and Hydroderm.

Competing against them would be strange. She hoped they wouldn't have to confront each other but was realistic enough to know that to get the points she needed to get into Wave and Wing, she had to beat everyone she faced. That didn't stop her from helping them. They were her friends.

The gossip about the Newcastles had died. Everyone had moved on to talking about which residential college would come out on top at Aquaticup. The gossip mill was fickle, and she was grateful it was working in her and Will's favor for now.

Everyone would wait out the weeks until term was over, and the inquiry would bring the topic front and center again. Will and Jet agreed to begin searching for Svashi and Viktor, spending every moment of their spare time doing it. The scholarch showed up unexpectedly every once in a while, so Jet told Will how to make his way from Svashi's grotto into the open water. He didn't find anything. Peppercorn went to the tunnel where Jet and Will discovered the dolphin but there wasn't any activity. She didn't care if the scholarch caught her. She had to get to the tombs after the tournament was over. She believed they'd find something there.

She didn't neglect anything, including Ruecroft's class.

The professor burdened her class with as much extra work as possible. Jet ignored the fury that welled in her every time she missed an hour of physical training because of a Ruecroft assignment. The best way to win would be on the tournament pitch. The professor would have to follow the rules then. Jet didn't delude herself, though. Even under the watchful eye of the scholarch, Ruecroft would try to teach her a lesson for entering the event without her blessing. She just didn't know how.

Jet finished her last stance, steeling her determination to win. After everything she'd been through, it was time for a fight. She met Charlie and Will in the Ordinary.

"Let's lighten up here," Jet said. "This isn't a funeral march. You two were the ones who told me how much fun this tournament is. I think a diversion may be just the thing we need."

"I'm sorry, but could you tell me where the real princess is?" Will asked. "She seems to be missing and in her place is an imposter, suggesting we have fun." He shook his head.

Charlie laughed, and Jet nudged her. "I'm sorry. I know I've been an insane person these last few days."

"That's quite an understatement, Jet. But we understand. Don't we, Will?"

"Sure we do. But what we don't understand is the sudden turnaround. Yesterday you left us, claiming your goal was to pulverize Morwenna into tiny pieces. Now we're supposed to have fun? I don't think I can handle the confusion."

"I've been self-absorbed about beating her, which ironically is just like her. I'm not comfortable with that."

"You aren't like her," Will said. "But I like the direction you're heading. We promise to have fun too. Okay?"

"What I'm really trying to say is, thank you both for…everything."

"We got it. Right back atcha, Princess."

~ * ~

The Aquaticup epitomized Pelagiana. Each tournament event celebrated a gift exclusive to the Pelagi people. There were matches for enComm, Hydroderm—which included rescue swimming, fin-swimming, and fin-diving—Movement, Hippocampi Show Riding and Jumping, Underwater Rugby, Archery, and Free Diving.

Open to every member of Pelagi society, the Aquaticup included different competition age brackets and requirements. Indigo City elite alongside members of the royal family attended and observed from special boxes. Many Pelagi lost quite a few shellbacks from ill-advised bets on the competitors, but it was all part of the fun.

Jet had attended the Aquaticup every year she could recall and watched from the royal box. She'd always longed to participate. She loved the pomp: flags waving, parading competitors, fireworks, and cheering crowds. Now, as she entered the field for the opening ceremony, she wore her growler colors with pride. Today she belonged on the field.

Her father stood, saluted the competitors, and bid them good fortune in the competition. As he took his seat, the event began.

Jet, Will, and Charlie, along with hundreds of other entrants, exited the main field to find the Boards, long, wooden signs where match assignments and results were posted each day. The tournament comprised ten events spanning four days. Guarded as a closely kept secret, the schedule of events was decided in advance and known only to the tournament committee.

Athletes had to come prepared for anything. Several students passed Jet as she made her way through the throng of contestants. A few even offered her support with an occasional "way to go, Princess."

"Does it seem like people are staring again?" Charlie asked.

"Yup," Will said.

"Wonder what I did or didn't do this time." Jet shrugged it off. "Let's find out where we're supposed to be."

"That sounds like a plan," Charlie said.

They all spotted Chace at the Boards. His eyes narrowed at Jet. "I knew you had a lot to prove, Jet, but this is extreme, even for you." He shook his head.

"What's that supposed to mean?" Will asked.

"As if you don't know, Newcastle."

"He doesn't know," Jet said. "None of us know what you're talking about."

"You entered all *ten* events, Your Highness." Chace bowed.

Charlie hissed in a breath, her eyes wide as she stared at Jet.

"But I didn't." She gulped. "There has to be some sort of mistake. I entered four events. I'm sure it's an oversight."

"Things just seem to keep happening to you, don't they?" Chace said.

"That isn't fair, Chace," Charlie said, coming up to stand close to Jet. "You know she isn't like that."

"Like what? What are people saying I'm like?"

Will put a hand on her shoulder. "Ignore it. It isn't important."

"I need to know what he means," she said. "What are people thinking I'm like, Chace?"

"I was the first to defend you, when people claimed you enrolled in Quad for attention. Even when people said you had something to do with Svashi and Viktor disappearing. But now this?" His face twisted into a sneer. "It's hard to believe you aren't attention seeking when you enter ten events."

"I already said I didn't enter ten events," she gritted out. "I entered *four*. There has been a mistake. Thank you for defending me in the past. People are going to think what they want no matter what I say. But can I ask why you care if I did enter ten events? Why are you so angry?"

"I believed in you. A lot of us did. We believed you were here to do something good and different. It sucks to feel like an idiot when you backed the wrong person. We put ourselves out there for you."

"I didn't realize there were sides chosen. I didn't realize people at school would care one way or the other."

"Well, they do." He rubbed the back of his neck. "And a lot of them believed in you without you doing anything to earn it."

"That's enough," Will said. "This isn't the time, Chace, and you have no idea what you're talking about. Jet had nothing to do with this."

"You didn't back the wrong person. I *am* at Quad to do something different. I'll fix this."

Chace shook his head. "You can't. Once your name is on the Boards, you have to compete or forfeit the whole competition."

"It's never easy, is it?" She sighed. A little crowd had gathered around them. "Looks like I'm going to be busy for the next four days."

"That's ridiculous, Jet!" Will stood in front of her. "You can't do this. You aren't prepared for every event. You need to talk to the scholarch and see if you can get out of this. Maybe you can appeal."

"That is out of the question. I'm not asking for an exception from the scholarch. I can't have the rules changed for me. You know how that would look." She was terrified and furious, but she wasn't going to quit.

"Whoever entered me into all ten events tried to get me out of the competition, and I'm not giving them the satisfaction. I will compete." Jet shouldered her way to the Boards to find her first event. Will, Charlie, and Chace followed.

Will began his protest again. "That's all well and good, but this is dangerous. People have died at Aquaticup!"

"I didn't spend sixteen years of my life at the castle just reading or playing piano. I'm pretty good at most of the events. I don't need to win anything except Movement. I'll figure it out, because there isn't another choice." She patted his shoulder. "I can do this."

"Who are you trying to convince?" he asked. "Me or yourself?"

"I think we can all assume who entered you," Charlie said then poked Will in the shoulder. "You can argue with her forever, but she isn't going to budge. I know it, and you know it. The next best thing we can do is help her. She's going to need it."

Chace piped in, "If you think Morwenna entered Jet into all ten events, you and I were on the same page there. But I checked, and someone entered Morwenna into all ten too. I think we agree that she wouldn't put herself in a bad position. She hasn't trained for all the events either. Charlie's right. We need to strategize."

Charlie put her hand on her hips. "Oh, it's 'we' now?"

"Yeah, it's 'we.'" He towered over her. "I made a mistake, Houndswood. Get over it. I know Jet isn't an attention-seeking, self-serving royal. I just temporarily forgot."

"Gee, thanks," Jet said with a sardonic grin. "First, I think it was Ruecroft who entered me into the ten events, not Morwenna. This is punishment, pure and simple. But I don't understand why she would enter Morwenna. Either way, we can't worry about that right now. Have there been others entered into all ten events? It's happened before, right?"

Will moved out of the way of an Alpha year looking for her sister. "Yes. A lot of people attempt it every year. Logistically it's almost impossible, because of the time constraints alone, but it can be done."

"Has it been done successfully?"

"If you mean has anyone won their age bracket in each of the ten events, then yes. In thousands of years, it was bound to happen once or twice."

"So not completely impossible?" she said, ignoring his sarcasm. "There must be a record of the winners in the library somewhere and probably ideas on why the winners were successful. Let's start there," she said. "Like Charlie said, I need any help I can get."

"I think we need to find out your schedule, don't you?" Charlie reminded her.

Heat spread across her cheeks. "Oh, yeah, that might help. I'm definitely going to need to know what I'm up against."

Thirty-Three

Ten events in four days seemed impossible. Jet would tackle each challenge one at a time. It wasn't possible for anyone to help her strategize, even though her friends tried their best. She waved them away. "Don't worry about me. Focus on your own events."

Everyone she knew was also competing, and they had their own problems to worry about. She bypassed the library and accessed her Elver for as much information as she could get on past Aquaticups.

Later that day, she made her way to her first event: hippocampi riding. Since it was a requirement for all able-bodied royals, she had trained in the show style of jumping and dressage, and she could get through each event with passing marks. But she had no delusions she would win any event she hadn't trained for.

The rules stated that only hippocampi trained in the royal school at Aurea Regia be used, but Jet didn't recognize her mount. Her bridle said *Stella. "Hello, Stella. You're looking fit today."* She had no misconception the creature would speak back to her. Hippocampi could be very aloof.

Terrified now and hoping she could get through this, Jet found the stable manager.

"Miss Lennox, please walk your mount to the arena."

Her heart raced as she took the reins and stepped to the arena entrance. She could see the feet of the spectators on the riser seating and hear the rumble of applause and the occasional gasp of shock when a rider missed a cue or jump. Finally, she and Stella made it to the rider entrance on the east end of the arena. The arena manager signaled her to mount.

She boosted herself onto Stella's back. Inside the stadium, seven judges sat, two she recognized as members of the Sagesse. Each judge was an expert in the event they adjudicated. She couldn't allow herself to focus on anything else, including her parents' questioning glances. They knew she had signed up for only four events and that this was not one of them.

Calming, she took deep breaths and shut out the crowd noise. Using the training techniques she practiced for Movement, she searched her mind for groundedness.

At the head judge's nod, Jet nudged Stella forward. "Here goes nothing."

~ * ~

"Unbelievable, Jet! I don't know how you pulled it off." Chace patted her back for what felt like the hundredth time, and she smiled at him.

Will, Charlie, and Jet followed him through the crowds toward the food and entertainment tents behind the center arena.

"I mean, wow," Chase continued. "You had four events today and you managed solid performances in each."

"I don't know either. I just did it," she said. "I wouldn't call falling off Stella on the last jump solid, though." Her backside stung but not as much as her pride.

"You still got a six," Will said. "So perhaps you weren't wasting all your time down in the palace these last sixteen years."

"Thanks. But we all know I just got by today, and these were the easiest events. I'm exhausted, and Movement is the last day." She had to be realistic. "I need to get some sleep, and I need to study. I haven't practiced free diving, and that's at dawn."

"That one will be easy. Just remember everything we've worked on. You just have to hold your breath and swim down. How hard can it be?" Charlie joked.

"Extremely hard since I'm not allowed to hydroshift for this event," Jet complained.

"You're too comfortable in the water to let that matter," Will said.

"I'd love to win, of course, but the focus is finishing without collapsing."

"You'll be great." He draped an arm around her shoulder. "Now let's all get something to eat and head back to our rooms. You're right about one thing—we all need sleep."

On her way back to Arctic Hall, with muscles aching, she dragged through the corridor by Neptune's fountain and had almost made it to her room before Professor Ruecroft blocked her path.

"Tired, Princess?" the professor asked.

Jet drew herself up. "Not in the least, Professor," she lied. "I thank you for your concern though." She was too tired to tamp down her fury with Ruecroft. "I can handle it. But you wouldn't know anything about that, would you?"

Her heart drummed when the professor moved closer and pointed a finger in her face. "I know more than you think, Princess."

"What's that supposed to mean?"

"Nothing to concern yourself with, Your Highness. Since you have such special abilities, you needn't worry over anything I know."

"Save your taunts for someone it matters to, Professor. I'm going to bed." Jet stepped aside and passed Ruecroft.

"Oh, it will matter to you, Princess. I'll make sure of it," Ruecroft promised.

~ * ~

Jet wouldn't find out the results for the free diving competition until the last day of the tournament. She thought she'd done okay. At least she had made it back to the surface without help from a spotter, but her time wouldn't get her anywhere near first place. After she found Will and Charlie that afternoon, she filled them in on the altercation with Ruecroft.

"I think you were right," Charlie said. "I think she entered your name for ten events just to teach you a lesson."

"I thought so too, but it still doesn't make sense that she would also enter Morwenna. She's her pet, and she isn't happy about this at all—if the rumors are true."

"We're due to be at the beach in ten minutes," Will interjected, "and you can see what kind of mood Morwenna's in when we get there."

Jet and her friends arrived at Quad beach, where the water-based competitions were staged. Huge stands had been erected in the sand in addition to the observation Aquatheater. Mr. Newcastle was responsible for inventing and designing the amphitheater along with viewing stands.

Will scowled. "They'll use my father's inventions to build bleachers in the water but then act as if they aren't convening an inquiry against him," he said. "Hypocrites."

"Don't let it ruin your concentration," Jet said. "We have to do one thing at a time."

Both found their places for the Hydroderm competition. The earlier heats were easy, and she was pitted against Chace, Will, and Morwenna in the final. Was Will bothered that he had to face her and Morwenna?

They warmed up next to one another. He stood first and said, "See you out there, Princess."

He took his place next to Morwenna. Jet and Chace met on the shore. Professor Hyde was supervising the event, and she gestured to all four of them. "Each of you will complete the same routine, and the judges will score you based on form, execution, and time. There are four components of the routine: First, you must complete a straight dive to five hundred meters as quickly as possible. Upon completion of the dive, your ascent will be scored for time as well. You will then execute three required forms—the three-sixty spin, an aerial water breach with flip, and, finally, the straight aerial breach from the water. This accurately measures your speed and power from water to air. We also measure your aerial height with the altimeter rod." Professor Hyde gestured to a protruding metal post towering above the surface of Indigo Lake.

"The routine will be scored on form, speed, and accuracy. Highest score wins. And be safe out there—the maneuvers required to win the semis are quite dangerous. Good luck to you all." Professor Hyde moved aside, motioning to the starter with her ceremonial conch shell horn.

"Miss Morwenna Saberton, please take your place."

She entered the water and swam to her mark. The judges signaled the starter, and off she went.

Jet thought her routine flawless, but the judges didn't agree. Morwenna scored well with a sixty-two overall, but Jet was confident she could beat her. Mr. Saberton sat in the stands. He did not appear pleased. In contrast, her own family and Will's sat together, waving and cheering them on. She couldn't feel sorry for Morwenna because of her father, but she understood why she was as ruthless as she was.

Will scored a sixty-six. Chace received a sixty-five. Jet had to beat Will for the overall win in this event. She could do this.

"Miss Lennox, please find your mark," the starter shouted.

The crowd roared. She waved as she entered the water. When she reached the buoy that served as her mark, she awaited the starter's conch bellow. At the deep bellow of the conch, she arced into the water and hydroshifted. Her heart thudded, the power of beyond the stars within her. Into the murky depths, she propelled herself downward. She navigated the rocks, brush, and looming obstacles. She couldn't go any faster. Reaching the five-hundred-meter mark, she swiveled and twisted then blasted upward until she breached the surface.

She couldn't stop the triumphant "Whoop!" as she performed the straight aerial breach. She'd killed it.

The three-sixty spin was meant to duplicate that of a dolphin's and must be performed in and out of the water. She plunged underwater again and twisted back up as she began the spin, bringing her arms in for a tighter twist. Driving her body, she shot out of the water and twirled in the air, flipped as she cleared and then dove back into the lake.

She swam to the original mark, transmuted her skin and heard the crowd for the first time. Still a bit winded, she waded to the beach and listened for her score. Professor Hyde smiled in the distance.

Belton, the head judge and a member of Sagesse, rose and used the microphone. "Ladies and gentlemen, we award Miss Lennox a perfect score of seventy!"

The crowd jumped to their feet. Jet lifted a triumphant fist in the air.

"Yes!" She had done it!

Will rushed to her side and screamed above the crowd, "That was amazing!"

Judge Belton extended both hands, and the crowd quieted. "The judges would also like to announce, pending official ruling, that Miss Lennox has broken the record for straight aerial breach by three meters. Excellent work, Miss Lennox."

She'd never forget this moment. She raised her fist again and shouted, "I did it!"

~ * ~

By the end of the third day of Aquaticup, she had medaled in three events and gotten a respectable score in six others. No one was more surprised at the results than Jet. She had expected to do well in Hydroderm and enComm, which she had. But she had also medaled in Fin-Diving, which was different from Free-Diving in that the entrants could hydroshift if they chose and use fins if they couldn't transmute to full tail. She proved herself adept once again at the task.

But her skills were more than challenged during the Archery and Underwater Rugby competitions. Having never practiced the events and given her natural clumsiness on land, these events were her lowest scores. They weren't terrible, but she needed work.

By the end of the third day and the first nine events, her body ached everywhere, and she also had a healing black eye from the Underwater Rugby competition. Given the Pelagi's extreme strength, she should have anticipated the ball wouldn't be slowed by water. She'd taken the hit from Chace well, but it still hurt.

The black eye was the least of her worries, though. As she readied for bed the night before her final event, nerves overtook her. From the corner of the room, Peppercorn's words entered her mind.

"Stop this nonsense. You're agitating the entire room. I can sense the vibrations of your fear."

"I can't stop. Fear is all I feel right now." She took a deep breath.

"You are ready for this competition."

"It isn't just Movement I am worried about. I've missed you, and I need to get back to work finding the animals. Please be careful. I don't want anyone to hurt you."

"If anyone tried to hurt me, I'd make them very sorry." He snorted.

"I have no doubt, but if someone tries or succeeds, try to enComm with me. No matter what, no matter where you are, don't stop trying. I'll never stop trying to find you, and when I'm close enough to you, I'll hear you. I'll always be listening."

"Of course you'll come for me, but for now stop this. You have enough to worry about without adding me to the mix. I am quite capable of taking care of myself." Peppercorn settled himself on his chair. *"You have done well these last weeks, finding your way—a balance. If you trust yourself, it will be no different tomorrow and all the days after. You will survive."*

"You're right. And after tomorrow, we can get back to work."

Thirty-Four

The arena, full to capacity and bursting with shouts and screams, beckoned Jet. A sense of dread she couldn't shake overwhelmed her. Everything she practiced came to this moment. She must have lost her memory, because suddenly, she couldn't recall any of her training. Her hands trembled, and sweat dotted her upper lip. Along with the other competitors in her age bracket, she sat on a hard, wooden stool. She had just beaten Chace in the semifinals, and now she rested her aching muscles as Morwenna fought Will.

When it was done, he hobbled to the mat's perimeter and took his seat next to her. Panting, he mopped the blood from below his left eye.

She wanted to hug him, but he'd see it as pity. She lifted an eyebrow as the blood trickled from several other wounds. "You'll live, Newcastle."

He shook with laughter. He winced as a specialist from the Eripium dabbed at the cut. "Don't make me laugh. I'm in pain, woman."

"Sorry, Will. Are you okay?"

"I'll be fine, don't worry," he muttered.

"You just hoped to finish her off so I wouldn't have to," Jet complained. "You and I both know I need the points. No one can save me."

"That isn't funny. This isn't about points anymore. Morwenna's out for blood. She's going to hurt you—badly. It's just a matter of whether you can hurt her too."

"I know." Jet heard her name called, and her stomach dropped.

He took her hand. "Remember in the power of the water. You got this, Princess."

She prayed he was right. As he released her, she viewed the judges' table. Six smiling faces, including Scholarch Wolverhampton. The seventh judge, Professor Ruecroft, sat like stone.

Jet met Morwenna in the center of the mat. The referee of the match, an Omega-year student named Wallace, nodded to both Jet and Morwenna. He towered over them. Jet, already taller than Morwenna by several inches, wondered if the other girl felt as dwarfed by his six-foot-seven-inch height as Jet did. But what Morwenna lacked in inches, she more than made up for in power and sheer resolve, not to mention fury.

He addressed them. "You will begin with Synchronized Fight Flow at half-time, please. Do not return to neutral upon completion, but initiate Hybrid Combat in real time."

At least Jet and Will had worked on Omega-year curriculum in their training, so she had background on the moves. Morwenna wiped a single drop of blood from the corner of her lip and smeared it onto her robe near her thigh. Will landed that particular blow.

The crowd screamed beyond them, but it was as if they were the only two people on the island at that moment. Jet ignored the fear coursing through her veins. There was no time to prepare any further. She assumed her position. Morwenna did the same. Jet tried to remember the water and called on a little help from Neptune. Without warning, her pearl glowed and warmed. Morwenna stared at it. Jet focused on bringing energy from the pearl to her movements. It reminded her of home and helped her concentrate.

As they finished Fight Flow, she knew she'd done well. She had worked hard enough, she told herself, but she wasn't finished yet. The worst was coming. Almost anything was allowed in Hybrid Combat, including strikes, kicks, and grappling.

Searing pain exploded in her cheek as Morwenna landed a punishing blow. Jet threw a cross to her jaw. Morwenna stumbled back, and Jet didn't give her time rest. Her bloody knuckles burned as she pummeled her face. Morwenna shook her off, and Jet fell with a thud onto the mat. She used the position to her advantage, spun then crouched into pouncing tiger stance. She kicked Morwenna off her feet then jumped to her feet. As she advanced on Morwenna, she swung her leg in a crescent. Morwenna's elbow smacked into Jet's temple. Silver-hot pain erupted, and she collapsed. She had thirty seconds to get up, or the match would go to Morwenna. Nausea swirled, making her want to throw up.

Through the haze of pain, there was a humming in her head. She pushed herself to her knees, gagging and panting. The buzzing went into overdrive. She gave in to the pain, collapsed back to the mat. At once, the noise went away, and she heard Will. He'd been trying to talk to her.

"Get up. Get up. You can do this. I know you're hurt, but you can do this."

He kept repeating it in her head like a balm, and she pushed up on her hands and knees. She could do this. Every muscle in her body screamed. Standing, she wiped her bloodied lip. *Focus, Jet! Be grounded.*

When Morwenna darted at her, Jet pirouetted and leveled a vicious kick. The strike to Morwenna's left shoulder propelled her across the mat. She screamed. As she struggled to right herself, Jet didn't hesitate. She followed with a left strike to her jaw. Triumph soared through her. Morwenna, returning to a standing position, punched Jet in the ribs.

Her own left upper cut landed squarely to Morwenna's jaw. Chest heaving, Jet bent over as Morwenna crumbled to the mat. Her eyes rolled back, and she passed out.

The arena was silent. After thirty seconds, she was still on the mat, and the crowd roared. Blood dripped from Jet's eyes, nose, and mouth, but she grinned at Will. Feeling the buzz in her head again, she let him in.

"Told ya you could do it, Princess."

Thirty-Five

"Poor Morwenna?" Will snapped at Jet two days later. "That girl almost killed half our graduation class, and you say 'poor Morwenna'?" He shook his head. "You have got to be kidding."

"I just said I felt bad for her when her parents ditched her while she was still lying on the mats. I mean, they didn't even stay for closing ceremonies, and she got a gold medal in two events. I can't help it, Will."

"I know, and you're a great person for feeling anything for her at this point."

"You feel bad for her too. Don't pretend."

"I do up to a point, but we need to get off this topic. It's getting us nowhere to hash over something we can't change. I told you a long time ago what kind of person Roger Saberton is. Nothing he does surprises me. He would do anything to protect Pelagiana. I just think his vision for the future is wrong. Morwenna not winning goes against his idea of Pelagian superiority."

They were in her dorm room, and Will sat on her bed, petting Peppercorn. Their bruises had begun to fade, and their cuts were healing. Both had hung several medals in their rooms.

Despite Ruecroft's insistence that her last punch to Morwenna had been illegal, Jet had won the Movement event in her age bracket. She still needed to pass the Movement final, but she was on her way to finishing with enough points in all her classes for Wave and Wing consideration.

She and Will were working on a plan to get to the tombs. It was the only place she could think they'd find new information.

She had also discovered a way into the Sabertons' indoor pool, which was like the Newcastles', but her father asked her not to go there. He didn't want to disrespect his friend by having Jet sneak into his home uninvited. Her father had also reminded her that the scholarch would be watching.

Using their Elvers, they accessed articles posted by the Intelligence System on Eelfare. They created a timeline of disappearances and, unbeknownst to Will, she used her Sagesse meeting notes to try to connect the disappearances with Sagesse activity over the past months. She hadn't made it to the last session because the scholarch had appeared outside her door when she tried to sneak out. Madame Wolverhampton had been pleasant, but Jet knew she wasn't going anywhere. So now they were stuck trying to find a way for her to leave her room.

She thought about what Will said about Saberton. "You know, my father thinks of Saberton as one of his closest friends, Will. My dad is a good judge of character. Besides, Saberton is the last person who would do anything to ruin any aspect of Pelagiana. I've never seen anyone more patriotic than he is. He would die to protect our heritage."

"You might be right, but just because the king likes him, doesn't mean I have to."

She lifted an eyebrow at him from her position stretched out on the floor. "I don't like him that much either. He's the whole reason I'm here in the first—" She couldn't believe she'd let that slip.

He frowned. "How does Saberton have anything to do with you being here?"

She bit her lip. She'd done it now. The reason didn't matter anymore anyway, so she decided to tell him. "He told my dad there were people in the Sagesse claiming the monarchy was out of touch. He said we needed to make a big move to convince people otherwise. My dad forced me to come to change people's minds." She shrugged.

"Oh, well. That isn't Saberton's fault either. He was just the messenger." He scratched his head. "I thought you liked it here."

"I do. Now. But at first I was terrified. I hated my father for taking me away from everything that was comfortable. Now I can see Saberton was right. I needed to do this to help my family. But it had the added benefit of showing me I have a lot to learn, more I could be doing, and I will."

"I'm glad you're here, whatever the reason."

"I'm just saying Saberton isn't the only possible suspect." She lifted some papers and found her Elver again. "Speaking of which, I'm searching the entire list of missing animals and am trying to get a sense if there is a pattern."

"What are you thinking?"

She took a breath. Something Professor Stemp mentioned in their last class had stuck in her mind, but she didn't connect the dots until the stress of Aquaticup was over. "So, the list of animals missing is: the sea minks, a kinkajou pair, a caiman, löwchens, two schipperkes, a honey bear, and Lilly's dog Onyx."

"Sounds right."

"Except for the dogs, a lot of these animals are either extinct in the human world or close to it."

"Yes."

"The missing animals were hunted by humans for their fur or hides. But we were able to save them."

"Yeah. So, what are you thinking?"

"I think we need to think about the possibility that whoever took these animals is trying to profit from them. That means selling hides and fur." She tilted her head.

"But you won't make a huge profit from selling one hide or fur."

"You would if you took a pair and bred them."

"It's illegal to sell hides and furs in Pelagiana."

"It isn't illegal everywhere else, though. A lot of places in the world don't protect animals the way we do. There are humans who hunt whales or elephants. Why wouldn't these types of people be interested in something extinct?"

"You think someone is breeding the animal pairs to sell out in the human world?" Will swung his legs to the side of her bed. "Jet, you could be right about this. But you have to know what this means!"

"What?"

"It means people will accuse my dad. Saberton can't be guilty—he hates human interaction. My dad has a lot of access to the human world, and he has free rein among the animals."

"Every one of us has access to the human world. We can swim off the island anytime. But you're right—they might blame him first," she said. Another idea sprang to mind, but now she was worried about his reaction. She reached out to Peppercorn instead.

"I trust him. I'd like to ask him. Should I?"

"Your dealings with the other one left you mistrustful of everyone. But not all are bad like her. You have to trust people in order to lead them, Jet, even if they aren't all deserving. Why not try with this one?"

As usual, he was right. Will wouldn't like it, but Jet had to ask. She took a breath and then said, "Will, how does your dad feel about the royal family?"

"My father is *not* sabotaging your family in the Sagesse. How could you think that?" He jumped from the bed.

"I have to consider every possibility, just like I know you would," Jet said.

He paced. "I can sort of see why you'd ask, but please trust me. He isn't doing this."

"I'm sorry."

"I know, but I'm still mad at you."

"You aren't being reasonable, though, and I understand because I'd be the same. For what it's worth, I don't think your dad is doing this either."

"It's worth a lot. Thanks. We both know people will still think of him first if we go with your selling-animals-for-profit theory."

"Not if we keep this a secret and find the culprit first."

"It's the best way until we can think of a better solution. But we can't breathe a word of this idea to anyone, not even Charlie, in case she slips to Morwenna. The Sabertons would go after my dad for sure."

"I won't say a word, but I was going to suggest we talk to Charlie about this because I have an idea, and she might be able to help." Jet shrugged.

"What is it?"

"If someone is selling animals for their hides, it makes getting into the tombs even more important. If the rumor of the Cloak and Veil trophy room is true, we have to look for it."

"But you can't sneak out, and what does Charlie have to do with this?" Will scratched his head.

"Charlie can cover for me, and say we are together, then you and I can slip out."

"What you're talking about is dangerous. I told you the tombs are so far beneath the lakebed average Pelagians start to panic from the pressure. It's like you're underwater but not, and you can't use the power of hydroshifting. It's terrifying. Not to mention that Cloak and Veil's members and where they meet are the best kept secrets at Quadrivium." He stopped pacing and settled on her bed again.

Peppercorn snorted his irritation.

"Well, I guess we give up then," Jet said.

"I'm not saying that, and I agree we have to get down there. I just wish there was a better way."

"I'll do whatever it I can to help. I care about those animals, especially Svashi and her babies. Atlas isn't related to Svashi and Viktor. If we find them all and Atlas finds a mate in one of Svashi's litter, there is hope for the future. If someone plans to sell them, we need to get to her fast. She's due soon," she pointed out. "We only have three more weeks before term ends and the Sagesse convenes for your father's inquiry."

"I know. What's the plan?"

"It's weird how it all keeps coming back to Morwenna, but I remember her saying she wanted an invite to Cloak and Veil back during the pledge period. I think we can both agree that if she wants something, she usually gets it."

"We can definitely agree on that point."

"I don't think it's a long shot that she's a member now. I think we should ask Charlie to let us know when Morwenna leaves their dorm room at night. We need to follow her and see where she goes. She could lead us to a Cloak and Veil meeting."

"It *would* save us a lot of time from snooping around, knocking on doors," Will agreed. "Charlie'll help us. She's on your side in this whole Morwenna thing. We need to be careful. We have three weeks of classes and finals to worry about, too. If we get caught, you're done at Quad."

"What about you? You have as much to lose as I do. Isn't this dangerous for you?"

"This isn't your fight. You don't have to do any of this," he said. "If you get caught on the wrong side of this, it could jeopardize your entire future—and even the monarchy."

"I'm not doing this just for you. I need people to know I'm willing to fight with them, not sit behind the palace walls."

"I hope you know…" He grabbed her hand and stared into her eyes. "Your help means a lot."

Jet swallowed hard. They got to work.

Thirty-Six

"No, I won't do it."

Charlie's harsh answer surprised both Will and Jet, who approached her the next day before Ruecroft's class.

"Why not, Charlie? I thought you were on our side with this?" Will asked.

"I think what Morwenna did to Jet was wrong, terribly wrong," she agreed. "But I still have to live with Morwenna for three more weeks and maybe next year. I'm not willing to spy on her. It kind of sets a bad tone."

His eyes widened. "I can't believe you'd live with her next year. Are you mental or just into the verbal abuse she throws your way?"

"That's hilarious coming from you, Will." Charlie stuck out her chin. "You've been defending 'Morrie' for years, then Jet comes along and now you see Morwenna for who she really is? Please, don't lecture me. She is the only person here who ever asked to live with me. There isn't a waiting list to be my roommate." Her eyes filled with tears.

"I'm sorry, Charlie. I was out of bounds. You're right. Jet did help me see what Morwenna had changed into. She wasn't always like this, so I understand your loyalty."

"I'm not thrilled with the idea of you taking sides between Morwenna and me anyway," Jet said. "But, Charlie, all we need to know is when she leaves. You're not the one spying on her."

"That's my second reason for not doing it. This is a crazy plan and very dangerous. You guys could get hurt. I care about you two, and neither one of you is sure if Cloak and Veil is part of it."

"It's the best we have to go on," he said. "If you care, why won't you help?"

Jet winced at the guilt trip. "What he means is that all he can think about is clearing his family's name and saving the animals. This is the best shot we have right now. Please don't make us stake out your dorm room every night, Charlie."

Her shoulders sagged. "Okay, but I hate this. I'll see what I can do and let you know."

She patted Charlie's shoulder. "This might shock you, but no one is lined up to live with me next year, either."

"What are you saying?"

"I'm saying that if you liked, we could room together next year. One of us would have to switch residential houses. I'm not sure if that's allowed. I know Peppercorn is opinionated, but you two seem to get along."

With unshed tears in her hazel eyes, Charlie stared at Jet.

Will rolled his eyes. "I will never understand women."

Both girls laughed. Charlie nodded at Jet. She nodded back. It was decided.

~ * ~

It was almost four days before Charlie marched up to Will and Jet as they sat in the Ordinary eating lunch.

"Tonight," she said. Gaze darting in all directions, she lowered herself into a chair next to Jet. "She got one of the notes she gets before she slips out when she thinks I'm sleeping. It should be about two o'clock this morning. It's never before one, but you should get to your spot early, just in case." She stopped her twitchy behavior and said, "How are you going to sneak out of Arctic and into Pacific without the scholarch knowing? I can't cover for you when you're supposed to sleeping."

"Peppercorn is going to help us," Jet said.

Her brow furrowed. "Please, be careful, you have no idea what you might run into." She looked at Will. "Take care of her."

"I am deeply resentful of the implication that I am unable to care for myself." Jet sniffed.

Charlie grinned. "There isn't a doubt in my mind that you can handle yourself, Jet, but it's nice to have backup. I was going to lecture you about taking care of Will too."

"We're a team," he said. "I think it's best if we just remember that."

~ * ~

"Are you ready?" Jet said. It was midnight. "Will?" she asked louder. "Are you ready?" She peeked under her bed.

He stared back at her. "You know, for a princess, you're really messy. Don't you let the house staff come in and clean? I counted three candy wrappers and more dust balls than I care to report."

"Thanks for the evaluation." She backed up as he rolled out from under her bed. She folded her arms. "Of course I let them clean. Things get overlooked sometimes." The conversation was getting weird. "Do you think you're ready to go or did you want to alphabetize my book collection and wash my windows first?"

"I'm just saying…you're a mess. It's kind of refreshing to catch you in regular moments."

"As opposed to?"

"You know, your 'perfectly princess' moments."

Her eyebrow winged up, and he held up his hands in surrender.

"Don't get huffy. And don't pretend you don't have times when you let your perfectionism take over. I was just remarking on the fact that you seem to be a combination of many different things. It's nice." He coughed. "Anyway, if we don't get caught and kicked out tonight, I'd get a broom under there." He gestured to the bed and cocked his head.

"While I find this conversation fascinating, why don't we focus on not getting caught and kicked out?"

He took a breath. "Okay, let's do this."

She looked at Peppercorn. Her pet twitched and jumped down from his perch on the bed. She opened the door and let him out. Then, she shut off all the lights in her room, and they waited. She wondered if Will was as nervous as she felt. Putting that aside, she focused on her pet and opened her mind to receive his message.

Will was standing so close their shoulders brushed. He stroked her arm and asked, "Are you sure?"

"Absolutely. Don't worry." Suddenly she heard the hum of Peppercorn trying to get into her head.

"The corridors are clear to the Ordinary."

"Okay, it's time." She reached for the door at the same time Will did. Feeling his hand on hers startled her, and she jumped, hitting him in the chin with her head and knocking him backward.

"See, this is one of your regular moments." He chuckled, and she groaned.

"Sorry. I guess 'perfect princesses' aren't clumsy."

"Perfection is overrated," he said. "Now let's go."

~ * ~

They both dressed in black. The darkened corridors cast few shadows, and they found it easy to stay out of the moonlight filtering in from the tops of the windows. Every once in a while, the top of Will's sandy-brown head shone in the glow from the moon.

"Crouch, Will. You're too tall," she whispered.

He grunted in reply and bent his knees. They reached the Ordinary. She brought him to the door that led to the tunnel down to the rehearsal room for Apollonian Octet.

"Peppercorn says we can access Pacific through here." She gestured to the door. "I know my way to the rehearsal room, and past that is the tunnel to the Sagesse Chambers."

"How do you know how to get to the chambers through the tunnels?"

She didn't see any reason to lie. "I've been spying for my family."

"That's great. Were you ever planning on saying something? My dad is head of the Sagesse."

"I can't apologize. It's no different than what we're doing tonight. I'm trying to help my family, just like you're helping yours. We can't be having this conversation right now. Don't worry so much."

"I'm not worried. I'm skulking around my school in the middle of the night, trying to follow a secret society into an unknown tomb to clear my family name with a princess who shouldn't be involved in the first place, all at the direction of a somewhat irritated pet sable. What could go wrong?" He shrugged, and she almost burst into laughter.

Instead she said, "Shush and follow me."

As she made to open the door, they heard footsteps. They couldn't make out who it was. He pushed Jet behind him against the stone wall, blocking her from being seen. She pinched his arm. Hard.

"Cut it out." His words were rough. "You can yell at me later."

The steps came closer, and she rose on her toes to peek over his shoulder. She gasped when she saw Ruecroft. Her head swiveled toward them, and her beady eyes squinted as she peered into the darkness shrouding Will and Jet. After long minutes, she shrugged her pointy shoulders and continued in the opposite direction. Jet gulped in some much-needed air.

When the coast was clear, she opened the door to the tunnel leading to the rehearsal room. Will closed it behind them and took a small lantern from his pack. "You're terrible at this."

"Gee, I'm sorry. It's my first time. I'll do it better next time. I promise. And what about you?" she asked. "What was that macho move back there, pushing me into the wall, trying to hide me?"

"I'm not apologizing for instinct. Trying to protect you is a gut reaction. You'll have to get used to it, because it's gonna happen again." He shoved hand through his hair. The lantern light played on his harsh features.

"We're a team, remember?"

"I remember," he said. "Again, I am not apologizing. You'll just have to deal with it." He picked up the lantern he left on the ground. "How about this? Next time I need protecting, I won't complain when you do it."

She didn't answer him. She heard Peppercorn trying to reach her.

"Where are you?" the sable asked.

"We need to move. Peppercorn's waiting." She led them down the stairs to the tunnel. They crept past the door leading to the rehearsal room. Jet and Will followed the corridor until they reached the fork in the tunnels where she ventured on to the Sagesse chambers.

"Take the right," Peppercorn instructed.

The pitch-dark tunnel sloped downward. If it weren't for the lantern, they would be blind to anything farther than three inches in front of them.

Will took the lead. "We must be under the east wing right now."

"I think we'll start to slope up here pretty soon." She could smell the damp in the tunnel, a reminder of how close they were to the water.

They came to a door almost identical to the one they opened to enter the tunnel from the Ordinary.

"What does Peppercorn have to say?"

"Peppercorn, we're at a door. Is it clear?" she asked the stubborn sable when he hadn't volunteered the information they needed.

After several minutes, her pet answered, *"Sorry, caught a mouse. Delicious."*

"That's disgusting."

"Go through the door, and you'll find yourself at Pacific's dining hall. Use the corridor on the west side exit. Go eleven doors down on the right. That is her room. There is spot outside, easily hidden in the shadows."

Jet and Will took Peppercorn's directions and crept through the vacant dining hall and corridors. Across from Morwenna and Charlie's dorm room, Jet discovered a curtained alcove to hide in three doors away with an excellent vantage point. Will gestured for her to sit on the little bench in the alcove. She shook her head.

He jerked his head and didn't budge. "I'll take the first watch. We're early. We'll rotate every hour," he murmured.

She plopped down onto the bench.

When it was her turn, he took her spot on the bench in the alcove, closed his eyes, and fell asleep at once. She rolled her eyes at his ability to relax at this moment. Several minutes passed, and then a form took shape from the shadows. A cloaked figure, covered from head to toe, approached Morwenna and Charlie's dorm room. A black-gloved hand reached out from beneath the cloak and rapped three times in quick succession.

The door opened, and another cloaked figure exited. The figures disappeared down the hall. Jet spun around to Will and nudged him in the foot. He jumped.

"Will," she said. "Morwenna is leaving. Someone came to get her."

He leapt off the bench. "Let's go."

They crept along the corridor behind the two figures. She contacted Peppercorn and put him on notice that they needed him again. He was circling the dining hall. They trailed the figures to the door they'd come through in Pacific's family dining room. The two people went through the door to the tunnel. As Jet was about to slip through the door, Will grabbed her arm.

"Let it close," he said. "Get Peppercorn to shadow them, and he can send us directions."

Soon they were backtracking through the same passage they had come, but instead of returning to the Ordinary, at the fork they took the opposite direction toward the Sagesse Chambers. She and Will didn't dare speak to one another, so she took the lead with Peppercorn's directions echoing in her head. Her palms were sweaty, and her breathing was unsteady. She needed to calm.

The passage led out to Indigo Beach. She recognized the ancient passage to Aurea Regia as the one where they discovered the dolphin. They stopped outside until Peppercorn issued the go-ahead.

"We might be on to something here. Cloak and Veil could have had something to do with the dolphin."

"Are you sure you want to keep going?" Will asked.

Jet didn't bother to answer.

"I had to ask."

She ignored him as she listened to Peppercorn. "It's time."

Thirty-Seven

Jet and Will hiked the familiar passage down under the lakebed. Ears popping from the pressure, she acclimated quickly as they descended. Instead of going up into Aurea Regia as they had weeks before, they took a side tunnel to the passage leading to Will's house. He gritted his teeth.

"Check off another box for team Will and Jet. They're heading for the tombs," he said. "Jet, you'll have to use all your training for this. I will too. The pressure is terrible down there, and you might not be able to hear Peppercorn. If we were in the water, it would be different because you could hydroshift and wouldn't feel it."

"I'll be fine. Let's go."

Peppercorn confirmed what Will and Jet had already figured out. They headed down the passage to the tombs, and she couldn't believe the pressure. It was hard to get a full breath. A crushing force weighed on her chest. Sweat broke out on her upper lip. She glanced over at Will as they traveled deeper.

His pale skin shone with beads of perspiration, giving him an unhealthy pallor. Before long, she could concentrate on nothing but the compression on her lungs.

He took her hand and panted. "It's just panic. Our bodies can handle this. We just have to acclimate."

If it was psychological, she would overcome it. She had no choice. Her vision blurred as they approached the door Peppercorn indicated. She blinked to clear her head. A small skeleton was embedded in the rock of the wall.

"Will," she said, "check this out." She gestured to the bones someone had so carefully placed in the wall. "It's a baby sea mink skeleton."

His jaw tightened, and then suddenly a grimace of pain crossed his face in the lantern light, and he crumpled to the ground. Before she could scream, a shaft of white-hot agony pierced her brain. She could think of nothing but the haze of pain in her head as she too fell hard onto the stone floor.

~ * ~

Jet awoke to the sound of whispering voices. Opening her eyes, she winced as pain sliced through her head again. She'd be sick if she even contemplated moving. Not able to think past the nausea, she let the pain overtake her and slept.

When she awoke again, she once more heard the voices. They were louder this time, and she heard enough to recognize an argument. She shook away the pain in her head. She had to get herself together. She had no idea where she was. Or if Will was with her. The cold stone of the floor scraped her bound hands. Someone had dropped her there, judging by her soreness. The voices were in the same room with her, so she peered through slitted eyelids to try to gauge her whereabouts.

Lantern light glowed on the ceiling. Her head hurt, but she had a concussion before this, courtesy of Morwenna's jab during the tournament. Jet was willing to bet Morwenna had something to do with this one as well.

Stifling the groan that fought to come from her lips as she opened her eyes a little wider, Jet took in more of the room. Forms took shape, and she wanted to vomit for a completely different reason than the concussion. This was the Society of Cloak and Veil's trophy room.

Skins of bear and zebra decorated the walls. Skulls from animals littered shelves and tables. Furs from sable, mink, and ermine were strewn across large chairs. The musty animal scent of the room made her gag at the waste of it all. These animals had not been used for food or their bones for weapons. They had been slaughtered for sport.

In the center of one of the walls was a massive stone altar adorned with more "trophies." Above the altar was one of the largest swords she had ever seen. She had to figure out a way to get to it.

At least she'd seen Will beside her. The pressure of the tombs still weighed on her lungs, and she could tell by his heavy breathing, it affected him as well. Her addled brain scrambled for a plan. She had to think! The whispers grew louder.

"We have no choice. It is the only way," a voice insisted.

"There has to be a different answer. They haven't seen us," another voice chimed in.

A third, "They know too much. They must be eliminated."

Her heart leapt to her throat. They were going to kill her and Will. She tried to nudge him to wake. She moved her leg in fraction-of-an-inch, not wanting to alert the three cloaked figures. He opened his eyes and peered at her. He mouthed the word *enComm*. Then he closed his eyes, and she let him into her mind.

"Any thoughts, Princess?"

"There's a sword on the wall behind your head. We need to get to it. All I know is that no one knows we can communicate this way, so let's use it to our advantage."

"I believe our guests have awakened." Ruecroft pulled off her hood. "Put them in the chairs, keep their hands tied."

Even suspecting it, she was shocked with the confirmation of Ruecroft's involvement.

The two other cloaked figures moved to where Jet and Will lay on the floor. They hoisted them up and dragged them to the chairs. He grunted in response, while she said nothing.

"I'm going to try to stall them, Jet. First, see if you can reach Peppercorn. He can sneak in here and chew through the ropes or go for help."

"He might have left by now; he wouldn't be able to handle the pressure long. Besides, I don't want him to get caught and killed. I'm not asking him to come in here. But I'll see if he's still out there, and I'll ask him to run for help."

"Sorry. Wasn't thinking straight."

She tried to reach Peppercorn. There was no answer.

"I can't say we aren't surprised you're this evil, Ruecroft," he said, "but surely you aren't planning on killing us just because you hate Jet so much?"

Ruecroft stood before Will. "No, that's just a little side benefit."

"How pathetic that makes you," Jet said, and Ruecroft charged up to the chair where she was tied. The blow, while expected, still shook her already aching head. She offered no response to it except to push her tongue against the inside of her cheek where it bled.

"If you and Newcastle had let well enough alone, none of this would be necessary."

Will poked into her head. *"Don't bait her. Get her to talk."*

"None of what would be necessary?" she asked.

"You know enough," Ruecroft snapped.

"But how did you know we were following you and Morwenna tonight? What are you doing down here, and where are the missing animals?"

"Let me answer your first question, as it will prove the most satisfying. You see, Princess, all is not as it seems." Ruecroft pivoted to the other two cloaked figures. "Show yourselves."

Morwenna pulled off her hood and sneered.

The other figure sobbed. Ruecroft strode over to the figure and ripped away the hood.

"Charlie!" Jet screamed as her best friend stood with tears streaming down her cheeks.

"I'm so sorry, Jet. I didn't have a choice," she stammered through her tears.

"You always have a choice, Charlie."

Ruecroft slapped Charlie so hard she stumbled across the room. "No, she didn't have a choice."

Jet stared at Charlie, who had fallen on the floor.

"Such a disappointment to me, just like her father. He was a jellyfish too," Ruecroft said.

"What is going on here?" Will demanded.

"Oh, allow me to introduce my daughter. You call her Charlie. I call her a curse."

Charlie's sobs grew quiet.

"Your daughter?"

"How I wish it wasn't true, Newcastle." Ruecroft nudged Charlie's prone body. "Charlotte is a disappointment. I knew it from the moment she was born. I gave her to her grandmother to raise. I longed for a girl such as Morwenna."

Morwenna smirked. Jet turned to Will.

"Will, I can't reach Peppercorn. The pressure is too much for me to use enComm outside the room. I'm trying to undo the ropes. Keep Ruecroft talking."

"On it, Princess. My ropes are coming along too."

Jet's lips curved.

Ruecroft noticed the smile and screamed, "What's so funny?"

He leaned back against his tied hands, giving the impression of complete boredom. "You, Ruecroft. You're what's so funny. You act as if scaring us and ruining your daughter is cause for a medal, when all I can figure is you're out of your mind. I get why Morwenna's here. She loves to be adored, and she probably enjoys whatever sick game you're playing. I even understand why Charlie's here—because she's afraid of you. But the real puzzle is, what the hell are you doing with the animals and why? Other than absolute insanity, I just don't get the motive."

Ruecroft drew herself up. "You shortchange both Morwenna and me if you believe this is a game."

"It seems like it's been a game to destroy Jet."

"In fact, Princess Jaiette altered plans already well in place. She didn't have to be involved at all if she hadn't decided to attend Quadrivium. She should have stayed where she belonged. She couldn't compete with Morwenna. She shouldn't have tried. So many instances when Miss Saberton bested you."

"Laying the princess out on her backside springs to mind as one of the best," Morwenna said.

Jet met her gaze. "You have a selective memory, *Morrie*. You seem to forget I laid you out in front of a crowd of thousands."

Rage burned in Morwenna's eyes. She snarled, "Ruecroft, end this game now. He's waiting."

"Who's waiting?" Will asked. "Come on, don't you think you owe me an explanation before you let her kill us? It was you who questioned my loyalty a few weeks ago, Morrie. For old time's sake."

She softened. "I don't want Ruecroft to kill you, but you're so stubborn."

"Tell me who's waiting for you and why."

"It doesn't matter either way now. My father. Ruecroft and I and a few others have been executing his plan for months now."

He laughed.

"What are you laughing at? The prospect of dying is so funny?"

"Actually no, that part's terrifying. I'm laughing because it's always been your father. He says jump, and you don't question." He took a breath then said, "How does he figure in all of this?"

Ruecroft's lips twitched. "It's simple. Roger Saberton knows what's best for our world. He wants to keep Pelagiana safe, and he will stop at nothing to get that. He had two problems. Declan Newcastle and the royal family."

Will shot up an eyebrow. Jet didn't know what Ruecroft meant.

Ruecroft paced. "He's been quietly suggesting for years that the royal family is useless to Pelagiana. When King Magnus began to trust Declan Newcastle and the ideas he brought from the human world, Roger used his influence in the Sagesse to start the small rumor that perhaps the king was losing his grip. That was step one. Roger needed the position on the Sagesse your father holds, Newcastle, so he could go about changing the laws the king supported. He needed to get rid of the king and Declan Newcastle." She stopped in front of Will and Jet.

"So Roger set about stealing animals, with our help, to discredit Newcastle and ultimately take his place. The idea was, once we got rid of Newcastle, the king would have gone along with anything Roger suggested to save face. After a while, the king would be forced to step down because of Roger's influence." Her eyes glazed. "Unfortunately, he believed he was losing the king's confidence, so he had to move faster to find a way to make the royal family appear even more inept. It was his idea to spur the king into sending the princess to Quadrivium.

"Roger asked Morwenna and me to keep the princess from completing Quadrivium. If the princess failed here and the Newcastles were ruined, control of Pelagiana would be his. As you can see, Roger Saberton is the best man for the job." Her expression grew hard. "The princess didn't cooperate. He assured us she was a mouse of a girl, spineless and uninterested in her role as heir." Ruecroft cocked her head. "For a while, the princess made it easy for us. You were such an easy target. Already so insecure, and Morwenna was able to play on that."

Jet said nothing because it was the simple truth. She had allowed herself to become a victim. Ruecroft paced the room again.

Charlie picked herself up off the floor. No one else had noticed.

"And now? Now that you've kidnapped the animals and are planning to kill us? What's the big plan? How do you"—Jet smiled, hoping to distract her— "I mean, how does *Roger* plan to explain away murder?"

Thirty-Eight

The door to the trophy room burst open, and the man himself strode in. "Masterfully done, ladies. Well, Princess Jaiette, my Morwenna couldn't beat you when I needed her to, but we'll rectify that tonight." He curled his lip.

"I'm so sorry, Daddy. I told you how sorry I was," Morwenna said.

He waved her away, dismissing her apology. "No matter now."

Will pushed forward in his chair. "How are you planning to pull this off with us dead, you sick, power-hungry idiot?"

"Will, do not bait him! He will kill you."

"He's going to anyway, and that will destroy my parents!"

"Where are my sea minks?" he screamed at Saberton.

"Oh, don't worry about the animals. I haven't harmed them. Now that you two have ruined my plans, I intend to put them to good use. Originally, I intended to make a fur for Morwenna; she so loves contraband. But now I realize we can't stay in Pelagiana anymore. My last bit of work here will be killing you two, and then we'll begin our new life with some others of a like mind."

"And the animals? How do they figure into this?"

"Those disgusting humans your father seems to think are worthy of our time will pay me a pretty penny for exotic animals. I'll use the money to buy an island. It is a pity. I planned to ruin both your fathers and watch it happen, but that was remarkably shortsighted of me. I find the idea of leaving them without their precious children an even better ending than I could have imagined. Pelagiana is a relic adhering to an outdated, irrelevant monarch who still clings to Neptune's gift, as if that alone will protect us."

Rage coursed through Jet.

"And, Princess, your parents began to favor Declan Newcastle over my vision. They never understood me." Spit shot across the room as he ranted. "Ruecroft, slit their throats. Leave them in the lake. Make it so they wash up on shore very soon. I will miss seeing their parents' grief. Pity. Once you are done, meet me at the Chateau. We'll gather the animals and leave tonight."

"Jet, I'm loose. How about you?"

"Just about there. Give me two minutes."

Will gave an imperceptible nod. "I have one more question, Saberton—why did you put Jet's name in for all ten events at Aquaticup?"

His eyes grew hard, and his lips thinned. "I was told"—he directed a look at Morwenna— "the princess would embarrass herself at the tournament. It provided another opportunity to disgrace the royal family. I hoped the tournament would illustrate how ill-suited the royals really were for the modern realities. We need a well-trained army in Pelagiana, not children playing." His body jerked. "Unfortunately, I was misinformed. The princess fared better than I was told she would, and our people began to believe in her." He waved his hand again. "It wasn't me who entered her. It was my dear Zephania."

Ruecroft blushed.

"We are of the same ilk, she and I. Zephania has been instrumental in gaining me access to Quadrivium and executing my plans. We also both share disappointment when our expectations are not met by our daughters."

"Tell me you're free," Will said.

"Yeah. I'm sick of listening to this guy talk about himself. Let's do it on three."

"Okay, but Saberton's mine," he said then counted. *"One...two...three!"*

At the same time as him, Jet sprang from her chair. She kicked Ruecroft in the midsection and sent her reeling into Charlie who sprang to life, picked up a skull from the table next to her, and whacked her mother over the head with it. Ruecroft crumbled to the ground with a groan.

Charlie reached for the sword above her. Morwenna came from behind her and kicked her in the back, sending her sprawling to the floor.

"You dirty little traitor! How can you do this to your own mother?" Morwenna screamed.

Will was holding his own against Saberton. Jet gauged that Charlie needed her more.

Charlie charged Morwenna. "My mother deserves a lot worse for what she's done to me." She landed a solid blow to Morwenna's abdomen, but she far outmatched Charlie. With one punch, Morwenna laid Charlie flat.

Jet jumped in front of Morwenna and met her gaze. "All right, Morwenna, now try that with me."

Wildly, Morwenna flew at Jet. She sidestepped and drove the heel of her hand into Morwenna's chin. Her head snapped back, and she stumbled. Too fast, she recovered and snatched up the sword.

Her evil smile terrified Jet. She handled the sword expertly, slicing through the air. Jet backed away, and Morwenna began to taunt her. "What's the matter, Princess, you didn't get this far in your Movement training? Don't you know how to use a blade?" Her question echoed through the chamber.

"How like you to have the only weapon in the room. Why am I not surprised?"

Her mouth thinned. "How like you, Princess, to expect a fair fight. That isn't the way the world spins. Don't you know that by now?"

"I know it isn't the way *your* world spins, but some of us have higher expectations." She jerked her head to gesture toward Will. "Like him. That's why you lost him, you know. He believes in something better too."

She tried to provoke the other girl to lose control. Morwenna had backed Jet into the wall. She had a view of Will and Saberton fighting behind Morwenna's back. Frantic for anything she could use, Jet searched for a weapon.

Will landed a well-placed punch. Morwenna, spun when she heard her father's cry. Jet advanced.

He screamed, "Jet! Move!"

She didn't think, she just reacted and jumped away as Morwenna raised her sword. His fist connected with Saberton's left cheekbone. Jet heard the crunch of bone, and he stumbled backward, falling onto Morwenna's raised sword.

"Daddy!" Her scream tore through the room.

Everything happened in slow motion. Morwenna falling to her father's side, the sword protruding grotesquely through his chest. Will wiping blood from his mouth. Charlie rising from the floor. They all stared at the girl mourning the father she killed.

The wracking sobs eased to a soft mewl. Jet knelt beside Morwenna. Before she could utter a word to console her, she stared up at her.

Hate radiated from her icy-blue eyes. "All of Pelagiana will pay for what you did here tonight. You murdered a genius, a visionary. If I could, I would kill you right here and now. I will destroy everything you love. Then, when everything and everyone you care about is gone, I'll kill you to avenge my father's death."

Will came to Jet, took her hand and helped her up. "Leave her. There isn't anything anyone can do."

Jet went to Charlie. She was whimpering in the corner, not far from where her mother still lay flat out on the floor. Jet couldn't believe Ruecroft was her mother. That shock would settle in later.

Charlie looked up. "Jet, you have to believe me. I didn't know about the animals, or their plans. Ruecroft made me become a member of Cloak and Veil, but I was never summoned to a meeting until tonight. I swear."

"Leave it. We'll talk after," she said. "Can you handle this?" She gestured to Ruecroft and Morwenna.

"I've got it." Charlie used the rope that tied Jet to bind her mother's hands. Ruecroft still didn't stir, and Morwenna hadn't moved from her father's side.

"As soon as I get out of the tombs," Jet said, "I'll be able to send help through Peppercorn."

She handed Charlie another length of rope from the floor. Nearby, Will stood behind Morwenna and secured his arms around her body so Charlie could tie the rope. Throughout the entire process, Morwenna said and did nothing but kneel by her father's lifeless form.

"Charlie, I don't want to leave you alone, but we don't know what we'll face from the other Cloak and Veil members when we find the animals. It makes more sense for Will and me to—"

"You and Will are the stronger fighters," Charlie interrupted, "so you have to go. Be careful. I don't know any Cloak and Veil members or if they are loyal to Saberton. He always demanded they wear hoods. I'm sure not all of them are bad…" She looked down at her hands.

"No one holds you responsible."

"You should, but we don't have time. You have to go." She gestured to Morwenna. "I don't think she even knows where she is right now, but I'll be careful."

Will and Jet clasped hands. Charlie called out to them. "Where are you two going?"

Jet and Will answered in chorus. "The Sabertons'."

They sped through the tombs and, once they reached the passage leading to Will's house, she enCommed with Peppercorn. *"Get Bevan and as many guards as you can find. Go to the tombs. Charlie is there, and she needs help!"*

She grabbed Will's hand. "Let's get to the water. We can get inside Saberton's chateau faster that way."

They raced to the grotto. Without a word, both jumped in.

"We need to make a quiet entrance. I don't want to warn Judith Saberton or any of the Cloak and Veil members who might be waiting for Saberton to show up."

"Yes." She hydroshifted and dove downward. *"I know which passage, but how do we know it's safe once we get to their pool?"*

"Try Svashi, Jet. Maybe she'll answer!"

She stopped swimming and reached out to Svashi. To her surprise, she got a reply. *"Follow me,"* she said as she heard the sea mink's instructions.

They took a small cave like the one that led to the Newcastles' grotto. As they followed the twisting cavern, they swam into a deep pool which led to the inside of the Saberton chateau. She and Will inched to the top to avoid detection.

They broke the surface of the pool at the same time. Jet peered above the rock perimeter of the pool. A small waterfall trickled down the wall of the cavern and into the pool. A beautiful, blue light reflected off the cave walls. She shook her head and scanned the area. She heard Svashi as she and Will exited the pool. They shifted their skin back for land. She led the way through the stone hallway to a garish great hall.

He grabbed her forearm. *"Jet, it's too quiet. Where is everyone?"*

"I don't know. Svashi said they left when Saberton went to the tombs. Let's worry about it later. We need to get to Svashi."

They followed the sea mink's directions until they found themselves in a narrow corridor lined with golden doors. She opened the third door. Lining the perimeter of the mirrored room were steel cages filled with the missing animals of Pelagiana. On the back wall, another steel cage held Svashi, her four cubs suckling.

She twitched her nose. *"It's about time."*

Thirty-Nine

By the time Jet and Will returned to Quadrivium, it was dawn. The animals had been released, but Svashi, Viktor, and their cubs needed to be evaluated before they could go home to the Newcastles' grotto.

The scholarch met Jet and Will at the Eripium. "Your friend Miss Houndswood is here and so is your keep, Peppercorn."

Jet gasped. "What happened? Are they all right?" Her stomach clenched.

"Calm down, Miss Lennox. I'm afraid the security team didn't arrive in time to apprehend Miss Saberton. Your keep arrived first. Even with tied hands, Miss Saberton was still able to grab Peppercorn around the neck. She threatened to strangle him unless Miss Houndswood untied her. Your friend saved Peppercorn, and her reward was a concussion inflicted by Miss Saberton." The scholarch shook her head.

Jet swallowed. "We weren't thinking, Will. We never should have left Charlie alone."

"There wasn't another choice. I couldn't have found the animals without you speaking to Svashi."

"She will be fine, and so will Peppercorn, thank goodness, and you can see for yourselves in a moment. Fortunately, security was able to keep hold of Professor Ruecroft. The rest of Saberton's followers, including Judith Saberton, have disappeared. Some members of Cloak and Veil have agreed to speak to me—confidentially, of course—but from what I have gleaned so far, they have little information to share. Apparently, as the head of Cloak and Veil, Saberton engaged in an environment of distrust. It helped him play members against one other." The scholarch folded her hands. "Ah, well. We shall get to the bottom of it, of that I have no doubt."

Jet and Will tried to leave to check on Charlie and Peppercorn. Scholarch Wolverhampton raised her hand. "Just a moment, you two. I'll need you to fill in some blanks for us, please. Your parents are here, and I think they'd very much appreciate seeing you. Besides that, as Morwenna Saberton is missing, any help you two could offer would be appreciated."

Exhaustion shadowed Will's gaze, yet he smiled. Throwing an arm around Jet's shoulder, he said, "Let's go tell them how we saved the world. It'll be annoying, but someone has to do it."

~ * ~

Two weeks later, Jet listened to the scholarch, who was speaking from the dais situated in the Atrium in front of the entire student body of Quadrivium. Classes and finals over, Jet managed to pass her Beta Year of Quadrivium with Optimum marks. The worry she experienced over accomplishing this goal seemed so silly after recent events, but she still had a sense of pride for the achievement. The scholarch herself taught the Movement class in Ruecroft's forced absence, and Jet's final exam was deemed outstanding. The scholarch also told Jet she wouldn't report to the Sagesse about her sneaking out. She figured it was moot since she and Will had saved the animals, but it was nice to know.

Morwenna had escaped and, of course, it was common knowledge she threatened Jet before she disappeared. She put it out of her head for now. Her family was up on the dais enjoying the graduation ceremony. Next to her in the audience, seated on either side of her, were Will and Charlie.

Charlie explained how Ruecroft had followed Saberton for years, and she had no choice but to obey her mother who used the fact she couldn't be dismissed from Quad as a way to stretch the rules. She'd been jailed by the Aurea Regia Guard, and she heard that even now her ex-professor kept ranting about the genius of Roger Saberton and the disappointment of Charlotte Houndswood, her only daughter.

Jet figured Charlie had suffered enough torment and forgave her. So did Will. The three friends vowed to keep truthful with one another from now on.

She applauded along with everyone else as the last Omega student's name was read and the diploma conferred. It seemed the ceremony might at last be over. The scholarch raised her hand for silence.

"And now, we come to a very important part of the proceedings," she announced. "Our dear friend Mr. Declan Newcastle will do the honors." Thunderous applause exploded in the Atrium. Will flew to his feet with the entire audience as his father took the stage. Jet stood with him, proud to have helped clear the Newcastle name.

Mr. Newcastle stood in front of the lectern. "Ladies and gentlemen, it is with so much joy I stand here today to announce the inductees for the new class of the Society of Wave and Wing."

The crowd cheered. The reception of the members of Civis Sagesse was quite interesting, since so many of them had decided to censure the Newcastles a few short weeks earlier. She smiled the cynical thought away, and her mother's words about "pompous politicians" echoed in her brain.

"For receiving highest honors among his peers, for exhibiting outstanding skill in Aquaticup, and, finally, for displaying bravery second to none, it is with deepest pride I offer William Newcastle membership to the Society of Wave and Wing."

She nudged Will. "I can't believe you scored higher than me."

"Even I can't believe it," he said. "Give a guy a break. It's a lot of work to keep up with someone like you." He trotted off to the stage to receive his robes.

The crowd quieted. Her stomach dropped. Mr. Newcastle cleared his throat. "For receiving the second highest marks among Beta students, for a stunning display in the Aquaticup, and for bravery in the face of many challenges, we offer a well-*earned* invitation to the Society of Wave and Wing to Miss Jaiette Lennox."

Stunned, she didn't move for a moment. Charlie patted her back and congratulated her. It all seemed to be happening in the distance around her. She did it! She'd earned a spot on her own. Not because she was a royal and not because someone else had done it for her. She had *earned* her place at Quadrivium. Suddenly, she felt a buzz in her head, and she let Will in.

"Hey, Princess, you wanna get up here on stage? You just sitting there is starting to look weird."

Jet jumped out of her seat, legs trembling as she reached the stage where Will stood applauding. She received her ceremonial robes as her family watched. As she waved at the student body still applauding them, she was comfortable on stage for the first time in her life. But she was still glad she didn't have to give a speech.

The crowd settled as they took their seats. Mr. Newcastle adjusted the microphone. "Thank you all for allowing me the privilege to represent this wonderful student organization. And before we let you go, the Noble Order of Fin and Feather request the presence of all members of Wave and Wing in a meeting immediately following this ceremony."

Will nudged her. "They probably want to welcome us properly."

"You know, for someone who didn't care all that much about getting in, you sure seem excited now."

His neck grew red. Jet circled to Charlie. "We're going to visit Svashi after this meeting. Meet us at the beach?"

A small smile twisted Charlie's lips. "Like I have a lot of other options right now. I don't know if you've heard, but I'm sort of an orphan now."

"You'll be visiting the palace next week, and I intend to keep you for as long as you can stand it."

Tears welled in Charlie's eyes, so Will hurried to say, "We've got to go, Houndswood. Indigo Beach in an hour."

She and Charlie shared a grin over his obvious discomfort with tears.

"I'll be there. Have fun, you two," Charlie said.

Before they could go, Jet's family found them. Her mother was holding Peppercorn. "We are taking this hero down to Aurealia with us. He deserves to ride in luxury."

Not surprisingly, he said nothing, but his snort indicated the praise was acceptable.

Queen Phoebe hugged Jet to her. "We are so proud of you."

Her father pulled her from her mother and peered deep into her eyes. "You will never know how important you are to me, Jet," he said. "Letting you go was the hardest thing I've ever done, but it was the best thing. You were always a light for us, but now you shine for yourself. You astound me, my daughter."

She swallowed. As she hugged her family close, she said, "Thank you for letting me find my own way. I needed to."

He kissed her forehead. "You've done what no other royal has since Indigo City was built. You've joined together the people of Aurealia and the city above it. You have united the Children of Neptune."

Epilogue

Jet and Will were led into a room that wasn't a room, but a long hallway leading to a stairway below the school. She hadn't been this way before, and she vowed to ask Peppercorn to help her find her way back here.

The Society of Wave and Wing currently had sixteen members, including Will and Jet. Her stomach fluttered with excitement as they proceeded to a doorway in the passage. They entered a room similar in size to the Apollonian Octet rehearsal room where Charlie had practiced.

That was where the similarity ended. Wall screens lined every available space. A rotating globe, with red lights glowing on various countries all over the planet, sat in the center of one of them. She had no idea what the red lights indicated.

Professor Stemp was in the room talking to Bevan, and she wondered why they were there. She recognized Bertie Cox as well, but no one else. She took a seat with the other members around a huge, round table in the center of the room.

A door opened, and Mr. Newcastle strode in with several people trailing him. She assumed them all to be members of Fin and Feather. He carried a file and threw it onto the table as he took his place at the head of it. She lifted her brows at Will, and he just shrugged.

Mr. Newcastle kept his voice low as he said, "I'd like to apologize to Newcastle and Lennox. Normally we throw a nice reception for new members." His expression tightened. "Unfortunately, we don't have that luxury today. Today we are under attack."

Tension fell over the room. What did he mean by attack?

"First, I think a brief background for Newcastle and Lennox before I explain further. Anything I share here today doesn't leave this room. You must accept this confidentiality as a tenet of your membership. Do we understand one another?" He spoke in a hard voice she barely recognized, and she nodded at once.

"You both are familiar with why the Society of Wave and Wing and its counterpart, Fin and Feather, were founded?"

She nodded again.

"We have broadened the scope of both societies to include defense. Wave and Wing members are recruited by the Noble Order of Fin and Feather as students at Quadrivium because they show special talents and abilities at a young age. These abilities are honed to supply Fin and Feather with new operatives."

Operatives? What did he mean?

"Fin and Feather operates one of the largest secret intelligence communities in the known world."

Her mouth fell open. Fin and Feather members were spies?

He pointed to the wall screen with the red dots on the globe. "Those dots indicate animals or Pelagi operatives placed by Fin and Feather across the world as intelligence gatherers. As opposed to some secret societies, we function as a political organization, but our motives are protection and defense. We do not operate for the good of Fin and Feather; we operate for the good of Pelagiana."

A shiver ran through her, and sweat trickled down her back. How did she not know this? She was a member of the royal family. She was the heir to the throne. "How is this even possible without the royal family's knowledge?"

"You are not privy to everything the royal family knows, but I realize that doesn't answer your question either. For now, we have work to do. You and Will need to know what's expected of you before you sign on."

"We're ready to hear it," Will said.

"As recruits of Wave and Wing, you will be trained to handle operations once you reach an age deemed appropriate. This age is never set in stone and depends on the individual recruit as well as his or her talents. Upon completion of your regular classes here at Quadrivium, along with specialized training, you will be evaluated for further advancement into Fin and Feather as a full operative. You must remember while we require absolute secrecy, you have a choice in this future. You may opt out at any time, if you respect the confidentiality. We have never had a problem with this in hundreds of years." He reached for a glass of water and drank deeply before moving on. "You are both here because you belong. If you are unsure about this path, you will not be judged or censured for leaving. I'll need your decisions now."

Jet didn't hesitate. "I'm in."

"Same here," Will said.

Mr. Newcastle's gaze warmed as he looked at his son. "Good. Now on to bigger problems." He opened the file in front of him. "Everyone in this room is about to receive classified information. This is not a training exercise for new recruits. We need to move fast. More heads are better in a situation like this, even if they happen to have little experience and training." He shook his head. "I am sorry to report that the Shield has been breached."

She gasped and reached for the necklace at her throat. It was missing. "Morwenna."

Mr. Newcastle shook his head. "That is our evaluation as well. Breaching the Shield compromises the safety of Aurealia and the Baroque. Now someone has a piece of the Shield. It will repair itself, thank goodness…this time." He let the threat hover in the air. "We have no idea how she might have gotten it or what she intends to do with it, but we have to get it back. If indeed it is Morwenna who stole it, we should assume she'll be back. Fin and Feather can't let that happen."

"I know how she got it," Jet said. Every head in the room rotated to her. Her face heated. "My necklace is missing. It must have come off in the fight with Morwenna. I didn't realize. It was a conch pearl made of—"

"Let me guess," Mr. Newcastle interrupted. "It was made of a small bit of the Baroque?"

She nodded.

"Well, that means all she had to do was scratch the surface of the Shield, and she could take a bit. Now that she has both, there is no telling what she might do with them."

"I'm so sorry," she said.

"Princess, there isn't a person here who hasn't made a mistake. While we appreciate the apology, it isn't necessary. If Morwenna Saberton wanted your necklace, she would have found a way to get it. Actually, this new information will help move things along. Information will be sent to your Elvers. We reconvene in forty-eight hours for another briefing."

Chairs scraped, and people rose to leave. Her head swirled with everything she just learned. Mr. Newcastle stopped her and Will.

"Newcastle and Lennox, your training and knowledge of Morwenna is going to be needed for this. I'm sorry to throw you in the deep end so quickly." He placed a hand on Will's shoulder. "I'm so proud of you." She tried to excuse herself, but he halted her again. "And you as well, Princess. You and Will make quite a team."

"Thanks, Mr. Newcastle. I have so many questions." She asked the first that came to mind, "Are the people who have been following me in Wave and Wing?"

Will's head swiveled. "What people following you?"

"We used several different people for your security, including students like Bertie," Mr. Newcastle said. "But we figured you had enough to worry about with going to school, so we didn't want to make you paranoid. The intel you provided about Saberton was very helpful. We hadn't even thought of him until you mentioned your concerns."

"I thought you said I was crazy for suspecting him, Jet," Will said.

"I didn't believe he'd betray my father, so I did think you were crazy." She turned back to Mr. Newcastle. "I still need to know so many things."

"I'm sure you do. But for now, go try and have some fun. You should celebrate a little. You've both earned it. Listen, you two, this mission isn't going to happen anytime soon. We have to find and interrogate his followers, including his wife. Unfortunately, most of the Cloak and Veil members remain a secret. Ultimately, we don't know how many supported him or just feared him. Remember, Morwenna Saberton is smart. She will plot and plan, but so will we. You have a busy summer ahead of you, so use the time you have now before you begin your training."

Will and Jet headed back through the tunnel. She reached the Atrium, still in a daze.

He caught her hand. "That was nothing like I expected."

"You think?"

"What do you think we should do?"

She knew she was meant to be at Quadrivium when Roger Saberton and Morwenna executed his plan. Morwenna wouldn't stop until she exacted revenge. Jet wasn't sure of all the reasons why yet, but she recognized fate when it smacked her in the face. She shrugged as they made their way to the beach.

"You know, for once it seems pretty simple to me. Morwenna has something that belongs to me, and I intend to get it back. She's coming for me at some point. Until then, we're going to train and we're going to learn everything we can. And when she comes, we'll be ready."

About the Author

Makenna Snow is the pen name for a collaboration between two sisters passionate about storytelling and the influence it has on people and decisions they make in their life. We hope that by diving headfirst into a character's motives we can tell their story and compel others to take the journey with them.

Readers can find more about Makenna at:

Website: http://www.makennasnow.com
Twitter: https://twitter.com/maksnowwrites
Facebook: https://www.facebook.com/maksnowwrites
Instagram: http://www.instagram/makennasnow

~ * ~

We hope you enjoyed *Children of Neptune*. If you did, please write a review, tell your friend, or even check out our other terrific offerings at Champagne Book Group (http://www.champagnebooks.com).

Interested in getting advance notice of great new books, author contests and giveaways, and only-to-subscriber goodies? Join https://www.facebook.com/groups/ChampagneBookClub/.

Made in the USA
Lexington, KY
14 November 2017